Song of
Yuan-Yuan

Song of Yuan–Yuan

Drama of 1644

Sidney Chan

Author of *Lord of Ten Thousand Years*

Archway Publishing books may be ordered through booksellers or by contacting:

Archway Publishing
1663 Liberty Drive
Bloomington, IN 47403
www.archwaypublishing.com
1 (888) 242-5904

Because of the dynamic nature of the Internet, any web addresses or
links contained in this book may have changed since publication and
may no longer be valid. The views expressed in this work are solely those
of the author and do not necessarily reflect the views of the publisher,
and the publisher hereby disclaims any responsibility for them.

Any people depicted in stock imagery provided by Thinkstock are models,
and such images are being used for illustrative purposes only.
Certain stock imagery © Thinkstock.

ISBN: 978-1-4808-4516-9 (sc)
ISBN: 978-1-4808-4514-5 (hc)
ISBN: 978-1-4808-4515-2 (e)

Library of Congress Control Number: 2017938403

Print information available on the last page.

Archway Publishing rev. date: 4/17/2017

To: T, D.J. and Cris

AUTHOR'S NOTE

In ancient Greece, there was a woman named Helen, whose face was so beautiful that it caused the Trojan War and helped launch a thousand ships that brought down the Kingdom of Troy.

In the seventeenth century, China also had a woman with a beautiful face, who helped launch a hundred thousand soldiers that brought down two dynasties.

In this novel, I tell the tale how this drama could have unfolded in the short period of forty-one days.

With regard to romanization of Chinese names and places, I chose, as I did for my first novel, *Lord of Ten Thousand Years*, to go with the traditional translation rather than the *pinyin* method, which is widely used today.

For example, I find it more appropriate in this story, to call Peking Peking, rather than Beijing, the current name. I find the flow of the story more fluid when using the old terminology.

C H A P T E R 1

Yuan-yuan

THE SONG OF LOVE IS A SAD SONG. SO IS A STORY OF LOVE.

The love story of Yuan-yuan, an exceptionally beautiful woman who lived during a tumultuous period in China, the early part of the seventeenth century, was no exception. She, along with many powerful men of the time, was swept into the center of a storm known as the Drama of 1644, a drama that had ended a once-mighty Chinese empire: the Ming Dynasty.

Like most ancient empires of the world, China had a male-dominated society. Women were seen as chattel and given a low social standing. For the common people, women were basically childbearers and domestic slaves. But for the wealthy, the gentry, and the political elites, a beautiful woman would assume a definitively higher standing. The most beautiful women were admired and treasured, and Yuan-yuan was one of those much-sought-after beautiful objects.

Yuan-yuan was born and raised in Soochow, an idyllic town located in the Yangtze River delta area, a fertile plain of eastern Asia. It was about four hundred miles south of Peking, the capital of the Ming dynasty. Soochow gained prominence primarily because it was near Nanking, a political center founded in the first century that became the capital of China for six short-lived dynasties. These dynasties, known as the Southern dynasties, were ethnically Han Chinese, the most populous of the five races in China.

The Han people were the dominant race because they were governed by a society based on letters and law, unlike the other four races, which were crude and nomadic. The Han Chinese branded the others "barbarians." For centuries, these barbarians occupied the vast mountain and desert regions in the north and coexisted with the Han Chinese living in the southeastern plain of the Asian continent. Historians called the region the Central Plain, or the Middle Kingdom, because it was more fertile and habitable than the treacherous terrain in the north.

The northern barbarians coveted the lifestyle and natural resources in the south and agitated to upset the balance of power. Over the next 350 years, they grew stronger, while the southern ruling class, living a soft and decadent life, became weaker. Two minor races, identified in history as the Northern dynasties, took up arms and wreaked havoc on the southerners. With the southern capital of Nanking being constantly threatened by their northern rivals, many of the southern political elites and scholars took on a "no tomorrow" attitude and chose the peaceful, good life that Soochow had to offer.

The climate in Soochow was moderate most of the year, with mostly pleasant temperatures in the spring and summer. The landscape of the city was unique and beautiful; streets were lined with trees, and a manmade waterway traversed its center. The waterway, called the Grand Canal, connected the Yangtze Valley with Tientsin, a seaport near the capital. On the west side of the canal resided the poorer people of Soochow; on the east side, the bank teemed for almost a mile with beautiful mansions and exotic night spots, such as saloons, teahouses, theaters, and brothels.

During Yuan-yuan's teenage years, the political fortune of the ruling class in Peking began to unravel. While the capital wallowed in a sea of trouble, Nanking and its infamous Chin-hwai River became the haven for the wealthy and the elites to have fun and escape from the turmoil—much like Soochow had been to Nanking, many centuries ago.

Yuan-yuan and her family lived on the west side of the canal because they belonged to the economically deprived class. The small wooden shed they lived in, nestled in the midst of many rundown houses, was only a few hundred yards from the shores of the canal. Looking down from the top of a grassy knoll, residents in that neighborhood could see the lights and hear the din and music emanating from the other side of the bank. It seemed that the noise and activities were interminable as the fine gentlemen of the day cruised the canal night after night to escape from their troubles and to enjoy the "good life."

Yuan-yuan's father was in his fifties. The locals called him the "old salesman" because he sold old merchandise for a living. He had a wife and two children, Yuan-yuan and her younger brother. Yuan-yuan was endowed with a beautiful face, a shapely body, and a free spirit. From age four, she started to sing and playact, even though she was still learning how to talk. As she grew older, her curiosity was roused by the sound of music from the distance. She took off to chase the sound and discovered the music was coming from the opposite shore of the canal, where many theaters and saloons were located. Thereafter, she frequently ran down to the shore with her little brother to listen to the music. Occasionally, she sneaked in to watch a show. In the beginning, her mother was concerned about the long absences of her children. But when she found out that they were down the canal, she only admonished Yuan-yuan to be careful and did not stop her adventure.

Over time, hiding in the corners of the theaters to watch the shows, Yuan-yuan became mesmerized by the actresses' colorful makeup and pretty costumes. She was especially impressed by one actress who was the star in a play. The play was about a young woman who was deeply in love with a dashing and handsome young man. When the young man went off to war, the young woman spent nights on end crying for his safe return and singing a song titled "Lover, Come Home!"

While the old salesman was busy every day trying to make ends meet, Yuan-yuan helped her mother tend to the household chores and watch over her younger brother. One evening, when Yuan-yuan was helping to prepare dinner, she cried out to her mother, who was busy sewing nearby, "Mother, our rice container is empty!"

"I know. We will have to wait and see if your father will bring rice home for our dinner tonight."

"We have not had rice for many days. I hope Father will answer your wish, Mother," Yuan-yuan said wistfully.

"Your father is working very hard to provide for us, and your brother is far too young to be helpful," lamented her mother.

"Mother, we cannot go on like this any longer. We must find a way to help Father." Although she was barely thirteen years old, Yuan-yuan knew the family could not survive indefinitely under such poor conditions.

"I understand," the mother answered dejectedly.

"Mother, I will work," said Yuan-yuan.

The mother, surprised, muttered, "A young girl like you will not be able to find work. What kind of work can you do?"

"Mother, I can sing!"

The mother did not respond; she shook her head and went back to her sewing. She was repairing a pair of worn-out pants for the old salesman.

When her mother didn't respond and appeared pensive,

Yuan-yuan walked out to the knoll and sang. Her voice was shrill but rather pleasing. While she was singing, her brother was playing nearby.

Suddenly, a singing voice echoed from a distance—a voice that Yuan-yuan had heard before. Within moments, she saw her father walking toward her and singing his favorite tune. The old salesman came from a poor family and was not educated. But he was endowed with a wonderful singing voice, and he thoroughly enjoyed music and singing. When he was not working, he stayed home and played on a broken violin, singing loudly by himself. He frequently boasted to his wife and friends that, given the opportunity, he'd succeed as a professional singer. But it was only a wild dream. Understanding that his dream could not be realized, the old salesman hoped that someday his daughter might fulfill his dream. In every spare moment, he taught his daughter how to read lyrics and use voice control. She was amazed that the old salesman, who was otherwise illiterate, could easily read lyrics. Was it fate that both the father and the daughter in this impoverished family shared an interest in music and singing?

The young woman rushed down the knoll to greet her father and interrupted his tune. "Father, did you bring rice home?" The father stopped singing and lumbered closer to his daughter, two heavy loads of merchandise teetering on his old back. He dropped them on the ground, wiped the sweat off his face with his sleeve, took a couple of deep breaths, and said haltingly, "Yes, I brought rice." He picked up a large bag from the basket and showed it to his daughter. "But rice is hard to come by!" he exclaimed. "It's very expensive! A lot of people are starving because they cannot afford to buy it even if they can find it."

Yuan-yuan did not expect her father to be so sullen, so she put on a happy face and said, "You must have had a hard day, Father. Nice to have you home!"

"My daughter, I bring more than rice for us." The father also assumed a happy expression. "I have a piece of pork and some vegetables in this bag!"

"What is the occasion, Father?"

"Nothing! I just had a good day in the market," the father said. "Let's go in and surprise your mother."

They walked inside the shed, Yuan-yuan's brother running behind them.

The mother was surprised and delighted to see the food her husband brought home. She left her sewing on the floor, rushed over to the cooking area, and began to prepare a sumptuous dinner—sumptuous by this hungry family's standards.

"Father," the daughter said. She nudged the father, who was sitting in a chair resting his old, tired body and eyes and waiting for dinner.

"Yes, my daughter?"

"I want to help you by providing for us," Yuan-yuan said softly.

"What?" His daughter's comment surprised the old salesman.

"Yes, Father," Yuan-yuan continued. "You have worked so hard and for so many years to provide for us. You are getting older, and I thought it was time for me to help."

"It is very good of you to offer." The father cracked a thin smile. "You are too young. Besides, there is no place in the working world for women."

"Father, I have been observing the singers and actresses in the theaters down the bank. They appear to be young like me, and they are performing and, I am sure, making money!"

"My daughter, I know you have been running down to the bank and watching the shows. I have warned your mother to be more careful about letting you out so often and so late," the old salesman lamented, shaking his head. "A young woman like you should not be seen in public places. Especially when you are not accompanied by anyone and do not pay to see the shows."

"I have my brother with me all the time," confessed the daughter.

"Your brother cannot be much help! That area is full of undesirable characters. All they do is indulge in immoral things: eating, drinking, and playing with women." The father shook his head. "With their education, they ought to be in Peking helping to restore order in our country!" He then turned to his wife and yelled, "Is dinner ready? I'm famished!"

The family gathered around a small rickety table and consumed the best meal of the month: pork and vegetables over rice.

After dinner, the old salesman invited his daughter to sing along with him. He picked up the violin and started playing some familiar tunes. Even though the instrument was out of tune, Yuan-yuan was able to spin out some beautiful lyrics. The father was pleased with his daughter's improvement, and the duo carried on merrily into the deep night, when the boy and his mother were soundly asleep. When Yuan-yuan began humming the tune she had picked up from the theater, the father muttered, "Where did you learn that? Isn't it … My love, where have … you gone?"

"No, Father," Yuan-yuan said with a smile, "it's called 'Lover, Come Home'!"

The father put down the instrument and turned and looked forlornly at the daughter. "It's a beautiful song, and a popular one, but a very sad one!" lamented the father. "Yuan-yuan, life will not be easy for us going forward, I am afraid!" After a pause, the father sighed and resumed his monologue. "Rumors abound in the marketplace that revolts are brewing all over the land. The rebels are winning their battles against the emperor's army. Lately, I have noticed that there are more beggars and homeless people on the streets. People are pilfering food from the merchants in broad daylight. The situation is chaotic, to say the least. With the country in such a mess, how does the emperor expect us poor people to continue to survive?"

The daughter noticed a trace of tears in the father's eyes. She lowered her head, leaned closer to him, and uttered softly, "Father, I will help you!"

The father did not respond to the daughter's offer, as if he had sunk into deep thoughts. Then he suddenly perked up and carried on with his tirade. "I hate to think of the day when the rebels finally land on our doorsteps. It would be a sad day for all the town folks when they have to endure the looting of their homes and raping of their wives and daughters by the rebels. Rumors have it that the rebels are mean and ruthless!"

"Father, we should have faith in our emperor to do the right things to protect us. The rebels' threats are not imminent; are they?

"You are young and beautiful! I dread to think of that day when it comes!"

"We cannot worry about things too far ahead. For us and many families, even tomorrow cannot be guaranteed," lamented Yuan-yuan. "Father, let me help you!"

Even though she was not sure how she could be helpful to the father, Yuan-yuan's voice projected an air of utmost determination. She had already made up her mind to be a singer. And her singing would earn sufficient money to take her family out of poverty. And, one day, she would be the best singer in China. And she would also be a most successful and beautiful actress—more successful and beautiful than the actress in that theater down the canal whom she had come to covet and admire. Moreover, she vowed to herself, one day she would find that handsome, dashing young lover of her dreams.

CHAPTER 2
The Malaise

THE COUNTRY WAS INDEED IN A BAD CONDITION, A CONDITION that set in motion the Drama of 1644.

In 1627, Chung-chen inherited the throne from his brother. He was to become the sixteenth emperor of the Ming dynasty at a time when the empire had already begun to spin out of control. The path of the impending collapse had been paved by his three predecessors, beginning with his grandfather, Wan-li. Emperor Wan-li was the thirteenth emperor of the dynasty, a dynasty founded in 1368 by a peasant, only the second commoner to have accomplished such a mighty feat in the history of China.

The Ming dynasty was unique. It was the last imperial dynasty belonging to the major race in China: the Han Chinese. It was also unique in that it was preceded and followed by two dynasties belonging to minor races in Asia: the Yuan Dynasty of the Mongols and the Ching Dynasty of the Manchus, respectively. These two dynasties were branded "barbaric" by Chinese historians, and they were considered "illegitimate" because their social structures were different from the Han Chinese. Their societies were not governed by letters and law.

In the beginning, the Ming dynasty ruled from Nanking. After the first emperor died, his grandson took the throne; his father had predeceased him. The new emperor, even though tender in age, was aware of the threats of usurpation he faced from the uncles and cousins who had inherited fiefdoms from his grandfather. So he began purging the ranks of the princes, trying to consolidate his power. However, a powerful uncle, named Ju Di, led a successful coup and usurped the throne from him. Since Ju Di's fiefdom was Peking, he moved the capital of the dynasty there.

Ju Di was an ambitious man. He took over an empire in his prime, full of energy and foresight; his vision was to make his empire a mighty one. With a brimming treasury after thirty-one years of peaceful rule by the founding emperor and many good harvest years, Ju Di embarked on many ambitious programs, both domestically and abroad. He restored the palaces in the Forbidden City and reformed the system for running the government. He rebuilt the Great Wall to protect his empire from intrusions by the Mongols from the steppes and the Manchus from the northeast. He also commissioned a team of engineers to build a fleet to explore the seas surrounding China. These seafaring programs expanded the empire's territorial reaches as far south as Southeast Asia and as far west as the Red Sea.

Ju Di died after ruling the Ming dynasty with great success for twenty-two years. A chain of mediocre emperors followed. Over the next 150 years, these rulers succeeded in bringing the dynasty slowly down the path to decay.

Emperor Wan-li was one of the mediocre rulers. He was a well-meaning but intellectually inadequate man. When he took over the country, it was at peace with the world, and the treasury brimmed with surplus. For that reason, he quickly became complacent and began to ignore matters of the court and not conduct regular court audiences. He finally abandoned the protocol altogether and opted to spend his time at leisure, indulging in the fun things in life: wine, women, and song. By delegating the running of the court to a few he favored, Wan-li sowed the seeds of the dynasty's demise.

Throughout the history of imperial China, rulers were insulated in an inner sanctum called the Great Within. The Great Within was staffed by manservants called eunuchs. The eunuchs' primary responsibility was to serve the emperors, but through the centuries they evolved into a form of secret police whose job was to isolate and shield the emperors from the outside world. In order to gain an audience with the emperor, all officials, regardless of rank, must pass through these gatekeepers. To qualify as a eunuch, a man must subject himself to castration. This rule had been made ostensibly to guarantee the emperor was the singularly virile man in his court.

In the latter years of his reign, Wan-li placed his trust in one particularly ambitious eunuch: Wei Chung-yan.

Wei Chung-yan was not educated, but he was sufficiently intelligent to have taught himself basic reading and writing. At age eighteen, he entered the corps of eunuchs merely for survival because he could not find work that would afford him a good life in the outside world. At first, he did menial duties as a junior eunuch. A few years later, opportunity beckoned: he was assigned to the chamber of a prince who happened to become the heir to the throne. When that prince became Emperor Wan-li, Wei gained his favor and grew in stature. As Wan-li became more withdrawn from his court, Wei founded a clique called the Eastern Factory and completely isolated the emperor.

The Eastern Factory, manned by mostly dishonest and aggressive officials personally chosen by Wei, wrested all power to run the court from the ministers that had been groomed by the imperial systems of examination. Under Wei, vacancies in the ministries were filled only by his friends or those who patronized him or not filled at all. A group of ministers loyal to the throne founded an opposition party called the East Forest Institute to combat the Eastern Factory, but it was no match for the brutal tactics employed by the treacherous characters of the Eastern Factory. Many of the ministers who had pledged loyalty to the East Forest were imprisoned and some were even executed summarily. Those who were allowed to remain were intimidated into submission or corrupted with cash, treasure, or sexual favors. Those who were fortunate enough to escape the purge disappeared underground, and many eventually moved to Nanking, the haven for exiled officials. In the absence of a capable and honest cadre of ministers to run the government, a state of anarchy prevailed in the court. With rampant corruption and waste and a failing tax system, the government was left in shambles!

Emperor Wan-li's reign came to an end after forty-three long and futile years. His son took over, and his reign lasted only thirty days. Many stories of palace intrigue surrounded the circumstances under which the new emperor suddenly died. Some accounts suggested that Wei Chung-yan had poisoned him because the new emperor despised him in favor of some ministers close to the East Forest fraction.

The next emperor was barely sixteen when he inherited the throne vacated by the sudden death of his father. Given the reign name of Tian-ti, he became the fifteenth ruler of the Ming dynasty. Mild in manner and meek in disposition, Tian-ti had not expected to be emperor so soon; he harbored no desire to be one. He had openly admitted that he would much rather be a carpenter. From an early age, he had spurned scholastic pursuit in favor of working with his hands. He was most happy when given the opportunity to build and paint wooden houses and furniture. Wei Chung-yan was happy with this young emperor and his laissez-faire attitude toward the governing of his empire.

One beautiful spring day, while Wei Chung-yan and his lover were strolling leisurely in his courtyard, enjoying the tweeting of the birds and the blooming of the flowers, he said playfully to his woman, "My dear, His Majesty has become quite an obedient child, much to my surprise."

"You should thank me for that," the woman, a rather good-looking woman in her late twenties, shot back.

The woman was one of eight chambermaids assigned to caring for the emperor when he had been merely an ordinary child-prince. The emperor's mother had been in poor health after giving birth to seven boys, so Tian-ti had been raised and cared for by a team of nursemaids. The boy was most attracted to the prettiest of the eight women serving him. Even though she was only six years older, the boy looked upon her as his surrogate mother and addressed her as his Ah Ma, meaning literally "my mother."

When Tian-ti ascended to the throne unexpectedly, Ah Ma's star rose, and she assumed the aura, if not the position, of the sitting empress. She was addressed as Empress Ah Ma in the palace, while the wife of Tian-ti was called Empress Gao, to distinguish between the real and the pseudo empresses. Empress Gao was not happy with the situation, but there was very little she could do to change it.

Ah Ma had met Wei Chung-yan when they were both working in Emperor Wan-li's private chamber. Wei was an obese man more than twenty years her senior. His obesity resulted from his imitation of the life of an emperor, including extreme indulgence in good food and fine wines. Even though he was close to many female workers in the court, especially Ah Ma, it was doubtful he could have engaged in carnal activities.

Once he became the power behind the throne, Ah Ma seized the opportunity to befriend him. Knowing that Ah Ma was the favorite of the prince, he, too, wanted to nurture the relationship. So the two opportunists forged a partnership in love, and in crime.

"Yesterday, I ordered six eunuchs to help him build a shed for his pet dogs. He was so happy that he awarded me the title chief minister," boasted Wei Chung-yan.

"Chief minister? A promotion?"

"Perhaps," Wei said proudly. "He told me that I have total say in running his court. Come to think of it, His Majesty seems to be very forgetful lately."

"You have been running the court ever since he took the throne—he would rather forget all the headaches of being an emperor. Besides, what's so important about a title?"

"It's important because the title puts more respect and fear into the hearts of the other ministers," Wei said with a wry grin. "You know what else His Majesty told me?"

"What?"

"He said that since he is the Lord of Ten Thousand Years, I should be named the Lord of Nine Thousand Years because I am his right-hand man!" Wei let out a loud laugh. But he was not laughing when he demanded that he be addressed formally as Chief Wei in and around the imperial household.

Five years into his reign, Emperor Tian-ti's health began to deteriorate due to an injury he had sustained in a mysterious near-drowning incident. Worse yet, his mental capacity took a turn for the worse. As the emperor's malaise persisted, Wei became more agitated because Tian-ti was a perfect puppet. The prospect of losing him was unthinkable. So he solicited the best medical minds to attend to Tian-ti, but the emperor's condition did not improve. In fact, he became worse.

Since Tian-ti's empress did not bear him a son, the thorny question of who would inherit the throne wreaked havoc in Chief Wei's mind. The person next in line for the throne was the emperor's sole surviving brother, Prince Shen, whom he detested. The prince was a person of high principles, and Wei knew that his position in the court would be greatly diminished if the prince became the emperor.

"We should have a plan to take care of the question of imperial succession." Chief Wei spoke with a serious face, pulling Ah Ma aside and into a pavilion. They sat on a bench and started to discuss the problem that would soon confront them.

"If His Majesty dies suddenly, his brother will ascend to the throne," Ah Ma said matter-of-factly. "Would he not?"

"That's precisely the problem!" Wei shouted.

"What exactly is the problem?"

Chief Wei was annoyed at his lover's casual attitude toward the problem, which he thought was most urgent. "You know that his brother has no love for me," Wei blurted. "He has been a thorn on my side. He takes the opposite view on almost every piece of advice I give to his brother."

"In other words, we will have to stop him from taking the throne?"

"Now you've got it! I know that he is a staunch backer of the East Forest Institute," Wei said, putting up a finger to his lips to signal the woman to speak softly. "People in the East Forest Institute are my mortal enemies!"

The two lovers stopped their dialogue for a prolonged moment, as though they were searching for a solution to this thorny problem. Suddenly, Ah Ma got up from the bench and said, "I have an idea that might work."

Wei jumped on his feet. "What's in your mind?"

"But it will take time to get it done."

"How much time?" Chief Wei asked, giving her an inquisitive but puzzled look.

"A minimum of nine months!" the woman said in a forceful tone. "Do you think His Majesty will live that long?"

"Nine months?" Wei was still puzzled.

"Yes, nine months!"

"I do not think he is in imminent danger of dying. His physical condition seems to be rather stable, even though his mental state is tenuous."

"In that case, my idea will work!" Ah Ma said with assurance.

"What exactly do you have in mind?" Wei was becoming impatient. "Why nine months?"

"His Majesty has not been in the company of women for many months, I notice," said Ah Ma.

"I don't understand! He's got a harem of hundreds of young, pretty women! How many more does he need to make him happy?" Wei was still puzzled by Ah Ma's idea.

"You miss my point. I know for fact that he has not been in bed with any of them for a long period of time."

"It's his loss!" Chief Wei chuckled. "What's wrong with him?"

"When I asked him about that, he shrugged me off by saying that he's either too tired or has no interest in sexual encounters."

"So where are we heading with your so-called idea?"

"I have two most beautiful young women to present to him. Hopefully, His Majesty will find them attractive and engage in some sexual activities with them."

"Your idea calls for positive results that are not guaranteed," Chief Wei muttered. "Can he do it?"

"Do not worry!" Ah Ma said confidently. "Give me nine months, and I will guarantee a positive result for you."

Chief Wei gave his lover a prolonged inquisitive look. "I

don't know!" He shook his head, and they walked out of the courtyard back to his luxurious bedchamber.

The next evening, Ah Ma paid an unannounced visit to the emperor while he was in his private chamber, in the company of only his attending eunuch. It was not unusual for her to show up unannounced because of her close relationship with him. She arrived with two young women, along with two of her own chambermaids. At a cue from Ah Ma, the eunuch left the room, and the five women lowered their knees and bowed to the emperor. Sitting erect on the edge of his bed, the emperor was perplexed by the impromptu visit of the women.

"Your Majesty, ten thousand years to you!" the women called out in unison.

"Rise!" The emperor waved his right hand.

The women rose.

"Your Majesty," Ah Ma said in her soft voice, smiling at the emperor and walking closer to him.

"Ah Ma, who are these young ladies?" the emperor inquired, not recognizing the two young women brought into his private chamber. He was a little surprised, to say the least.

"Your Majesty, I've noticed that you have not been entertained by pretty young ladies for quite a while." Ah Ma waved the two young women closer to her. "These two will keep you happy this evening." At the end of her comment, Ah Ma gestured for her maids to leave the chamber. They complied.

"Ah Ma, I'd like to thank you for your good intentions, but you know I have not been well lately," the emperor responded in a low voice. He took a quick glance at the two young women and found them rather beautiful and alluring.

"I will beg Your Majesty's forgiveness and take leave now." Ah Ma lowered her knees and bowed to the emperor. While the emperor fixed his sight on the two young ladies, he did not notice that Ah Ma had left. He was left alone with the two young women. Without any fanfare, the two women joined the emperor in his bed. After undressing the emperor and then themselves, they quickly sank under the bedcovers. The emperor was completely consumed by the voluptuous bodies of the two women. For the first time in many months, he drowned himself in a heavy session of sexual play.

The emperor was delighted with the newfound companions, so they moved in with him as his new consorts, much to the irritation of the reigning empress and the other consorts. Five months passed after the new consorts entered the harem, though neither woman showed any signs of pregnancy. Apparently, the new sexual adventures had been unproductive because the emperor lacked sexual potency.

"Your big idea is not working!" Chief Wei blurted out, lying in bed with Ah Ma one evening. "We've got to do something about that woman!"

"We cannot punish the women for His Majesty's impotency!" argued Ah Ma, pushing his large hulk away from her.

"No, no, no! I don't mean them," responded Wei, sitting up in the bed.

"Who do you mean then?"

"Empress Gao!"

Even with all his power, Wei was insecure because he felt threatened by the empress. To him, the threat was real because she was very close to Prince Shen.

"His Majesty's health is failing fast, and your plan is not working," Wei continued. "Even if one of the women is pregnant, we cannot wait for the child to be born." He got off the bed and started pacing the room like an expecting father. "Besides, who can guarantee that it will be a boy?"

Ah Ma was speechless, and she gave her man a blank look.

"We must act quickly to prevent his brother from taking the throne!"

"I have an idea." Ah Ma raised her hand to stop the nervous man from pacing.

"What other fancy idea have you come up with now?"

"We will find a little boy!"

"What kind of idiotic idea is that?"

"We will bring a male child in to show the empress."

He shook his head slowly and then paused for a long moment. "Well, I suppose we have nothing to lose in trying."

The next day, Ah Ma requested a visit with Empress Gao. Her request was reluctantly granted by the empress. Entering the empress's chamber, Ah Ma quickly knelt to pay homage to the woman who waited impatiently in a large teakwood chair.

The empress waved her right hand to invite Ah Ma to a seat opposite hers. "Is His Majesty well?" Empress Gao inquired in a soft tone.

"Your Highness," Ah Ma answered softly, placing herself in the chair. "You have not seen His Majesty in recent days?" She feigned ignorance of the empress's estranged relationship with her husband.

"I have not seen His Majesty for many a moon," lamented the empress. "I presume that he has been in your company."

"Oh, no! Your Highness, I have not had the pleasure of seeing His Majesty for just as long."

"Really?" The empress was genuinely bewildered. "Then he must be keeping company with the other consorts."

"I heard rumors in the court that His Majesty took in two young and very beautiful consorts," said Ah Ma. "He must have been busy enjoying their company."

The empress grunted loudly, and she pursed her lips.

"Your Highness, I heard that His Majesty's health is failing.

I am here to see if Your Highness can tell me more about his condition."

"I am very much kept in the dark about His Majesty's condition. I am equally concerned about the state of His Majesty's well-being."

"If His Majesty's health takes a turn for the worse, who is going to succeed him on the throne?"

Empress Gao was taken back by Ah Ma's question. She was especially curious over the concubine's intrusion into the issue of imperial succession. On second thought, she assumed that the chief minister must be the one who had dispatched Ah Ma to see her. So she held back her curiosity and said rather calmly, "Yes, I have thought of that also. But only His Majesty can make that decision. It is not a matter of concern for us women."

"His Majesty has not designated a successor; is that not correct?"

"As far as I know, he has not even broached the subject."

"I do not want to step out of line," responded Ah Ma, hiding behind a facade of subservience, "but I have some information to offer that might help in settling the issue of the imperial succession."

The empress's curiosity turned to annoyance. She took a long pause and then asked, "What would that information be?"

"I understand that the brother of His Majesty, Prince Shen, has been considered as the successor."

"I have no knowledge of that," Empress Gao said, pretending ignorance. But, in fact, she met with the prince frequently. The matter of imperial succession had been a subject of quiet concern for both the empress and the prince, albeit for different reasons.

"Your Highness, I appreciate your trust, but I really have no interest in becoming the emperor," Prince Shen had said in a recent audience with Empress Gao. "Besides, I believe that His Majesty will recover from his ailments quickly. So there is no urgency to the question of appointing his successor."

"Your Excellency, I'd like to be optimistic about His Majesty's condition, but in reality, we have to be prepared in case the worse were to happen. Since His Majesty has no male issue of his own, you would be the natural choice as his successor."

"Is His Majesty's condition dire? If not, there is time for us to reassess the matter at a later date, is there not?" The prince wanted to avoid the subject altogether.

"Your Excellency, I'd like to err on the side of caution. You know that there are people close to His Majesty who are scheming for an advantage in naming a successor to the throne?"

Prince Shen was the fifth of seven brothers, the emperor being the eldest. Save the emperor and the prince, the other brothers had died young. The prince, barely sixteen years of age, was more mature and intellectual than the emperor, who was seven years his senior. The prince was well aware of the designs of the Eastern Factory and the chief minister, but he truly hoped that his brother was not in imminent danger of dying so the question of succession would not become a pressing issue.

"Your Excellency, as a devout student of Confucian teaching, you should know the importance of guarding the imperial temple of your honorable ancestors," the empress said, trying to arouse the prince's sense of filial piety.

"Your Highness, I truly appreciate your concern. But I need time to reconsider this matter," Prince Shen said while rising and bowing to the empress. "Have you consulted with the Grand Council on this matter?"

"I have thought of getting in touch with the grand councilors, but I did not want to tip my hand to the Eastern Factory." The empress sighed.

Prince Shen shook his head and bowed once more to bid the empress farewell. "I will give more consideration to this matter, Your Highness." He turned and departed the empress's chamber.

The news of Prince Shen's visit with the empress quickly reached Wei Chung-yan.

"If in fact Prince Shen is designated as the imperial successor, then he would be looked upon as a usurper," Ah Ma stated boldly, jolting the empress back to reality.

Empress Gao was really annoyed, but she paused again to compose herself before answering. "What is the foundation for your accusation?"

Ah Ma decided to commence her attack. "You do not know that two of His Majesty's concubines have given birth to baby boys recently?"

"What …?" The only word that the empress could utter came out loudly.

"The throne rightfully belongs to one of these babies!"

"What are you talking about?"

"His Majesty's fifth and seventh concubines have presented him with two sons!"

"Is His Majesty aware of these events?" the empress asked, momentarily stunned. "If His Majesty knows, he would have informed me and the court, I am sure."

"His Majesty's mental state has not been strong." Ah Ma pressed on. "Perhaps he did not remember to inform Your Highness and the Grand Council?"

"Even if His Majesty does not remember, surely there are people around him who would announce the good news!" retorted the empress.

"His Majesty, as emperor, enjoys the company of many consorts and concubines. It is not easy for him to keep tabs on all his liaisons with them."

The empress, searching for an answer, was slow to react to Ah Ma's comment. She had a strong suspicion that the chief minister was cooking up a scheme to steal the throne from Prince Shen.

"If you do not believe me, I will bring the babies here to visit with Your Highness," Ah Ma pushed on.

"How can we prove the legitimacy of the boys?" The empress decided to challenge Ah Ma.

"Your Highness, do you mean to question His Majesty's manhood?" retorted Ah Ma.

The empress was again speechless, but her demeanor showed controlled anger.

"Your Highness, I will bring the boys to you, and perhaps you will see fit to anoint one of them as the heir-apparent to the throne."

"I have no authority to appoint the heir-apparent to the throne," the empress said with a stern expression. "The decision rests with His Majesty!"

"But I am sure His Majesty will take your recommendation with utmost respect," Ah Ma said as she rose from her chair. Then she bowed and asked to be excused. She left the empress's palace thinking that she had succeeded in duping her into the scheme. While Ah Ma was working feverishly to locate infant boys to show the empress, Chief Wei was busy lining up support in the court, by means of bribes or intimidation, for his plan.

"We must stop his brother from taking the throne," the chief minister said urgently in a hastily called meeting of his close associates. "His Majesty's health is deteriorating quickly!" He then related the meeting Ah Ma had had with the empress to his coconspirators.

Yuan Da-siang, his closest adviser, spoke first, as was his usual habit. A devious and ambitious man in his late fifties, Yuan had been a member of the inner circle of the court for more than twenty years. He always had his way with his colleagues because of his brash manners, and he pushed his weight around most people, except the chief minister.

"Chief Minister, Prince Shen is no threat to us!" Yuan said with a smirk. "Since we already have a crown prince-in-waiting, we should just tell His Majesty to install him as the heir-apparent."

Wei was inclined to agree with Yuan, but, deep down, he did not want to provoke the prince, knowing that he was influential with the emperor. He also knew that even though Prince Shen wore a nonchalant facade in all matters relating to the court, he was of the bloodline of the imperial family. Most of the officials present were reticent, so Wei turned and looked with piercing eyes at his other close associate, Tian Wang-yu. "Minister Tian, what do you think?"

Tian Wang-yu, over sixty years in age, was a career bureaucrat. He began as a lowly administrator in Emperor Wan-li's court, but due to his shrewdness and his keen political instinct, he had wormed his way up the ranks and become the deputy minister of finance. In that rather influential position, he was put in charge of setting rates and collecting taxes. He had to answer only to the finance minister and the emperor. And the finance minister happened to be the brother of his father-in-law.

Tian Wang-yu hated eunuchs. In his view, they were meddlesome and vindictive. But, more importantly, in his view they were not "men," in the true meaning of the word. Unlike him, they could not consummate acts of love, even though they were surrounded by many desirable young women. But, for political expediency, he had to kowtow to one of these abnormalities: Wei Chung-yan. Oddly, Chief Wei trusted him because the eunuch recognized the political reality that Tian was a senior official with a significant loyal following. And Wei had a soft heart for the old minister because he continued to funnel vast amounts of cash from the imperial treasury to facilitate the needs of the Eastern Factory and his own lavish lifestyle.

"Your Excellency, I tend to agree with Minister Yuan, but I also agree with you. We should be mindful of Prince Shen." Tian seemed to be hedging his bet for a good reason. Even though he was accepted into the Eastern Factory, he had maintained a strong clandestine relationship with the prince. It was important to the old minister that whoever won the ultimate power struggle, he would remain in a position to survive and maintain special interests in the court. His many years in the Ming court had taught him the advantage of playing all his cards to the fullest. Prince Shen, on the other hand, played along with the old minister because he wanted a conduit into the working of the Wei network. Tian Wang-yu quietly played on both sides.

"If we are to survive, we must act without delay!" Yuan cut in when the chief minister was slow in responding to Tian.

"We still have to get His Majesty to sign the edict to appoint his heir-apparent, even if we get past the empress," Tian said haltingly.

"With the condition His Majesty is in, I do not think that will be difficult to do," asserted Yuan while darting a look of disdain at the old minister.

"I think Da-siang is right," Wei said forcefully. "We will bring one of the babies to see the empress without delay."

"How can we produce two babies out of nowhere?" Tian queried.

"Ah Ma has seen to that already," Wei said matter-of-factly.

The old minister assumed an innocent look and asked a logical question. "Are these babies' mothers really His Majesty's concubines or consorts?"

"How does it matter? If we do not act fast, your good life will be over quickly, Minister Tian," Yuan said sarcastically. "I suggest that we move without delay!"

Wei scanned the men surrounding him and saw many heads nodding in agreement with Yuan's comment. So he declared confidently, "Go home and wait for the good news to come!" He waved his right hand and dismissed his associates.

After the group had disbanded, the chief minister returned quickly to his chamber to work with Ah Ma to carry out their plan.

The empress wasted little time in summoning Prince Shen to an urgent meeting in her chamber. Obeying the summons, the prince appeared promptly.

The empress got to the point as soon as the prince completed his verbal respects to her. "Your Excellency, Ah Ma came and told me that two of His Majesty's concubines have recently given birth to two sons."

The prince displayed a lack of emotion as Empress Gao proceeded to relate the recent conversation that she'd had with Ah Ma.

The prince seemed to be sinking into deep thoughts, and the empress looked at him in bewilderment. "Your Excellency, are you not surprised or concerned over what Wei Chung-yan and his Eastern Factory are planning to do?"

The empress did not realize that the prince had received a secret report from Tian Wang-yu before she'd summoned him.

"Your Highness, I have been informed by some sources that their plan is about to unfold," Prince Shen said icily. "Let it play out."

"I am really concerned for His Majesty's health and safety," Empress Gao said.

"I visited with His Majesty before coming here," Prince Shen responded in a soft but caring voice. "His Majesty has given me his blessings to do whatever is needed to take care of matters."

The empress let out a sigh of relief. "Your Excellency, are you telling me that you are not adverse to being appointed the heir-apparent to the throne?"

"It will not get to that," the prince said, "but if need be, I will not dishonor the wish of His Majesty. And more importantly, it is my solemn duty to uphold the temple of our illustrious ancestors."

The empress found comfort in the prince's statement.

Two days later, on a day suggested by Ah Ma and granted by the empress, two infant babies were brought to the empress's chamber. Accompanying Ah Ma were the two concubines who purported to be the mothers of the babies, along with two maids from the concubines' chambers.

"Your Highness." Ah Ma lowered her knees to the floor to pay respect to the empress, who was perched on her chair, two ladies-in-waiting standing behind her. The other women followed Ah Ma and also knelt.

"Rise!" uttered the empress without emotion.

Ah Ma got on her feet and immediately beckoned the maids who were cuddling the babies to come forward. "Your Highness, these are the sons of His Majesty. They are here to pay respect to you!"

The empress motioned her two servants to step forward and bring the babies closer to her. The servants obeyed the order. The empress looked at the babies briefly, with an expression of indifference. She then put on a facade of feigned interest and smiled. "I will have to congratulate His Majesty personally. Incidentally, is the Grand Council aware of the birth of these two boys?"

"Chief Wei surely has informed the Grand Council of the good news," said Ah Ma.

"I want to thank you for coming to present me with such

wonderful surprises," the empress said while rising from her seat. "I will consult with His Majesty on the matter of designating one of these boys as heir to the throne." She raised her right hand to dismiss the party from her chamber.

Ah Ma was pleased that the empress did not challenge the legitimacy of the babies, but she was not confident that her mission had been successfully accomplished; the meeting was brief and the empress's demeanor curt. She gathered the group and left the empress's chamber with a very uneasy feeling.

CHAPTER 3

The Emperor

AN ATMOSPHERE OF SUSPENSE SHROUDED THE FORBIDDEN CITY. While Wei Chung-yan was waiting for the empress and the emperor to make a move to designate one of the boys he had picked as an heir-apparent, Prince Shen and the empress were waiting for Wei to make his move. It remained quiet on both fronts for more than a month. The impasse was finally broken when the emperor's health took a turn for the worse. Suddenly, he died.

While Wei moved quickly to urge the Grand Council to place one of his boys on the throne, Tian Wang-yu worked feverishly behind the scene to enlist the help of the ministers who were loyal to the prince to assert their influence on the Grand Council. Tian knew that the political winds were blowing in favor of the prince taking the throne, so he adroitly swayed his loyalty toward the prince and gradually severed his ties with the Eastern Factory. Working behind the scene, he succeeded in persuading the Grand Council to delay Wei's motion by saying that the court must take a recess from all official business during the mourning period to pay final tribute to the late emperor. Wei was infuriated by the Grand Council's decision, so he boldly made his move and proclaimed that the older of the two boys was to be installed as the new emperor.

Meanwhile, in lightning fashion, Prince Shen made a countermove that surprised everyone, including Wei and his Eastern Factory. The prince called the Grand Council to a brief meeting and announced that the emperor had left an edict designating an heir to the throne. And that the heir was himself. Upon hearing the reading of the edict, Wei went ballistic. But his challenge to the edict was to no avail since the Grand Council certified the authenticity of the document. Thus, the balance of power in the court began to swing against Wei, with Tian Wang-yu and the East Forest Institute working feverishly behind the scene to dismantle his network.

Realizing the gravity of the matter at hand, the prince took the throne after observing a brief period of mourning. The coronation ceremony was solemn and businesslike, lacking the traditional imperial prom and circumstance. So it was under these most unusual and trying circumstances that a reluctant prince became the emperor of a failing empire.

Prince Shen took the reign name Chung-chen. He ascended the throne purely by accident. He was not in the order of succession; he had become emperor because of the short lives of his father and all his brothers. After taking the throne, he vowed to give his all to save the empire. Unfortunately, Chung-chen had two tragic flaws: he was narcissistic, and he trusted no one. These personal traits eventually caused both his failure and the demise of the Ming empire.

"Your Majesty," announced Chung-chen's attending eunuch Wang Tung-yin. He lowered his body and continued, "Chief Minister Wei requests an audience with Your Majesty."

Chung-chen was preoccupied with reading the reports he had received from his officials when the eunuch interrupted him. He was testy because many of the reports contained bad tidings, and he had wished not to be disturbed. More importantly, he was not interested in seeing Wei Chung-yan. So he ignored the eunuch and turned his attention back to reading.

"Your Majesty, he is waiting outside your chamber now." the eunuch insisted, rather gently.

The emperor was annoyed but managed to say, "Do you know what he wants?"

"I do not know, Your Majesty," the eunuch answered in a soft tone. "He said it is most urgent. He insisted on seeing Your Majesty at once."

"Well, bring him in," the emperor muttered unhappily, dropping the report he was reading on the desk.

The eunuch rose and left the chamber. Shortly, Chief Wei entered alone. He walked in with his trademark gait, swaggering in huge strides, bordering on pompous. He was dressed meticulously, as usual, in his dragon-embroidered gown and a jade headpiece. He did not hide his disdain for Chung-chen as he marched close to where he was sitting and grudgingly lowered his knees. He said in a loud voice, "May peace be with you … Your … Majesty!"

"Minister Wei." The emperor greeted him with equal ambivalence.

"Your Majesty, a report came to my attention that you have ordered the finance ministry to change our tax collection policy in the provinces."

"Indeed I did!"

"Your Majesty should consult with me before making such an important decision."

"I am the emperor, Minister Wei." Chung-chen was fuming within, and he could barely complete his sentence. "Do I need to get permission from anyone before acting?"

"The finance minister works closely under my supervision. I would suppose that I would be informed by Your Majesty before an order is issued." Chief Wei cocked his head and opened his eyes wide. "Besides, it is my duty to issue the order. Not Your Majesty's."

Chung-chen was really burning inside, but he suppressed his anger. There was a moment of silence; the emperor thought, *I should not be intimidated by him.* "I should have summarily fired him," Chung-chen mumbled under his breath. But, as a realist, he knew that Wei still wielded sufficient power in the court, especially with the Eastern Factory behind him. Wei would be difficult to take down. So the emperor held back and bided his time. Since assuming reign, Chung-chen had tried to build a power base. Even with the help of many loyal ministers, including Tian Wang-yu, his base was slow in forming and reaching the level where it could take on Wei and his well-entrenched Eastern Factory.

"Our treasury is depleted to a level not seen in many years. I understand that our troops have not been paid for a long time. With internal and foreign threats mounting against us, how are we to defend our capital without financial resources?"

"Reports I received on a daily basis indicated that all fronts were quiet." Chief Wei was spinning a lie to deflect the emperor from his efforts to change the tax-collecting process. "I believe Your Majesty should not interfere with the daily operation of the court."

The emperor spoke in a loud and deliberate voice. "I have also received reports from the provincial governors in the southwest saying that revolts are brewing in many of their towns and villages. Without financial help from the central government, these governors will not be able to build up their defense to quell the uprisings."

"Your Majesty," Wei shot back, "the revolts are a result of the people in these towns and villages opposing the increase in tax rates. For that reason, I would not have ordered the tax increase, but Your Majesty unilaterally made an unthinkable move!"

"Minister, it is my solemn duty to guard against the deterioration of the empire. Lack of funds to run the government and lack of a well-trained and well-fed army would surely result in a major disaster for our country."

"Your Majesty, our empire has enjoyed more than sixty years of peace and prosperity under your grandfather, your father, and your brother. I submit that it will go on with or without Your Majesty," Chief Wei, in a feisty mood, said. Perhaps he had begun to feel his position was being threatened.

"Chief Minister, I thank you for that reminder, but if you want to continue to hold the position of chief administrator of my court, you'd better get me involved in the decision-making process from now on." The emperor was also getting into a fighting mood.

"Do I understand that I must get Your Majesty's permission for every move in the day-to-day running of the court?"

"Yes, Chief Minister!"

"Does Your Majesty know that some actions must be taken promptly, and waiting for permission from Your Majesty could invite unnecessary delays and dire consequences?"

Emperor Chung-chen found it difficult to mask his anger any longer. He decided to put an end to the outrageous dialogue, a dialogue that demonstrated amply that his chief minister was a devious and aggressive man who despised him. "From this point on, Chief Minister, you are to report to me on all actions to be taken before orders are issued to your subordinates."

"All matters, Your Majesty?" Chief Wei was livid, and he flavored his remark with a trace of sarcasm.

"Yes, Chief Minister. Without exceptions!"

"I will take Your Majesty's order under advisement."

"My order has been given, so it shall be obeyed … Minister!"

"May peace be with you … Your Majesty!" In one quick motion, Chief Wei dipped his head slightly and turned on his heels. He committed the ultimate disrespect by showing his back to the emperor, without taking the usual slow backward steps away from the throne.

The emperor did not miss the disrespect heaped upon him. He could not wait to put an end to the cancer that had caused the malaise in his court.

As the emperor agonized over his plight and tried to build up sufficient support to eradicate the cancer, Wei Chung-yan became bolder. He blatantly ignored the emperor and carried on with programs that would only benefit his clique, the Eastern Factory, and, more importantly, himself. The lawlessness and corruption that prevailed within the Forbidden City far exceeded those perpetrated by the Wan-li regime, which was well known for its decadence and perversion. Wei's closest associate, Yuan Da-siang, was especially brutal in his dealings with those who opposed him and his superior. He'd routinely incarcerate or dismiss ministers who spoke up in favor of the emperor.

Two years into his reign, Chung-chen had seen and endured enough Wei misdeeds, so he decided to go on the offense by issuing a "take no prisoners" order.

The order to execute the purge of Wei Chung-yan and his Eastern Factory fell on the lap of none other than Tian Wang-yu. After secret planning and many clandestine moves, Tian quietly solicited the help of several officials loyal to the emperor, and he also recruited many to help his cause who had been alienated by Wei. They'd become comfortable and complacent after having their way with the emperor for so long, and Wei and Yuan were caught totally off guard by the coup. With his plan nearing a successful end, Tian Wang-yu requested a visit with the emperor.

Tian Wang-yu knelt and uttered the usual words of praise to the emperor when he was granted an audience. The emperor gave him permission to rise. Tian Wang-yu rose and explained, "Our plan is coming to an end very shortly. We have found and arrested the women who claimed to be the mothers of the make-believe princes. They led us to Ah Ma, Wei's accomplice, who was the chief architect of the scheme. We placed her under house arrest pending a trial by the Grand Council."

The emperor stated the obvious. "Wei Chung-yan was obviously behind the scheme. Are you able to identify who else in the Eastern Factory played a vital role?"

"Your Majesty, Yuan Da-siang was one of them, but our people are having some difficulty locating him. The last we heard, he is in Nanking tending to some personal business."

"Where is Wei Chung-yan now?" the emperor asked urgently. "To finished what we set out to do, we must get him!"

"We have a team working on finding and arresting him," answered Tian, "but I have not heard the latest on that yet."

"A job well done, Minister!"

"I consulted with the chief councilor of the Grand Council," reported Minister Tian. "He is in the process of gathering evidence to bring charges against Wei Chung-yan, once we have him in custody."

"Charges?"

"Yes, Your Majesty." Minister Tian put on a stern expression. "Charges for the crimes of treason, corruption, and subversion of the throne."

"If these crimes are successfully established, what will the penalty be, Minister Tian?"

"Death by decapitation for subversion of the throne alone!"

While the emperor seemed to sink into deep thoughts, the old minister continued. "Your Majesty, we are working hard to end

Wei Chung-yan and the Easter Factory's treacheries, but we are also trying to maintain an atmosphere of normalcy in the court. I believe Wei Chung-yan still has no clue that the ax is about to fall on him. We should be able to nab him without great difficulty."

"I believe your observation might be correct, Minister," said the emperor. "Otherwise he would not have continued to act so pompously toward me."

"Your Majesty, we must continue to keep everything under the lid until the deed is completely done."

"How did you manage to arrest Ah Ma and her accomplices without raising Wei Chung-yan's suspicions?"

"Believe me, Your Majesty," the old minister smiled wanly and continued, "it was not easy. I must have done a great selling job all these years to earn Wei's unconditional trust."

"Minister Tian, I appreciate your loyalty. If we succeed in eradicating the evil in our court, you will be rewarded handsomely!"

The audience ended with the emperor and his minister exchanging hearty laughs.

When his mortal enemies were busily hunting down his co-conspirators and dismantling his network, Wei Chung-yan was busy enjoying his good life outside of the Forbidden City. Under China's imperial protocol, eunuchs were not allowed outside of the Forbidden City. But Wei Chang-yan was an exception because he controlled the court, so he could do as his heart desired. One fateful summer day, he was being entertained by some friends in Peking. Actually, he was busy selling official positions and his influence to some wealthy patrons.

After completing some lucrative deals, he was ready to leave for the Forbidden City with his entourage. Suddenly, an aide rushed into the restaurant and stopped in front of him. The aide did not want to speak in front of others, so he pulled Wei aside and mumbled to him breathlessly, "Sir, we have … trouble back home!" He completed his message by whispering it into Wei's ear. The chief minister's face instantly became ashen. The aide had informed him that the emperor's palace guards had taken over his mansion. And everyone in the mansion was taken away.

His closest associate Yuan Da-siang was also caught off guard by the coup. He, like his boss, had left the Forbidden City, busy selling his influence to his "friends" in Nanking, his base of operation. So when he learned of the events in Peking, he had no problem hiding his identity and settling underground there. Wei Chung-yan was not as fortunate because he had no other base of operation outside of the capital. All his earthly possessions were in his mansion, and the emperor had confiscated them all.

Reality finally sank in. Wei muttered to himself, "I'd better get out of here before they catch up with me." Without a moment of hesitation, he turned on his heels and directed his aides to take him to the closest hostel on the outskirts of town. There, he gave some money to one of his aides and asked him to buy some civilian garments for him. He then handed a small bag of coins to the others and dismissed them from the scene. When the aide came back with the clothes, Wei quickly took off his opulent official outfit and put on the drab civilian garment. After staying with his aide for a restless night in the hostel, he gave him some coins and sent him off the next morning,

Sitting alone in the spartan room of the hostel, Wei Chung-yan found himself dropped from the zenith of wealth and power to the abyss of misfortune. Now he had only the clothes on his back and a small bag containing a few hundred ounces' worth of silver coins, the price he had exacted from his patrons the day before.

Wei Chang-yan did not stay in Peking for long. He'd heard rumors that he was on the top of the emperor's most wanted list,

which included Yuan Da-siang and all of his closest associates. So
he moved stealthily out of the capital and found a deserted temple
in a small hamlet, where he settled in for many nights.

Sharing the temple with him were some people who were
displaced by the poor economic condition that had affected the
capital and much of China. Wei endured sleepless nights, fighting
the cold and hunger. One morning he awakened to find two thugs
standing in front of him in a threatening manner. One of them
bent over menacingly and asked, "Hey, fat man, what have you
got in that small bag?"

Wei sat up and clutched the bag tightly against his chest. "Oh,
my clothes!"

The thug said loudly, "Your bag is too small to hold any clothes.
Look, fat man. We are all skinny and sickly. You don't look like
any of us. We have not eaten for many days!"

"You said it, brother," the other thug echoed. "He looks well
fed! We should see what he has in that bag."

The first thug started pulling the bag away from Wei. Wei got
to his feet and started to struggle with the aggressor. After a few
pushes and tucks, he finally realized that he'd better make peace
with the two younger men.

"All right. Stop pulling, and I will give you something from
this bag," Wei said.

The two thugs paused while Wei opened the bag, reached in
with his right hand, and produced some silver coins. The eyes of
the two thugs opened wide, and they reached for the coins simultaneously. Wei let go, and the coins dropped and scattered on the
ground. While the two thugs bent down to pick up the coins, they
were joined by other hobos trying to do likewise. Wei took the
opportunity and fled the scene.

For someone like Wei Chung-yan who was used to the good
life, descending to the bottom of hell was devastating. For many

nights thereafter, while lying in an open-field or in a rickety shed, he could only dream of the glory of the past and pity himself. More often, though, his haunting thought was his mistake in trusting Tian Wang-yu and the thought that he and Yuan Da-siang had not maintained vigilance on Tian and his followers.

As rumors of the manhunt intensified, Wei thought that he had better get out of the province and head farther south to Nanking or Soochow. To avoid detection, he shunned public transportation and opted to travel on foot. Unable to walk for long because of his obesity and weakened physical condition, he had to find means to cover the long distance ahead of him. As a last resort, he grudgingly parted with some of his silver and bought an old donkey from a poor farmer and rode it toward the south. On his way to the next province, he took circuitous routes to bypass towns with dense population. Even though he was traveling in plain clothes, Wei was fearful that he would arouse attention. After more than ten days on the road, his donkey succumbed from the lack of food. Walking again, Wei landed in another hamlet and found an empty, rundown house where he settled in for more than ten days.

Wei Chung-yan knew that constant running was not a permanent solution. He'd have to find a place to settle down and work if he were to survive. So, again, he proceeded farther south. After a difficult journey lasting over two months, hitching rides on small boats and beating the mountain paths, he finally landed in the Yangtze Valley. He thought again of settling in Nanking or Soochow, but he chose not to because he knew many displaced officials from Peking had nestled in those two cities. Some might be his former associates, and some might be his erstwhile enemies. For sure, someone would recognize him.

After more than six months his bag of silver was dwindling, as were his body and spirit. For someone who had been used to an easy and comfortable life, Wei Chung-yan finally found himself at the end of his rope. Another month had gone by, and with no end to his suffering in sight, Wei Chung-yan chose an easy way out of his misery. One quiet and lonely evening, he hanged himself on a small tree behind the broken house where he had lived, ending his once-glorious life unceremoniously, by his own hand.

Back in Peking, Emperor Chung-chen was grateful for Tian Wang-yu's efforts in taking down Wei Chung-yan and his network. He rewarded the old minister lavishly: promoted him to the first rank and gave him a posh mansion and a large cache of gold. With the ouster of Wei and the Eastern Factory, Tian Wang-yu basked in glory and grew in stature. He quickly filled the vacuum by becoming the most powerful minister in Chung-chen's court.

Over the next few years, the emperor was liberated, able to keep his court temporarily in order. He worked diligently and insisted that his officials do the same. As time passed, though, he found it more difficult to run his court because the treasury was under severe strain. Famine and natural disasters in most provinces in China had taken their toll on tax collection. Waste and the corruption of officials throughout the land had begun to rear their ugly heads, which contributed heavily to the financial woes of the country. Even Tian Wang-yu, once a staunchly upright minister, had turned greedy and dishonest. His advanced age did not deter him from indulging in excess carnal activities as he inducted many young women into his opulent mansion. To add to his stature and influence in the court, he had his daughter brought into the emperor's palace to become his new consort.

As the court and the empire were spinning out of his control, Emperor Chung-chen gradually adopted a laissez-faire attitude, much like his father and brother had under similar conditions. In reality, even if he had wanted to right the ship, onrushing events, both external and internal, were out of his control. In short, his empire was doomed.

CHAPTER 4
The Singer

WHILE PEKING WAS IN A CONSTANT STATE OF TURMOIL, LIFE had become worse for many impoverished families in China. The family of Yuan-yuan in Soochow was no exception.

One winter, Yuan-yuan's father, the old salesman, was struck down with a virus. Ill for many months, he was unable to tend to his selling. Finally, the sickness got worse, and he died. The old salesman's passing put the family on the brink of starvation. Desperate, Yuan-yuan's mother turned to her only relative, a brother named Chen Wan, for help. She visited the brother, who also lived in Soochow, and begged to move her family in with him. Chen Wan and his family of five were also living on the edge of poverty, so it was difficult for him to take on his sister and her two children. But, after much pleading by her, the brother accepted her family into his small home.

Life under the roof of the Chen household was grim. Food was at a minimum, and there was no relief in sight. Chen Wan was a carpenter, but work was hard to find. After eking by for a few months, the widow approached her brother and offered to move out to help ease his burden. Not knowing how she could take care of the family going forward, she pleaded to the brother to let her daughter stay with him. Since there was no other option open to them, Chen Wan agreed. At the tearful parting, Yuan-yuan would see her mother and brother for the last time.

Life continued to be difficult for the family, but Chen Wan was pleased to have Yuan-yuan stay on because he had discovered that they shared a mutual interest: music. The uncle, like her father, was uneducated but loved to sing. In their spare time, which they had a lot of, Chen Wan practiced singing with his niece or took her to watch shows in town. They got along so well that he decided to adopt her as a daughter and bestowed on her his surname. Thus, she became known as Chen Yuan-yuan.

Chen Wan had worked for a man who happened to own an opera house in Soochow. The opera house was a popular gathering place for professional singers and those who wanted to be. Chen Wan and the owner drank and sang together for many years and had become good friends. One afternoon, after watching a free show with Yuan-yuan in the opera house, Chen Wan introduced her to the owner. The owner was taken by Yuan-yuan's good looks, and so he beckoned her to sing with some of his pupils. After hearing Yuan-yuan sing, he was completely captivated by her beauty and talent. Thereafter, he opened his door widely and frequently for his good friend and Yuan-yuan.

Within a year spent in the Chen household, tragedy struck Yuan-yuan again. Unable to find work, Chen Wan began to accumulate debts and had a difficult time providing for the family. He tried to struggle on, but things quickly reached a breaking point. With no relief in sight, Chen Wan approached the opera house owner, trying to find a solution to his plight. The owner jumped on the opportunity and offered to take Yuan-yuan in, paying a price of ten ounces of gold to his friend. At first, Chen Wan resisted the temptation, but after enduring more economic hardship, he reluctantly accepted the offer. Even though she had wanted to be an actress or a singer, Yuan-yuan objected when the uncle approached her about the deal. Thinking that the uncle had betrayed her mother's trust, she refused to leave. However, after much soul searching, she decided that since the uncle had made the deal, she could not alter the fait accompli. So, tearfully, she packed her few belongings and left the uncle's house. Holding her head high, she walked to the opera house without looking back.

The opera house owner was delighted over getting Yuan-yuan. More importantly, he knew that he could turn the deal into a most profitable one. He put Yuan-yuan through a strict program of voice and acting training. She resented the hard work, but, realizing this could be her only chance to be free from bondage, she went through the daily routine without complaint. At first the opera house owner worked her into the nightly programs as a standby performer. Even in that role, Yuan-yuan began to attract a following. It did not take long for her opportunity to arrive.

One evening the leading actress was ill, so the owner called on Yuan-yuan to take over her role. He knew Yuan-yuan had the ability to perform, but he was uncertain whether she was ready to step up on the stage in front of a packed audience. But he had no other options. When the name Chen Yuan-yuan was announced, the audience reacted unenthusiastically; they had come to see the star actress, not a replacement. The owner was on pins and needles; he had too much at stake and did not want to disappoint the customers.

The curtain opened. The lights shone on the eighteen-year-old acting novice. To the delight and surprise of the audience, the new actress was beautiful to behold. To most, she had more stage presence than the actress she had replaced. As the music began, Yuan-yuan spun out the most pleasing and melodic tunes, which completely captivated the audience. At the end of the last act, the whole audience stood and applauded, demanding an encore. Yuan-yuan complied, and the demand began once more. The show finally ended after three encores.

Yuan-yuan was exhausted, but this was her personal triumph at last. Thereafter, Yuan-yuan became the star performer by popular demand. The opera house owner was on cloud nine, and he thanked heaven for bestowing upon him a fortune called Chen Yuan-yuan.

But disaster was soon to strike again. Unbeknownst to the opera house owner, in the audience on the night of Yuan-yuan's debut were two prominent rival gang leaders, one from Nanking and one from Soochow. The owner and most of the residents of Soochow had known or heard of these thugs, but none would foresee what was to come for the opera house owner, and, more importantly, for Yuan-yuan.

Ma Yi was a thirty-two-year-old who had spent most of his adult life gambling, drinking, and womanizing. A hunk of a man with a hairy face, he appeared intimidating to most people and made a living by scamming and extorting them. His base of operation was in Soochow, where he controlled an organization of more than two hundred thugs.

"Hey, Big Brother," yelled one of the thugs who was sitting around a table with Ma and five others in a teahouse in the heart of Soochow. "Do you know that there is a beautiful new actress in town?" Ma Yi was commonly addressed as Big Brother by his associates, a title of respect usually reserved for the head of a gang.

"Of course I know," barked Ma Yi. "I was there when she debuted the other night."

"What do you think of her?" asked another thug.

"What? Her acting?" said Ma Yi.

"Of course not ... her body!" the first thug said, chuckling loudly.

"How in hell do I know? I have not gotten close enough to feel her out yet!" Ma said, moving his hands in an obscene manner.

"Have you gone back to see her? I mean up close?" the second thug teased.

"Seriously, Big Brother, I heard rumors that Wang Kuang is showing up frequently in the theater lately," a third thug said after packing his belly full with two bowls of rice porridge. Then he let out a loud burp.

Big Brother suddenly perked up and thundered, "What the hell is he doing here?"

"My source told me that he visited with the actress backstage after the show the other night," the third thug continued.

"I thought I saw that son of a bitch the night the actress did her first performance. Did any of you see him?" Big Brother said, and he glanced around the table. No one responded. "Go check him out." Big Brother pointed at two thugs sitting closest to him. "Find out if that son of a bitch is camping out at Soochow. If so, where in hell is he staying?"

"Okay, Big Brother," said the two thugs, who then left hurriedly.

"Let's get out of here," yelled Big Brother. "We've got a job to do on the other side of the canal." He threw some coins on the table and pushed his cohort out of the teahouse before him.

Wang Kuang's base of operation was in Nanking, even though he was born and raised and lived in Peking, where his father was a high court official. An antithesis of Ma Yi in looks, he was rather clean-cut and good-looking. He, too, like Ma Yi, resorted to extortion for a living. In reality, he did it more for fun than for basic needs.

He was in his midtwenties and educated, and he could have made it as a successful bureaucrat or a businessman. Instead, he professed that he found more fun and satisfaction in pursuing a life in the lower rungs of society. When he was a teenager, he'd spend his after-school hours indulging in petty theft, visiting houses of ill-repute, and gambling with money he had stolen from others.

He was in attendance the night Yuan-yuan made her debut. Like Ma Yi and many others in the audience, he was beguiled by the beauty of the new actress. From that evening on, he vowed he would not stop until he had gained possession of her.

As it turned out, Ma Yi was a step ahead of him. After a performance one evening, Ma Yi went backstage and confronted the opera house owner, demanding to see the actress. The owner knew that Ma Yi was not one to be denied, so he hesitantly brought Yuan-yuan out to meet him. Upon seeing the actress up close, Ma Yi salivated and could not contain his lust for her. He grabbed the woman and dragged her away. With the help of two thugs, he hustled her into a waiting sedan. The opera house owner was helpless. Yuan-yuan tried to resist, but she was subdued by brute force. She tearfully pleaded her case with Ma Yi, but he imposed his thick lips on her mouth, nearly suffocating her. As they both struggled in the sedan, the horse galloped full speed ahead. From that night on, Ma Yi would personally escort Yuan-yuan to the theater to perform, and at the end of each performance he brought her back to his residence.

When Wang Kuang learned that the woman he coveted had been abducted by Ma Yi, he blew his stack. "You imbeciles! Why didn't you tell me that asshole stole my woman?" He vented his displeasure on his two closest assistants, who sat with him eating lunch at an opulent restaurant in the center of Nanking.

"Well, sir ..." One of the assistants nearly choked on his

mouthful of food, trying to answer his master, "I told you a few days ago, and you—"

"You fool," yelled Wang Kuang. "You didn't tell me it was Yuan-yuan who was taken by that son of a bitch!"

"Sir," volunteered the other assistant, trying to defend his friend, "you were quite drunk when we told you. As a matter of fact, you pushed us aside and said that you were busy laying a woman."

"Stupid man—you should have pulled me aside and told me." Wang Kuang yelled so loudly that he attracted the unwanted attention of many patrons in the restaurant.

"But, sir," the first assistant said, "you and the woman were naked in bed, and you were fucking her. We were afraid to disturb you, but ..." His voice was so loud that it aroused more people.

"You know I am not taking a backseat to anyone when it comes to owning a beautiful woman, especially that one!" Wang Kuang's tirade was not to be stopped. "I don't give a shit if it's the emperor or Ma Yi!"

The owner of the restaurant finally heard the commotion. He came over to the table and tried to calm things down. "Master Wang, what seems to be the trouble? Is the food not to your liking?"

"Take the damned food away," Wang Kuang yelled, and in one motion, he swept all the dishes from the table. Broken porcelain and food scraps flew, provoking an ugly scene in the dining area.

The owner was upset, but he knew better than to show his irritation. So he swallowed hard and waved some waiters over to clean up the mess. "Sir, is there anything else I can do for you?"

"Get the hell out of my face!" Wang Kuang stood up, pushed the owner aside, and stormed out of the restaurant, his assistants chasing after him.

The owner shook his head dejectedly. Not only had he suffered a humiliation in front of his customers, he'd also lost the cost of the food eaten by the thugs.

While Ma Yi continued to drown in the joy of his prey, Wang Kuang endured sleepless nights trying to devise a plan to steal the actress.

One morning, having porridge for breakfast with his close assistants, Wang Kuang again took his displeasure out on them. "Can't you boneheads come up with a solution to help me?"

"Well," mumbled one of the companions around a mouthful, "why don't you offer five hundred ounces of gold to him and see if he will let you have the woman?" He chuckled and at the same time tried to swallow the food.

"I don't find it very funny!" barked Wang Kuang. He slapped the assistant across his face, and he nearly choked.

"Sir," the other assistant muttered, "let's kill that son of a bitch at sundown. I know just the person to do it for us."

Wang Kuang perked up; the idea of killing Ma Yi might be the best solution. But, on second thought, there was no assurance that would guarantee his getting the woman.

The three men paused for a prolonged moment while they consumed the food on the table. While the other men were busy picking and cleaning their teeth, Wang Kuang suddenly cried, "I have an idea! Let's go to Soochow tonight for the last show."

They left the restaurant quickly. Wang Kuang scattered some coins on the table. This time he paid for his food.

The boat ride on the Yangtze River took almost a day, and Wang Kuang and his band of twenty men arrived at Soochow barely in time for the last performance. Wang Kuang and two of his men were in the audience to take in the show, and the others waited outside for his order.

One of the men elbowed Wang Kuang and swayed his head to

the right. Wang Kuang moved his gaze to the right and saw Ma
Yi sitting in the front row. With him was one other thug. As the
last act approached, one of Wang Kuang's men rose and left the
auditorium. He went outside to gather his gang and found most
of them sleeping on a knoll nearby. He roused them, and they all
headed toward the back of the theater with him.

The show ended with Yuan-yuan making her final curtain call.
Ma Yi jumped off his seat and dashed toward the backstage. When
he tried to enter, the door was bolted tight, which was unusual. He
normally gained easy entry. While he tried to shake the door open,
Wang Kuang found his way backstage to join his men.

"Get the woman!" Ma Yi heard a voice yelling from inside
the room.

"Go out the backstage door!" another voice blurted.

"Quickly, quickly!" Some sounds of pushing and shuffling
ensued.

When Ma Yi heard the commotions, he knew that something
very bad was taking place inside the locked room, but he was
helpless. He pushed one of his thugs and pointed toward the exit
to their right. The thug nodded and rushed out quickly. Outside,
he went directly toward his gang, hanging out in a shack across
from the theater, and led them to the backstage area. Wang Kuang
and a few of his men were pulling Yuan-yuan out of her dressing
room toward the door. The opera house owner tried to stop them,
but he was too old and weak and could not fend off the onrushing crowd. When he heard the charge of the Ma gang heading
backstage, he found a table and ducked under it for protection,
peeking out curiously. He was very interested in the outcome of
the upcoming battle.

When the two gangs met, it was indeed holy terror. Wang
Kuang was trying to escape from the scene, but he found it difficult
with Yuan-yuan in tow. Soon Ma Yi found his way circuitously to

the backstage and landed squarely in front of Wang Kuang. With no choice but to slug his way out, Wang Kuang let go of Yuan-yuan and took on Ma Yi in a fist fight. Ma Yi was a larger and stronger man than Wang Kuang, and as the fight went on, it was clear that Ma Yi was gaining the upper hand. Nearby, trapped in the corner observing, was Yuan-yuan. When she noticed that Ma Yi was about to land a mortal blow on Wang Kuang, she picked up a club lying on the floor and swung it at Ma Yi with all the force she could muster. The blow hit Ma Yi in the back of his neck, and he fell forward, stunned. Even though she did not know or like Wang Kuang, she hated Ma Yi more for all the sexual abuse that he had inflicted on her. Given a reprieve, Wang Kuang quickly gathered himself, pushed through the crowd, and pulled Yuan-yuan out the back door with him. Once outside, he jumped on a waiting horse with her and galloped away.

The melee came to an end when the men saw their masters, one lying flat on the floor and the other fleeing the premises. A few of the Ma thugs stayed behind and tended to their fallen leader, while the others fled into the darkness.

Wang Kuang found a small hostel in the outskirts of Soochow for the night. He chose to stay in a seedy neighborhood to avoid detection, even though the accommodation was not up to the standards he was accustomed to. Yuan-yuan was tired and wanted to sleep, but her captor could not contain his lust; he forcefully undressed her and sexually molested her throughout the night. While Wang Kuang continued the foray, Yuan-yuan could only lie in bed; she swallowed her tears and took the abuse. Barely eighteen years old, Yuan-yuan had already endured the ravages heaped on her by two lecherous thugs.

The sun finally rose. Wang Kuang promptly took Yuan-yuan with him to a nearby dock. Waiting there for them were ten men with a boat. Once Wang Kuang and Yuan-yuan had boarded, the

CHAPTER 5

The False Prince

BACK IN THE THEATER, MA YI OPENED HIS EYES AND SAW FOUR or five of his men hovering over him. He tried to lift his body, but pain overwhelmed him, so he fell on his back again.

"Where is my woman?" he yelled.

One of the men responded, "Wang Kuang took her away!"

"That son of a bitch!" barked Ma Yi. "Help me up ... hurry!"

Two of the men pulled Ma Yi up and placed him on a chair.

"You!" Ma Yi pointed at the opera house owner, who was standing near the exit to the backstage area.

The owner meandered over and bowed to Ma Yi. "Can I get you a cup of tea, sir?"

"You get my woman back, you hear?" yelled Ma Yi.

"Sir, I am not responsible for her disappearance. I am just as ... eager to get her back as you are. I need her to perform tomorrow!"

"I don't care if she is going to perform again or not. I just want her back with me!" Ma Yi yelled louder.

The owner could not reason with Ma Yi, so he stood by quietly, waiting for the ax to fall.

"Well, don't stand there—do something!" Ma Yi tried to get at the owner.

The owner thought that this would be a good time to escape from the raging gangster while he was still disabled, so he turned and left, saying, "I will see what I can do, sir!"

Ma Yi gathered himself and appeared to sink into deep thoughts. Within a few moments, he jumped up and demanded, "Get a boat! I have got to go to Nanking."

"Big Brother, it's too late to leave now," said one of the men. "Let's get some food and a good night's sleep and go tomorrow. Besides, you've got to rest!"

After much prodding, Ma Yi grudgingly agreed. The men asked the owner to provide a bed for Ma Yi, and after some snacks they scattered around the floor and slumbered away.

The next morning, Ma Yi took ten men and departed the theater hastily. They boarded a boat on the Yangtze and headed west for Nanking. Upon arriving, Ma Yi and his men made a beeline for Wang Kuang's mansion. They forced their way in, even though they were blocked by two guards in front of the house.

Ma Yi pushed the guards away and yelled at the top of his voice, "Wang Kuang, you son of a bitch, you can't hide from me." No one responded, so Ma issued the order: "Search this damned house." Except for one man who stayed with Ma Yi in the foyer, the others rushed inside to look for Wang Kuang and Yuan-yuan. Moments later, they reappeared with ten young women and five manservants.

Ma Yi took a quick glance at the group and barked, "Where is my woman? Where is the son of a bitch Wang Kuang?"

"Big Brother, there was no one else inside except this bunch!"

"You." Ma Yi pointed at one of the young women, the one with the prettiest face and the best-looking dress. "What is your name?"

"I am Orchid, the number one mistress of this household!"

"Number one, huh? Where is your number one master?"

"Master Wang is not here. I have not seen him for more than ten days."

"Do you know where I can find him?"

"I do not know where he is. It is not my place to know!"

"Who's number two here?"

Number one pointed over to another pretty lady standing behind her and said, "She is number two. Her name is Peony."

"Orchid, Peony—I suppose there is a Rose here too." Big Brother let out a robust laugh.

"I am Rose," volunteered one of the other ladies.

"Really?" Ma Yi looked over to where the voice had come from and saw another pretty face. He began to wonder how Wang Kuang could have used so many pretty young women. With all these beauties at his disposal, why did he insist on taking Yuanyuan? Ma Yi mumbled to himself. He turned his thoughts back to the problem at hand and barked, "If you don't tell me where he is, you will pay a dear price for that." He issued a threat, hoping to coax an answer from someone. Hearing no response, he grabbed a sword out of the hand of one of his men and swung it wildly to show his seriousness. The servants and the women were all frightened, and some quickly hid behind furniture for cover.

"Where are the money and the jewels?" demanded Ma Yi.

No one dared speak.

Ma Yi became agitated. He grabbed Orchid by her waist and pulled her out of the foyer into the main chamber. While doing so, he waved his gang along, and they went inside the other chambers in the back of the mansion. Some dragged the women along with them. The manservants took the opportunity to escape from the scene. Ma Yi and his gang raped the women, ransacked the mansion, and merrily left with the loot.

Ma Yi jumped onto his horse and went in one direction with

an escort. His gang went in another direction in two horse-drawn wagons loaded full of treasures. Even though he'd had the satisfaction of ransacking his enemy's house and abusing his women, Ma Yi was upset about not finding Wang Kuang and his woman. Unhappy, he wasted no time and headed straight to the famous House of Soong in an upscale district in Nanking.

As they arrived at the house, a guard by the front entrance greeted him with a wide smile. "Big Brother, what wind blows you here?"

"Brother, is the prince in?" Ma Yi said, returning a faint smile and reaching for the guard's hand.

The guard shook Ma Yi's hand, pleased that Big Brother had taken care of him. "Sorry, Big Brother, my master is out," the guard said.

"Where did he go?"

It was normal protocol that the guard was not allowed to divulge the whereabouts of his master. Since Ma Yi had greased his palm, the guard whispered into his ear. Besides, he knew that Ma Yi and his master were good friends.

"Thanks, brother!" Ma Yi said, jumping back onto his horse, and he galloped off with his man.

Prince Soong was not a genuine prince. He hated the name that was given to him, so he chose to be called Prince—a name more befitting to his ego and his whim.

Prince Soong's father had been appointed by the emperor to the post of tax minister for the rich Yangtze River delta area, which included Nanking, Soochow, Hangchow, and Kaifeng, to name a few of the major townships in that district. It was a reward for the senior Soong's efforts in helping to bring down the Eastern Factory and Wei Chung-yan. The fact that the senior Soong was a close friend of Tian Wang-yu greatly facilitated his rise in the new order of the court.

The prince had grown up in a well-to-do environment and was more educated than most of his contemporaries, but he still loathed books and chose to indulge in the life of a playboy instead. When he was younger, he'd spent a lot of his time traveling with his father on his business trips.

When he was with his father on a tax-collecting mission, he would say, "Father, when I grow up, I want to be like you and collect a lot of money!"

"My son, the money belongs to the emperor. We are only collecting it for him."

"Father, I know the money belongs to the emperor, but I saw that a lot of it stayed in our vault in the house, not sent to Peking."

"Quiet!" The old man put his right palm over the son's mouth. He then pulled him aside and chastised him. "You are too young to understand. Do not speak like that anymore." Upon arriving at their destination, the senior Soong led a squad of men to a rather opulent house in town, the little boy trailing along.

The owner of the house was a wealthy landowner in Kaifeng. He leased his land to local farmers who not only paid him rent but also the taxes that were levied by Peking and the provincial government. The taxes were then turned over to the imperial tax collector: in this case, Minister Soong. Taxes were payable to the imperial collector quarterly, but the Kaifeng landowner was late in his payment. Minister Soong took the case personally due to the large sum involved and also because he had a large vested interest in it.

"Hon, you've got to get on top of your debts," Minister Soong admonished his good friend as soon as they met. "You have been habitually late with your payments, and I cannot cover for you much longer."

"Minister, I am good for my money. You know that!" Hon Wun chose to address his good friend in a formal manner to hide their dubious relationship in front of others.

"Peking is pressing me for more and quicker collection because the government is in dire financial troubles."

"I know, but my tenants are having financial troubles of their own. Their crops are failing, and as a result their income suffered." Hon Wun was telling the truth, even though he was also trying to dodge the pressure from his good friend.

"Regardless, you are more than three quarters behind," Minister Soong retorted.

Hon Wun tried to find an excuse and deflect attention from his problem. "I heard that the situation in the south is far worse than here. The droughts down there have wreaked havoc with harvesting. I bet you that their tax delinquencies are far worse than mine."

"Hon, I understand. But that's their problem! I have to answer to the tax minister in Peking. He is riding me pretty hard lately."

Hon Wun pulled his friend aside and whispered, "I scratched your back, and you've got to scratch mine!"

The minister blushed. When the son overheard Hon Wun's comment, he lowered his head as though he were ashamed of his father's enterprising behavior. But if not for the father's enterprising behavior, he would not be living the good life that he had come to enjoy so greatly.

"Hon, if Peking gets wind of what we have been doing, we will both be in deep trouble!" Minister Soong shot back. "For that reason, we've got to come up with some money from your end. I have to make the revenue report in our province look better so that we can keep Peking off our backs!"

The landowner thought of a compromise. "Can you live with a smaller cut for the last three quarters?"

The minister was taken aback by the proposal, so he hesitated.

If he did not take a reduced rebate, the revenue reports he must submit to his superiors would look very bad, the minister rationalized. That would reflect on his efficiency as the provincial tax minister. If he took a cut, it would squeeze his personal situation. The minister thought before he finally spoke. "What is a small cut?

"Well ..." Hon Wun suddenly found it hard to come up with a precise amount or percentage. "Our usual holdback is 20 percent each. Would 10 percent be workable for you?"

"Er ... are you willing to take the same cut?"

Hon Wun did not expect that from the minister. He pondered the question and countered, "I will go with 15 percent, and you will temporarily take 10."

"Hon, be honest. That's not fair!"

"Minister, I am the one who has to work very hard to collect the revenue from the suffering farmers. Most of the time, I have to resort to force to get the money. God knows I was nearly killed the last time I confronted one of them!"

Hon Wun's response struck a chord in the minister's mind. It was true that the hard work was done by the one who had to face the taxpayers. But then he rationalized that without him covering for them, the landowners would have a difficult time dealing with Peking.

"Hon, we've got to settle the score here and now. Peking is expecting some revenue from us in quick order," the minister said, trying to find a middle-ground solution. "If I were to take ten for the last quarter only, would it work for you?"

So the bargaining went on, the minister finally accepting a 10 percent cut for the last quarter and Hon Wun a 5 percent reduction. It was indeed sad that these types of corruption were rampant in provinces throughout China while the national treasury was teetering on the brink of bankruptcy.

Prince Soong observed the transaction between his father and his friend with keen interest, even though he was only a teenager. By the time he was an adult, he had become a successful schemer in his own right, plying his trade using methods learned from his father.

The day when Ma Yi came calling at his residence, the prince was out enjoying a warm spring afternoon with three of his good friends in the busy market of Nanking.

While Peking was wallowing in the throes of economic depression and in fear of enemy attacks from the north and south, Nanking became the paradise for the wealthy, the displaced politicos, and the men of letters. These middle-aged men spent a significant amount of their daytime drinking and wailing about current events and their misfortunes. At night, they cruised along the infamous Chin-hwai River to sing, listen to music, or sink into the arms of hired women.

Prince Soong frequented teahouses and saloons in the daytime and brothels at night. He especially favored a brothel called the Greenhouse on the east shore of the Chin-hwai River. His favorite girl plied her trade in that brothel.

One evening, while they lay in bed enjoying a beautiful moonlit evening and listening to some soft music filtering through the window from across the other shore, the girl nudged the prince and said, "Honey, we have been together for many months now. Do you still find me desirable?"

Prince Soong mumbled casually, "Of course I do!" He was somewhat intoxicated after downing a few glasses of fine wine. "You are young and beautiful." He kissed her on the cheek and fondled her breasts. A moment later, he suddenly perked up and asked, "Why are you asking such inane questions?"

"Your reputation precedes you. I heard rumors that you like

beautiful women and that you like to play with many of them at the same time."

The prince was caught off guard by the girl's comment. He murmured, "Er … that must have come from people who are jealous of me."

"Hey! I heard there is a woman who is supposed to be the most beautiful in Soochow," the girl said teasingly. "Some say she is the most beautiful woman in China."

"Really?"

"Are you interested in seeing her?"

"If you are not jealous, I'd like to see her and judge her beauty personally." The prince smiled. "Who is she?"

"She is an actress in a Soochow opera house. I heard a fight broke out between two gang leaders over her recently."

"Wow! She must really be very beautiful." The prince was wondering if one of the gang leaders was his good friend Ma Yi. If Ma was indeed involved in the fight, then the woman must truly be a beauty, the prince thought. "I'd like to see her," he said again.

"I should not have told you about her," the girl protested gently, regretting that her lover might soon leave her in pursuit of the actress.

True to her prediction, the prince rose early the next morning and left on his new mission. Traveling down the river to land at his favorite teahouse, he hoped to find two close friends there who could shed more light on the gang fight over the actress.

He entered the teahouse, and before he could scan the whole scene in front of him a voice called out from his left. "Hey, Prince!" He looked over and moved in the direction of the voice. The voice said, "Sit here." A man pointed at a seat across the table from where he was sitting. He had located the two friends he was looking for, former officials who had worked for his father while he was in Peking.

The prince obliged.

"Hou, you've got to help me." The prince sounded urgent as he nudged the first friend.

Hou ignored the prince's remark and asked, "Hey, how is your love life these days?"

He poured some wine into an empty cup and handed it to the prince. "Let's drink to the good times!"

"Hear, hear!" echoed Lin, the second friend, who was also holding up his cup.

Prince Soong's heart was not into drinking. He was more interested in learning about the fight between the gang leaders over that beautiful woman. So he picked up his cup and went through the motions of drinking. "Have either one of you heard of a fight over an actress in Soochow recently?"

"You mean you have not heard that yourself?" queried Lin. "Where have you been?"

"I have just been laying low lately," answered the prince. "I guess I have not been keeping up with current events."

"You are probably too busy laying your beautiful lover," chuckled Lin. "The fight over Chen Yuan-yuan is a big news item in Soochow, and in Nanking."

"Tell me more about it," urged the prince. "Who is Chen Yuan-yuan? Is she really as beautiful as everyone says she is?"

Prince Soong knew that his two good friends were the best sources for up-to-the-minute news because his own father had relied on them as his eyes and ears in Peking. They were once members of the East Forest Institute that opposed Wei Chung-yan. Membership in the East Forest Institute was exclusive: the group consisted mainly of higher-ranking officials and their offspring and scholars who had passed the highest levels of the civil examinations. Hou and Lin were among these exceptional scholars. When Chief Wei made his preemptive strike to take down the East Forest Institute, most of its members were executed; some were fortunate enough to have escaped the purge. Hou and Lin were among the fortunate few. They'd escaped incognito and quietly settled in Nanking.

Hou hurriedly downed the wine in his cup, wiped his lips, and proceeded to relate the Ma-Wang episode over the possession of Chen Yuan-yuan. When he finished telling the story, he shook his head and said, "In the end, no one will win. There is an old saying. 'A beautiful woman is like troubled water!' Brother, I suggest that you stay away from Yuan-yuan. Nothing good will come of that!" He refilled his cup, raised it, and said, "Let's drink to the good life! And good friendship!"

The prince continued to probe for the whereabouts of Yuan-yuan, and Lin and Hou tried to divert him from the subject. While they were carrying on their disjointed conversation, a loud voice interrupted them.

"Hey, is this empty seat for this old man?" An elderly man who had walked slowly into the teahouse approached.

"Master Soo." The prince looked up. "What a surprise!"

"I've been looking high and low for you, Prince. So you are hiding here." Soo mumbled the words because of a denture problem. He promptly sat on the empty chair.

"I was looking for you yesterday, but your servant said you went to Soochow," Hou said, pouring some wine for the old man. "What were you doing there?"

"That son of a bitch Yuan Da-siang is giving me trouble again," said Master Soo.

"We all had troubles with him," claimed Hou. "What's so special about you?"

"I want to hunt him down and settle the score with him, once and for all," said the old man.

"What kind of trouble is he giving you now?" asked the prince.

"I have many friends and former associates living in Nanking.

That son of a bitch is hunting them down and using strong-arm tactics to extort them," the old master responded.

It appeared that after his escape from the purge of the emperor, Yuan had also settled in Nanking. Over time, as the danger of retribution subsided, he'd resurfaced in Nanking high society, after changing his appearance and name. He had become prosperous by extorting the middle-class citizens and merchants there.

Soo and Yuan shared a mutual hatred. Not only had they belonged to opposite ends of the political spectrum during their days in Peking, but their moral characters were polar opposites. For many years, Soo had tried to foil Yuan's profiteering in Nanking, but he'd failed, though he persisted as a thorn on his enemy's side. Not to be denied, Yuan decided on a counteroffensive and engaged a local gang to harass the old master. Yuan's attempts had failed because Soo was equally as cunning as his rival.

"Do you think he is hiding from you, Master Soo?" asked the prince.

Soo was widely known as "master" because he was both a calisthenics expert and a musician. He taught classes in both disciplines for the upper-class citizens in Nanking. Even though he was over sixty years of age, he was fit as a fiddle. Yuan, also over sixty, was a physical specimen in his own right.

"Prince, I want to ask a favor of you." Master Soo turned to the prince.

"Master, anything—I am at your disposal," Prince Soong said courteously.

"You and Ma Yi are good friends, aren't you?" the old master asked.

The prince was surprised that Soo knew that he and Ma Yi were friends. Why did the master want to see Ma Yi? the prince wondered. After a brief pause, the prince said softly, "Yes, but I have little to do with him lately."

Master Soo came directly to the point. "I would like to see him."

"To be frank with you, I have not seen him for many months." the prince offered. "As a matter of fact, I wouldn't mind seeing him myself."

Wonders never ceased. As his name was being tossed about, Ma Yi barged onto the scene. "Prince, I am hunting all over for you!" Ma Yi yelled breathlessly once he spotted the prince in the crowd. "I am glad I've found you!"

"Well, Master, here is your man, speaking of the devil!" said the prince jokingly. He was more than surprised and glad to see Ma standing in front of him.

Master Soo was completely befuddled. He looked at Ma Yi and then turned back to the prince. "Are you going to introduce me to Mr. Ma?"

Ma was equally befuddled. He turned and looked at the old master and said to the prince, "I really need your help quickly!"

"Well, let me introduce you to Master Soo," he said, pointing to the old master. "This is Ma Yi, the man you were asking about." He then pointed at Ma Yi.

The two men bowed to each other.

Since the focus of the gathering had turned to more serious business, Hou and Lin thought it was time for them to take leave. They stood up, and Hou said, "Gentlemen, we beg to be excused. We have some business to take care of in town."

The prince nodded and said with a smile, "Good day! I will call on you in a few days."

The men all stood and bowed to one another.

"Nice to meet you, Mr. Ma," Lin said, nudging Hou away. They did not have any business to conduct, so they leisurely meandered toward the Chin-hwai River to indulge in more of the so-called good life.

Back in the teahouse, the three remaining men sat back down

and started to address the matters at hand. The prince opened by asking Soo why he wanted to see Ma Yi. Before Soo could answer, Ma Yi blurted, "Prince, I must talk to you about my problem—alone."

"Well, Big Brother, I understand," Prince Soong muttered uncomfortably, "but Master Soo has an urgent matter he wants to consult you about."

"All right, let's get with it," Ma Yi said, revealing his lack of sophistication in human relations and self-control.

"Mr. Ma, your reputation is sterling in some circles in Nanking," said Soo, smiling, in the understatement of the century. "I have a job that I believe only you can do for me."

Ma Yi felt flattered. He blurted, "A job?"

"I want you to take someone down," said the master bluntly.

Ma Yi was not surprised at the request; he was only curious as to whom the target might be.

"Who might that someone be?" asked Ma Yi impatiently.

"Yuan Da-siang!" the old master said very softly, for fear of being overheard by others in the teahouse.

A loud yell came out of Ma Yi's mouth. "W-h-a-t?"

"Yes, Yuan Da-siang!" Soo reiterated resolutely, still in a very soft tone.

Ma Yi was speechless, as was Prince Soong.

"When ... will ... it ... be?" asked Ma Yi slowly.

"As soon as possible," the old master answered, putting his right hand up to his mouth to muffle his voice.

Ma Yi knew of Yuan Da-siang's reputation through the underworld channels. For more than ten years, Yuan had built an infrastructure in Nanking that was unrivaled by anyone, even his formidable archrival Wang Kuang.

"I have a plan." Soo turned to Ma and whispered at length into his left ear. The prince was curious, but he did not see fit to pry.

"Well, do you know where he is now?" Ma Yi inquired.

"I have not seen or heard of him for quite a while," said Soo. "Why don't you come to my house tomorrow morning, and we will talk more about the details of the plan." He stood and bowed slightly to both young men. He left with these parting words: "Keep our conversation to yourselves. The prince will give you directions to my home." He left, taking huge strides.

Ma Yi turned to his friend. "Prince, you have handed me a very hot potato! You are really a good friend."

"I did not recommend you for the job. He came asking for you. If you don't believe me, ask my friends who were here with me the next time you see them."

"Never mind! Do you know how much he is willing to pay for the job?"

"You are asking me?"

"He left in a huff. I did not have a chance to ask him."

"Well, did he not mention the price when he whispered to you?"

"No! No mention of money!"

"Incidentally, what did he whisper to you?"

"Something about a plan."

"What is the plan?"

"Search me! I have no idea!"

"You are really funny. You have accepted a job, a big job, and you don't know what he was telling you?"

"I guess I will find out tomorrow." Ma Yi shrugged. "Prince, I need your help badly!"

"Now it's my turn?"

"Tell me where in hell is Wang Kuang?"

"How in hell do I know! He was in Soochow like you, wasn't he?"

"His home is here in Nanking. I went there and could not find him."

"What do you want him for?"

"That son of a bitch stole my woman!"

"What?"

"He stole my woman, I said!"

"So … go get another one. What's the big deal about that? There are plenty of pretty young women in the Chin-hwai River area."

"I don't want those bitches! I want her!"

"Who's 'her'?" The prince already knew who she was, and he put on an act to hide his own desire for the same woman.

"Chen Yuan-yuan!"

"Chen Yuan-yuan is your … woman?"

"Yes!"

"Since when?" The prince continued to act dumb.

"I had her for over a year. And now that Wang Kuang son of a bitch stole her from me, in broad daylight."

"That's funny! A tough guy like you cannot take care of a woman? Wang Kuang is a weakling. He is no match for you!!"

"That son of a bitch made a surprise move on me."

"What you want me to do?"

"Prince, I know you have connections in Peking. Wang Kuang's father-in-law, old man Tian Wang-yu, is also the father-in-law of the emperor. I cannot take on that old man by myself!"

"Neither can I. You want Wang Kuang, not Tian Wang-yu!"

"But I am sure that son of a bitch is hiding under Tian's roof. I want you to find out if he is hiding my woman there."

"A rather tall order, I must say."

"Please, Prince! If you help me get my Yuan-yuan back, I will do anything and pay any price you ask."

"All right. I will see what I can do," muttered the prince. "I will sleep on it. Come to my house in the morning, and we will visit with Master Soo together."

The two men went their separate ways.

That evening, lying in bed, the prince thought he should help his friend. First, he must pry the woman away from Wang Kuang. After that, he could deal with Ma Yi instead of having to fight a battle on two fronts. Full of anxiety and anticipation, he went to bed dreaming of the sweet taste of kissing that beautiful woman named Yuan-yuan.

The next morning, Ma Yi met the prince in his mansion, and they went together in a sedan to Soo's house. Soo lived in a modest house, even though he was a man with some wealth. Once inside, they indulged in some porridge and pastries. Between bites, the old master handed an envelope over to Ma. "I want you to follow the plan inside this envelope I have laid out."

"Yes, sir!" said Ma around a mouthful of food. He paused, swallowed, and inquired, "What are you paying me for this job?"

The master was not surprised by the question. He was rather surprised that Ma Yi had posed the question in front of the prince. "Fifty ounces of gold … if the job is a success."

Ma Yi swallowed hard. "What if it is not successful?"

"Then the price you have to pay would be unthinkable!"

The prince darted a quizzical look at Soo and Ma. He uttered not a word.

After the meeting, the two young men rose and bade farewell to the old master.

Soo waved. "Good luck, Mister Ma. I will wait anxiously and hopefully for the good news to come!"

On the return trip to the Soong mansion, Ma Yi nudged the prince, who was dozing, and asked, "Have you decided to help me or not?"

"Yes, I have."

"Well?"

"I will help you. But it will take time."

"How much time?"

"I have to go to Peking and do some digging."

"When are you leaving?"

"Shortly!"

"Prince, I beg of you! Please go quickly. I cannot wait any longer," Ma Yi pleaded.

"Don't worry! I promise you I will take care of matters for you, Big Brother. When will you be doing the job?"

"I will know after I read what's inside this envelope," Ma Yi said, waving the envelope he held.

Soon, the sedan arrived at the Soong residence. The prince got off instructed the driver, "Take Mister Ma to his hostel." He then turned to Ma. "Good day, Big Brother! Good luck! We will be in touch." He walked slowly inside the house.

At his hostel, Ma Yi went inside and ripped open the envelope. He found a large piece of paper showing a map of the location where his "job" was to take place. Ma Yi did not have an education, but he was smart enough to have learned some basic Chinese characters. Using his limited reading skills, he was able to ascertain the date and time of the job and the number of men needed to accomplish it. Without delay, he checked out of the hostel and took the next boat back to Soochow to gather his men and logistics. According to the plan, he was to do it five days later. Soo had gotten a report that his target would be back in Nanking by that time.

Yuan Da-siang's spies had tailed the old master to the teahouse and discovered that he had met up with Prince Soong and Ma Yi. When he got the report of the meeting, Yuan's instincts told him that some plot against him was in the works. So he quickly gathered his brain trust and devised some plans to counter what he knew was an assault on him by the old master. After much debating and planning, the Yuan gang was prepared for action. The only uncertainties were the time and the date of the assault.

On the evening of the fifth day, Ma Yi and a gang of fifty strong mounted a raid on the Yuan residence. They had gotten inside the compound without obstruction, but when they were about to penetrate the mansion, two groups of men stormed out from the bushes. The ambush by Yuan's force of more than a hundred men took the Ma contingent totally by surprise. After a prolonged scrimmage, many of Ma Yi's men were killed, and he was one of the fatalities. The Yuan gang suffered minor casualties because the battle had been fought in their own ground. More importantly, Yuan had a better network of spies, so he was more prepared for battle than the raiders.

The news of the failed foray reached Master Soo. He was saddened by the death of Ma Yi, but he was more disappointed by the loss to his archrival. He moved out of Nanking in a hurry to avoid Yuan's retribution. Thereafter, Master Soo was not heard from or seen in Nanking!

Prince Soong was also saddened by the death of Ma Yi, but secretly he was happy that the first step in his quest for Yuan-yuan had gone his way. He gathered a few men, boarded a luxurious boat, and cruised merrily up the Grand Canal to Peking.

CHAPTER 6
The General

As THE EVENTS SURROUNDING YUAN-YUAN WERE UNFOLDING, the Ming Commandant of the Northeast Garrison was keeping a keen eye on them. The commandant, who had received the title and position from Emperor Chung-chen, was a widely respected young general named Wu San-kuei.

Wu San-kuei had yet to meet Chen Yuan-yuan. But after learning much from news and gossip about her beauty, he had begun to fantasize having a liaison with her. Even though he was married and had many concubines, Wu believed that he still had not found the love of his life. More importantly, he was frustrated that with his youth, power, and charisma, he still had not possessed a woman beautiful enough to match his stature. He spent many sleepless nights pondering his fate and trying to find ways to reverse his fortune.

While he was preoccupied with the important tasks of guarding the gateway to Peking and defending the northeast frontier from invaders, Wu still devoted a lot of his time to the pursuit of this personal quest. Gathering information and news about Yuan-yuan was a painstaking task because he had to deploy a network of messengers to accomplish that goal. As a matter of operational procedure of his command, messengers were dispatched between his headquarters and the capital on routine basis. Wu increased the frequency of the trips in order to step up his surveillance on his woman. He even assigned an officer, a lieutenant named Pei, to the carrier team as his personal spy, solely to keep track of Yuan-yuan's activities.

By the late 1630s, the Northeast Garrison had built its strength to forty thousand troops under Wu's command. The garrison was located about two hundred miles northeast of Peking, near the first gateway in the Great Wall of China. The fortress was named Shan-hai-kuan: the Gateway of Mountain and Sea. The gateway was located to the west of the China Sea and opposite the Liaotung Peninsula; it separated China proper from the territory called Manchuria. From the fortress, the wall stretched for hundreds of miles westward, protecting China proper from incursions by the non-Chinese races in Asia. Over one and a half millennia, the wall was rebuilt and reinforced by successive Chinese dynasties. At last, the great Ming emperor, Ju Di, completed the project in the late fifteenth century. Until the seventeenth century, the wall succeeded in keeping invaders out of north China, save the Mongols in the thirteenth century. Throughout the history of China, the Chinese coexisted with the belligerent non-Chinese races, keeping them north of the Great Wall.

Between the late 1630s and the early 1640s, Wu's army in the northeast was the last force available to the emperor in his defense against his enemies. The rest of his armed forces were either decimated by his lack of support or had surrendered to the rebel forces coming from the south and west of China. With the Manchus constantly threatening from the northeast, Wu's forces were preoccupied and unable to assist in the defense of the other fronts. For decades, the Manchus had made sporadic attempts to break through the fortress, without success. In the early 1640s, with Peking in disarray, they stepped up their harassments with incessant raids at Shan-hai-kuan. Time and again, it was Wu San-kuei who repelled them.

Wu grew up in a middle-class military family. His father, Wu Shang, was a military officer with a moderately successful career. Because the father's posting was mostly in the northeast region of China, he was born in Liaotung Peninsula. At a young age, he showed disinterest in the pursuit of books; he was instead attracted to the lifestyle of his father and an uncle who was also a military officer. That lifestyle meant leading men into battles. At the tender age of seventeen, Wu San-kuei enlisted in the army led by his uncle, Ju Da-sou. At eighteen, he was posted as a junior officer in Shan-hai-kuan with them. During one of the Manchu raids, he and his uncle were observing from a watchtower high above the fortress as Wu Shang battled the Manchus. His father's unit was outnumbered by the Manchus, yet it fought on relentlessly. As the battle raged on, it was apparent that Wu Shang's troops were losing and that he was at risk of being killed or captured by the enemy.

"Uncle, I must rescue Father," screamed young Wu.

"My nephew, we are powerless! Our troops are very thin in the garrison. We need to save them for a potential siege by the enemy," the uncle responded desperately.

"No, sir, I cannot bear to see my father killed or captured," the young man persisted. As he was crying out, he reached for his weapon, ready to jump on his horse, which waited nearby. His uncle tried to hold him back, but Wu was quickly in the saddle. He then roused his platoon to follow him out the gate.

As soon as he and his platoon rode past the gate, they charged at the enemy on two flanks with the force of a violent gust and slaughtered hundreds of tired and unsuspecting enemy soldiers. While focusing his gaze on his father, he suddenly felt a pain in his face, and the blood that spewed out of the wound nearly blinded him. He had apparently been cut by a sword, but he fought on unrelentingly. With whirlwind quickness, he picked his father off his horse and onto his own in one mighty motion. With equal quickness, he turned and galloped back to the fort, bringing his father to safety. Without hesitation, he dashed back out the gate and resumed his battle alongside his soldiers. His sudden and courageous intervention thoroughly disrupted the Manchus, and they reluctantly withdrew after another unsuccessful foray.

It was with such gallantry that Wu San-kuei won the admiration not only of his uncle and father but his comrades and the people of Shan-hai-kuan. Thereafter, Wu continued to demonstrate bravery and extraordinary leadership qualities at all levels of his military assignments, and he rose steadily through the ranks to become a general in his own right in the late 1630s.

One warm afternoon, while napping in the office in his mansion, Wu San-kuei was awakened by Lieutenant Pei, who had returned from Peking with news about Yuan-yuan.

The lieutenant nudged the general and reported softly. "General, I have some ... not-so-good news for you." Since he had been given the special assignment, the lieutenant was allowed direct access to the general, avoiding normal military protocol.

The general rubbed his eyes, straightened up, and asked, "How bad?"

"There was a fight recently in Soochow between two gang leaders over the woman." Pei spoke at a rapid pace and suddenly stopped to catch his breath.

"Go on!" The general was most curious to hear the story.

"One is called Ma Yi and the other ... Er ..." Pei had to reach deep to come up with the other name.

"I don't care what their names are—just tell me the outcome of the fight!"

"Oh, yes, Wang Kuang was his name. He won the fight and took the woman."

"What did he do with the woman?" The general was anxious. "Who is Wang Kuang?" Now that he knew that Wang had gotten his woman, he became interested not only in his name but who he was. He got off his chair and pounded his right fist on the top of the desk.

Pei was slow to complete the story. Wu fumed for a few seconds and turned back to the lieutenant, who was trailing him by a few steps. "Tell me what happened next."

"The one who did not get the woman was killed in a raid on Yuan Da-siang," the lieutenant continued, but the general interrupted again.

"Who cares about him!" the general yelled impatiently. "So where did the Wang thug take the woman? And what did he do with her?"

"I found out that Wang happens to be the son-in-law of Tian Wang-yu, the chief minister of the court," the lieutenant continued. "After kidnapping her, he took her directly to Peking ... to the Tian mansion."

"Why Peking?"

"Apparently, Wang was afraid to stay in Soochow or Nanking for fear of revenge by the other thug, so he chose to hide under Tian's roof for protection."

The general was listening intently. The lieutenant slowed to catch another breath. "In the meantime, there is another man with a bad reputation in pursuit of the woman ..."

"Another one?" General Wu was aroused by this new turn in the story.

"Apparently, the son of the provincial financial minister of

Nanking, who calls himself the prince. My contact told me that he is also in Peking now."

"So what then?" The general was worried about the situation his woman was in. He waited anxiously for more from the young lieutenant.

"Sir, I could not find out more because our team leader said we had to come back here quickly. Apparently, he has some bad news on the military front to report to you."

Wu was annoyed that his lieutenant did not get more information about the plight of his woman. But he grudgingly realized that official business should also be important to him.

"I am sure the team captain will bring the official report to you quickly," Pei said, turning to leave.

"Wait! Lieutenant, when is the next messenger trip leaving?"

"I believe within the next ten days."

"I will talk to your team captain about that when he brings his report to me," the general said resolutely, and he waved his hand to relieve the young officer, who quickly made an about-face and left.

Before the team captain arrived with his report, Wu San-kuei walked out of his office, back to his bedchamber. When he walked in, he was surprised to see his wife there, who greeted him with a smile and said softly, "Your Excellency, did you have a good day?"

The general and his wife had become rather formal with one another over the past few years, since he became preoccupied with the Yuan-yuan affair. She did not know what was causing his aloofness toward her, but as a traditional Chinese woman, she thought it was not her place to mind his business. Besides, she knew that defending the frontier against the ever-threatening Manchus was a grave burden for her husband to bear. So she opted to leave him alone almost all the time.

The general shook his head and furrowed his eyebrows as he absentmindedly answered his wife, "Not so good!"

She tried to converse with him. "The Manchus are causing us trouble again?"

But the general did not answer her. Instead, he hurried into the washroom and proceeded to splash water on his face. Walking back out to the chamber, he wiped his face dry. He then picked up his cap from a table near the bed, put it on, and ran out of the room without uttering another word. The wife knew better than to stop or question him.

Wu San-kuei ran directly from his chamber to the fortress lookout tower. As he marched up to the top of the fortress, two guards at the gate saluted him. But he seemed preoccupied and did not return the salutes. Upon reaching the top, he stood between two ramparts and focused his sight to the right, in the southwesterly direction, at Peking. How unfortunate, he thought, to have all his power and position and still he could not save the woman of his dreams from the ravages by thugs like Ma Yi and Wang Kuang. To add insult to injury, he thought there was the likelihood that an old lecher would gain possession of her. With Tian Wang-yu's position in the court, it would be near impossible to wrest Yuan-yuan from his grasp. *I have got to stop that from happening*, Wu told himself. *I have got to go to Peking quickly to take her away before it is too late*, he rationalized. *But without an imperial order, I simply cannot walk off my post and go to the capital.* So he found himself in a predicament. He turned and paced from one end of the fortress to the other circuitously. His mind wandered to the day he would meet Yuan-yuan and the joy of getting to hold her in his arms. *That joy must be overwhelmingly pleasurable! If not, why would so many men fight so hard, and even die, for her?* As he continued to pace and daydream, a voice jolted him out of his reverie.

"General, I have been looking for you!" said a young officer who stopped a few steps away, maintaining his salute.

"Oh, Captain." Wu snapped out of his daze and returned the salute to the leader of his messenger team.

"Sir, I have a message from the Grand Council. It is marked Most Urgent!" the captain said in a serious tone. He handed a scroll to the general.

Wu opened it, read it rapidly, and yelled at the captain, "Go! Go get my command staff to meet me at my office at once." He then turned and dashed from the tower with the young officer trailing him. He made a detour to his private chamber to pick up some papers. By the time he arrived at his office, the four high-ranking officers who made up his command staff were waiting for him.

Seeing the general walking in with huge strides, the staff officers all stood erect and sang out in unison, "General!"

"As you were," General Wu answered. "Take your seats."

As soon as the general placed himself at the head of an oval table, the others found their usual seats.

"I have here an urgent message from Peking," announced the general, waving the scroll in his left hand. "Apparently the rebel armies are surging toward the capital, and our troops are unable to hold their defensive positions in the southern and western provinces."

"Are they asking for our help, sir?" queried one of the officers.

"Not yet," responded Wu, "but the tone of the message foretells the dire situation that Peking is about to face."

"Sir, perhaps we should send a message back to them and ask if we should lend some troops to help them," said a second officer.

"Sir, the colonel is right," volunteered the third officer, seated next to the colonel. "It is our sworn duty to protect the emperor and his capital when they are facing a menacing situation!"

"I beg to disagree," averred the fourth officer. "Our responsibility is to safeguard this fortress and prevent the Manchu devils from invading the capital."

Wu put down the scroll in his left hand and picked up another one he had brought from his private chamber. "Read this one!" He handed it over to the colonel, who was his senior staffer.

The colonel unrolled the scroll, pored over it, and yelled, "Oh my God!" He then passed it over to the officer sitting next to him. As the scroll completed its circulation, the faces around the table turned stoic. The scroll contained a report that the Manchus had amassed an unusually large army north of the fortress. Their intentions were not known, but it was apparent that they were aiming to take Ningyuan, a major garrison town near Shan-hai-kuan.

"I'd like to make a visit to Peking," the general suddenly declared.

"Sir," the colonel said hurriedly, stopping the general in his tracks. "I do not believe that you should take leave of our post because of the threat posed by the Manchus!"

All the other officers murmured, but none spoke up for or against the general's wish.

"I suppose you are right, Colonel," murmured Wu. "Without an imperial summons, it would be difficult to explain my taking leave from this important post!" He shook his head dejectedly; he could not divulge his real intention for wanting to go to Peking. "Gentlemen, I will order the team captain to take his team for another run to Peking for an up-to-date surveillance of the situation." He then waved his hand and dismissed the staffers. They stood up, saluted him, and left his office. The young general had more pressing problems on his mind than those he was charged with in his official capacity.

Wu San-kuei summoned the team captain to his office and ordered him to make another journey to Peking the next day. Before the team left his garrison the next morning, he called for his trusted lieutenant and instructed him to track down Yuan-yuan's whereabouts. He was most concerned that Tian Wang-yu might have taken his woman away from him.

In the next thirty days, Wu spent more sleepless nights thinking about his woman and not much about the military problems confronting him and his emperor. He fantasized about how sweet it would be to place his lips on hers while holding her in his arms. In the daytime, he spent many hours pacing the fortress, looking between the ramparts toward Peking and waiting impatiently for the return of the traveling team.

For this young general would not rest until he had gained sole possession of the woman of his life: Chen Yuan-yuan.

CHAPTER 7

The Double Cross

PRINCE SOONG AND HIS MEN ARRIVED AT PEKING AND HEADED directly to Wang Kuang's mansion. He was determined to find and get to Yuan-yuan. Reaching the mansion, the prince stepped forward and stopped in front of the entrance, but two guards blocked his way.

"Is your master in? I have to see him on some business," said the prince impatiently. "I came all the way from Nanking to see him."

"My master is not in," answered one of the guards; the word *Nanking* hit a chord in him. He gave a hand signal to his partner, and the other guard rushed quickly toward the back of the house.

"Do you know where I can find him?" Prince Soong inquired.

"I am under strict orders not to divulge his whereabouts!" the guard responded curtly.

"As I said, I came from Nanking, and I must see … him!" The prince could barely complete his sentence before two groups of men rushed toward him and his men, coming from the back of the house, wielding swords and clubs. They started to swing their weapons at the visitors as soon as they encountered them. Prince Soong's men also drew their weapons, but since they were surprised and outnumbered by the Wang group, they were easily overcome. Prince Soong was caught in the middle of the battle, and he was killed, along with all his men.

It was most unfortunate that the false prince was killed because of a false identification. Apparently, Wang Kuang had left instructions to his guards that should anyone come from Nanking or Soochow looking for him, the guards were to kill him without questions. Wang Kuang thought that a man from Nanking or Soochow would be Ma Yi. The false prince was the farthest from his mind. But since the prince had not identified himself and the guards did not ask for his name, Prince Soong paid a dear price for coveting a beautiful woman named Yuan-yuan. Upon learning that the man who was killed on his doorstep was not Ma Yi but Prince Soong, Wang Kuang ordered a cover-up of the wrongful killing.

The long absence of Prince Soong aroused his father back in Nanking. His son had not told him that he was going to the capital, which deepened the mystery. After many efforts to hunt for his son failed, the prince's father reluctantly dropped the search. The case of the missing false prince faded with time.

While Wang Kuang had survived the ordeals of Ma Yi and Prince Soong, he could not survive the wrath of his wife when he brought his woman back home from Soochow. Wang Kuang's wife was the older of Tian Wang-yu's two daughters. She was beautiful in her own right, but she lacked the sex appeal of Yuan-yuan that most men desired. When Wang Kuang told her he wished to have Yuan-yuan as his new concubine, the wife exploded into a rage.

"You already have two consorts serving you in our home— why do we need another one?" She was indignant and apparently jealous of Yuan-yuan's beauty.

"If we don't take her in, she'll be without a home!" lamented Wang Kuang.

"That's not my concern, and neither is it yours!" yelled the wife.

"I beg of you to be kind and reasonable," pleaded the husband.

"I will let her stay for two days. Then you must move her out of our house."

"Where do you expect her to go!" Wang Kuang shot back, holding down his temper.

"I don't care where she's going; I just want her out of my sight as soon as possible!" the wife cried.

"Don't be unreasonable. Give me a month to find a place for her," Wang Kuang pleaded again.

Yuan-yuan stood by silently, witnessing the family feud. She felt sorry for him, but she also understood the wife's position. Most of all, though, she felt the deepest sorrow for herself. *I have got to find a way to get out from under these unpleasant situations,* she thought.

While Wang Kuang and his wife continued to argue, Yuan-yuan's mind wandered into never-never land.

"I was fortunate to escape from Ma Yi, but now I am in the throes of another terrible experience," she mumbled to herself. "There's got to be a man out there who could rescue me from these untenable situations." As her mind sank deeper into dreamland, she suddenly thought of one man who had the power to save her. That man would be Wu San-kuei, the young general in the northeast she had heard so much about. She began to fantasize that one day he would come and save her.

Yuan-yuan had not met him, but her heart had been longing for him. In her mind, Wu San-kuei would fit the role of that handsome young man she coveted, the man in that play she had watched in the Soochow opera house. She heard rumors that Wu was not only handsome and young but also dashing and powerful. Little did she know that the young man was also fantasizing about her!

As the indistinct noise of the fight between Wang and his wife continued, Yuan-yuan's mind drifted deeper into the abyss. She agonized over the misfortune that had befallen on her: the sexual abuse heaped on her by Ma Yi and Wang Kuang. These men were thugs who had no concept of love. They were animals that only knew how to use her body to sate their sexual appetites. *I've got to get myself out from under these predicaments*, she reasoned again. *My beauty and youth are fading quickly with time!*

"Yuan-yuan!" Wang Kuang's loud voice jolted her out of her daydreams.

Yuan-yuan felt a sudden surge of energy as she turned to face Wang Kuang and saw that his wife had disappeared from the scene.

"Come with me!" he commanded.

"Where are we going?"

"We are staying here tonight," said Wang Kuang softly, "and we will have to move you out of here in two days." Apparently, he and his wife had come to an uneasy truce.

Wang Kuang spent a mostly sleepless night in bed with Yuan-yuan. He rose early the next morning and ran out of the house before Yuan-yuan could ask him where he was going. He was heading off to his father-in-law's mansion to ask for his help. He was hoping that Tian Wang-yu could help ease his tension and find a place to settle his woman.

The guard at the front door of the Tian mansion recognized him, so he let him in without obstruction. As he stepped inside the foyer, a young female servant greeted him with a smile and said, "The master is still in bed, sir."

"Do not awaken him." Wang Kuang returned an awkward smile. "I will wait here for him." He promptly flopped in a chair near the parlor door. The maid smiled and handed him a cup of tea before leaving him alone. For more than an hour, Wang Kuang fidgeted, alternating between standing and sitting many times.

As the sound of approaching footsteps finally gained Wang Kuang's attention, he looked toward the source of the noise and saw the old minister walking toward him, a manservant holding a cup following behind.

"Kuang, what a surprise!" said the old minister, now standing two feet from his son-in-law.

"Good morning, sir," Wang Kuang said while bowing to the minister.

Tian pointed to a chair near a large round table and beckoned the young man to sit. He then took the seat on the opposite side of the table; the servant handed the cup to him and left the scene.

"I heard that you came back to town yesterday," Tian said with a wan smile.

"Yes, sir," answered Wang Kuang, "but it was too late in the day, so I did not see fit to come and pay my respects to you."

"I also heard that you did not come home alone," the old minister said with a slight smile. "I understand that your companion is a rather ... beautiful ... young woman!"

Wang Kuang did not respond immediately. He was thinking, *What an efficient spy network!* He did not know that, after their argument the night before, his wife had sent a confidential message to her father apprising him of the situation.

After a moment of hesitation, while the old minister was sipping his tea, the young man mumbled, "Yes, sir. She is a rather ... beautiful young woman!"

"Oh! How did you come upon her?"

"She is a popular actress from Soochow. I met her through a good friend. I had a hand in rescuing her from some unfortunate circumstances—"

"Unfortunate circumstances?" the old minister interrupted.

"Yes, sir. She was being abused and threatened by some thugs in Soochow."

"How should that involve you?"

"I happened to walk onto the scene. It was at a theater in Soochow City."

"Oh ...?"

"A local gang leader barged backstage and tried to abduct her." Wang Kuang tried to play down the story. "The theater owner asked for my help to save her."

"To help save her, I can understand. But how did you end up with her?"

"The thug did not give up. I had to fight with him, and after knocking him out, I took her with me, out of danger."

"Well, why did you bring her all the way here to Peking?"

"The thug refused to give up, as I said." Wang Kuang began to feel the pressure put on him by his father-in-law. "And I didn't want to stay in Soochow or Nanking, where he could easily hunt me down. I thought Peking would be a safer place to hide from him."

Wang Kuang became more uncomfortable. He had wanted to ask Tian to help relocate Yuan-yuan from his own home, but the old minister seemed to be more interested in the young woman than his problem. "Sir, I must find a place for her to stay. Your daughter, my wife, will not allow her to stay in our home."

"Where is she now?"

"She is still at my house. But she must leave within two days."

"Two days?" mused the old minister. He massaged his graying beard with his left hand as if he were calculating.

"Can you take her in until I find a place to move her?"

Tian had heard a lot about Yuan-yuan. Since he was the most powerful official in Emperor Chung-chen's court, his spy network was very efficient. Also, since he was a man who admired women, especially young and beautiful ones, his acute interest in Yuan-yuan was not unusual. At the advanced age of seventy-two, he still welcomed an opportunity to gain possession of a beauty of Yuan-yuan's quality. He paused for a moment, feigning indifference in the matter, and then said, "All right! Tomorrow ... bring her here tomorrow."

Wang was happy to hear the offer. Little did he know that his father-in-law had an ulterior motive of his own.

The next day, Wang Kuang escorted Yuan-yuan to the Tian residence. She was captivated by the opulence of the mansion. She had heard that Tian Wang-yu was the most powerful man in Peking, so she was delighted that the old minister had accepted her into his house. Since her primary aim was to escape from Wang Kuang, settling in an older man's household seemed a viable solution.

Wang Kuang introduced her to Tian Wang-yu when the old man greeted them in the antechamber. "This is Yuan-yuan, Minister." Yuan-yuan lowered her body to pay respects to the old minister without saying a word.

When the old minister's eyes landed on the young woman's beautiful face, he found himself speechless. When he moved his gaze down her shapely body, he could only say, "Oh! Yuan ... Yuan!"

"Minister, will you let Yuan-yuan stay for a short duration, until I can find a suitable place to move her?" inquired the son-in-law.

"Of course! Of course!" The question was music to the ears of the lecherous old man. "She is most welcome to stay as long as she wishes."

Wang found his father-in-law's response pleasing to his ears, but he was reluctant to let go of her, even on a temporary basis. But since he was in dire straits, he really did not have a choice in the matter. He thanked the old minister again, bowed to him, and bade farewell to him and the woman.

Wang Kuang moved back with his wife, briefly restoring peace at home. He paid frequent visits to Yuan-yuan, but under the watchful eyes of the old minister, Wang Kuang found it impossible to spend intimate time with his woman.

Months turned into a year. Yuan-yuan settled comfortably in the good life given her by Tian. Even though the old man had made frequent advances on her, fondling her, kissing her, and embracing her, Yuan-yuan accepted the advances without overt objections. In her mind, life with Tian Wang-yu was a lesser evil than with Ma Yi or Wang Kuang. More importantly to her, living with a powerful man like Tian would eventually afford her the best chance to extricate herself from bondage. So she placated his whims and desires without rancor.

"Minister," she said one evening while lying in his sumptuous bed with him, "how are things in the court?"

"It is not your place to mind the business of government," the old minister chastised in a loving manner. "Beautiful woman like you should only be concerned with the well-being and happiness of an old gentleman like me!" He then pressed his mustached lips on hers. She gently turned her face, and his lips landed on her right cheek instead.

Yuan-yuan smiled and said, "Minister, you have many young and beautiful women in your household. How do you find the time and energy to tend to official business and still take care of them all?"

"My love," Tian said while his wandering hands roamed all over her soft body, "now I have only you to take care of! The others can wait."

Yuan-yuan gently wiggled out of his grasp and continued to ask questions that the old minister found impertinent. "I heard that the rebels are marching closer to our capital. Are we in danger of being overrun by them?"

"What's new? It has been that way for many months!" the old

minister replied in a very nonchalant way, as though the problem of
the empire coming under attack by rebel forces was not a concern
or worry. "I guess our generals and their armies will take care of
the threats!"

"But you are the chief minister of the court—would you not
be concerned with these threats?"

"Let's not worry about such mundane things now," the old
man muttered. "Besides, my intelligence reports tell me that our
generals in the field are holding their lines. A real threat from
the rebels is not imminent!" Tian's assessment of the situation
was grossly inaccurate: most units in the Ming army had either
been routed by the rebel forces or had put down their arms and
surrendered.

Yuan-yuan was more than observant; she was also cunning,
for she had a plan of her own, a plan that would free her not only
from Wang Kuang but also from Tian Wang-yu. "Minister, I
heard that the Manchus have begun to threaten our borders up
north once again. Are they not another threat that our emperor
must face?"

"Oh, that is the least of our worries!"

"Why?" She persisted in carrying on with the conversation,
but the old man had other motives on his lecherous mind.

"Let's not continue with this kind of conversation. Besides,
a woman should not meddle in official business. Let's have some
fun!" His hands began to fondle her breasts again.

"You are the highest-ranking minister in the court. If you don't
get on top of these pressing problems, the emperor will be upset
with you, and he might even dismiss you from your high position!"

"He would not dare!" the old minister declared, sitting up from
his reclined position. "His Majesty owes me too much. If I had
not helped him destroy Wei Chung-yan and his Eastern Factory,
he would not be sitting on his throne now! Let me give you an

example of my relationship with His Majesty." He began a monologue about his recent meeting with the emperor.

"Your Majesty, how have you been these past few days?" Tian
Wang-yu knelt to pay his respects to the emperor.

"Minister Tian, I am well!" the emperor said softly, waving
his hand to allow the old man to rise. "However, I am still quite
worried over the rebels coming closer to our capital."

"Your Majesty, reports from some of our generals in the field
tell us that things are under control." The minister stressed the
word "some" to lessen the accuracy of his statement. He did not
want to be caught for not being diligent on his duty and truthful
to the throne.

"Minister, I am not as optimistic as you are. I've received reports that our troops are not up to the task of holding back the
advances of the rebel armies."

How and from whom does he get this news? Tian wondered. He
put up a brave front and said, "Your Majesty, those reports are not
accurate!"

The emperor shook his head repeatedly and muttered,
"Minister, I'd like to believe you. I hope you are right!"

"Sir, I would not dare tell a lie to the throne! My subordinates
know that giving a false report carries a harsh penalty," the old
minister asserted with confidence.

Emperor Chung-chen found a level of uneasy comfort in Tian's
remarks. "Minister, you are the pillar of our court, and I rely on
you and those who work for you to keep order and security in our
empire."

It appeared that the emperor and the "pillar of the court" he
leaned on had both been living in dream worlds of their creation.

The old minister seized the calm moment and continued. "Your

Majesty, have you been enjoying the company of my daughter?"
He had presented his younger daughter recently to the emperor as
his new consort.

"Consort Tian has been most attentive to my needs. I'd like to
thank you for giving me the pleasure of enjoying her beauty and
talent," the emperor answered the old minister in a halfhearted
manner. Lately, his mind had not been on female company, let
alone into carnal pleasures.

"Your Majesty must let your mind relax and enjoy some of the
pleasures that are available to you," Tian said. "Matters of daily
operation of the court should be left to me and my subordinates."

"I suppose you are right," said the emperor. His comment
seemed to lack a degree of confidence.

Tian Wang-yu turned back to Yuan-yuan and boasted, "You
see, I've got him in the palm of my hand!" He held up his right
palm to stress his point. "Let's have some fun and some sleep!"

"Minister, I understand there is a general in the northeast who
is instrumental in the defense of our capital. Can you tell me more
about him?" The young woman persisted with the conversation.

"Wu San-kuei?" The minister casually mentioned the general's
name.

"Yes, General Wu!"

"He commands the Northeast Garrison and has the responsibility for defending the fortress of Shan-hai-kuan from being
penetrated by the Manchus. If the fortress is penetrated, Peking
will fall to the Manchus."

"He has a very heavy responsibility," Yuan-yuan said in an ad-
miring voice. "Can you tell me more about him, Minister Tian?"

Tian was annoyed, as he very much wanted to engage in some
intimate time with the young woman. "Let's get on with some fun

things!" He sank back under the bed cover and tried to pull her down with him.

Yuan-yuan gently resisted and continued to ask questions. "How old is he?"

"Oh … thirty, thirty-five. I am not sure," the old man mumbled. "Give me a big kiss!"

"He is very young to have accomplished so much!" she said with admiration. "Have you met him?"

"I have not had the opportunity to meet him, but I know his father quite well."

"Does he have a family of his own?" Yuan-yuan was most interested in the general's personal life.

"I heard he has a wife who's living with him in the garrison. I do not believe he has any children," said the minister. "His father is a retired military officer who lives in the capital, not far from here." The old minister was curious why the young woman showed so much interest in Wu San-kuei. While Yuan-yuan sank into a dream world of her own, the old minister finally pulled the blanket over his head and slumbered away.

Wang Kuang was becoming more irritable over not being able to see more of Yuan-yuan. He had finally located a house closer to him and wanted to take her out of the Tian mansion. Since his father-in-law's reputation with young women preceded him, he had become suspicious of his woman's safety in Tian's house. So he gathered all his courage and decided to confront his father-in-law.

Wang Kuang announced his intention to the old minister when he visited with him one afternoon. "Minister, I'd like to thank you for keeping Yuan-yuan in your home for so many months. I have found a place to move her, and I will come and pick her up in a few days."

Tian was taken back by the announcement and was temporarily speechless.

At the lack of a response from the minister, the son-in-law pressed on. "Is there a problem with that, Minister?"

"Well ..." the minister mumbled. He really did not want to part with Yuan-yuan because he had become accustomed to his wonderful life with her. He finally found words to counter the young man's demand. "Oh, I have a plan for her."

"A plan?"

"Yes, I am planning to present Yuan-yuan as a gift to His Majesty, the emperor," declared the old minister. The truth was that he did not want to let her out of his sight, so he used the emperor to intimidate his son-in-law into giving up the woman.

"You are not serious about that, are you?" Wang was not about to give up without a fight, so he pressed on. "She is coming with me now, and you'll have to find another woman to present to His Majesty. As a matter of fact, you presented him with your own daughter recently."

Tian realized that he was engaging in a bitter fight with his own son-in-law over Yuan-yuan. To win the battle, he would have to play the last card he was holding. So he struck the final blow. "You'd better take care of yourself and not cause trouble for others."

"What do you mean by that, sir?" Wang found his father-in-law's comment odd.

"I mean ... you should leave Yuan-yuan alone!" Tian said resolutely.

"But she's my woman!" Wang said awkwardly. "I brought her here ... and I should be able to take her away."

Tian was so smitten by Yuan-yuan that he did not want to part with her either. The two men continued the unpleasant dialogue. Finally, the old man had no choice but to break the impasse by saying, "If Minister Soong finds out that you killed his son, you'll be in more trouble than you can handle!"

"W-h-a-t?" Wang's face turned white, and no other words came out of his wide-open mouth. He was stunned that his father-in-law had knowledge of the killing. *It had to be his daughter, my wife, who spilled the beans on me*, Wang Kuang thought.

Seeing his son-in-law's reaction, Tian quickly drove a nail into the coffin. "If you relinquish Yuan-yuan to me, I will make sure that Minister Soong will not learn who murdered his son!"

Wang Kuang was trapped. He knew that if he did not give up Yuan-yuan, he'd be signing his own death warrant. After a long pause to take stock of the situation, he hung his head low, licked his wounds, and walked out of the Tian mansion.

Wang Kuang was not heard from or seen in public again.

CHAPTER 8
The Willow

TIAN WANG-YU WAS GLAD TO HAVE GOTTEN HIS SON-IN-LAW out of Yuan-yuan's life so he could continue to keep her to himself. But he could never have imagined that the pretense that he had used to win Yuan-yuan was about to come back to haunt him. He had lied to Wang Kuang about wishing to present Yuan-yuan to the emperor as a consort. Much to his dismay, after Consort Tian, his daughter, learned that he had taken on another young and beautiful woman as a consort, she had a surprise in store for him.

One day, after he had an audience with the emperor in the Forbidden City, Tian paid a visit to his daughter. After a pleasant lunch in her chamber, the consort approached her father and said, "Father, I heard that you have adopted another young woman as a concubine. Rumor has it that she is the most beautiful woman in China. Is it true?"

The old minister was momentarily dumbfounded by his daughter's comment, but he soon regained his composure. "Oh, yes! Your brother-in-law brought her to my home from Soochow and thought that I would enjoy her talent ... singing, that is. So he asked me to take her in for as long as I wished."

"Father, I congratulate you! I'd like to meet her, so I can judge her beauty and her talent personally."

Tian could not find a good reason to deny the daughter's request, so he acceded to her wish. Meeting Yuan-yuan the next day in the Tian mansion, the consort was taken by her beauty. Without hesitation, she declared, "Father, I'd like to present her to His Majesty as a new consort!"

Tian Wang-yu was shaken by his daughter's declaration; as his face turned white, and he was at a loss for words. In contrast, Yuan-yuan, standing nearby, found the proposition very pleasing to her ears. Her heart jumped a few beats when she thought her chance to escape captivity by undesirable men might come soon.

The old minister finally found a response to the daughter's proposal. "His Majesty has a harem full of pretty young women, and with you as his new love, I'd venture to say that he does not need another consort."

"Lately His Majesty has been working too hard. His mood has been quite foul because of the pressures exerted on him by events out of his control. I think Yuan-yuan will greatly help to lessen his stress and worries."

Tian knew the emperor well, and he knew that Chung-chen was unlike his three predecessors, who had indulged in debauched lifestyles to the neglect of their duties. In his spare time, Chung-chen would rather enjoy being by himself, reading books or tending to his garden. When he was tired from reading the official documents that inundated him, he'd turn to books on history and horticulture. When he was tired from reading, he'd opt to spend days on end tilling the soil and planting flowers in his garden.

Chung-chen had inherited the throne of a dying empire. In the beginning, he buried himself in the task of trying to reverse the fortunes of the dynasty. With a dysfunctional court that was in the making for decades, he found himself unable to right the ship of state. To complicate matters, the court, for all intents and purposes, was controlled by someone other than himself. In the beginning, it was Wei Chung-yan. Later, it was Tian Wang-yu. Outside of the court, he was threatened by the rebel uprisings in the southwest and the Manchu intrusion in the northeast. As the empire began to slip out of his control, Chung-chen had become more disillusioned and tended to sink into frequent periods of deep depression. It was in his nature not to trust anyone, so he gradually began to keep to himself and take matters into his own hands by not seeking counsel and assistance from his ministers. But in reality, even if he had called on them, they were incapable or unwilling to help him.

"I think His Majesty will not have the heart or the leisure to take on another consort in these difficult times," Tian finally rebutted. His assessment of the emperor's mood was rather accurate.

Deep down, Consort Tian agreed with her father's assessment, but she had her own reason for wanting to present Chung-chen with a new consort. She was a beautiful woman in her own right. And with her pleasing personality, she had quickly become the favorite of the emperor. As a result, some higher-ranking consorts felt that they were being neglected by the emperor, so they became jealous and banded together to undermine his relationship with Consort Tian. To counter her antagonists, Consort Tian thought that having a more beautiful woman on her side could alter the balance in her favor. Sensing that her father was reluctant to give up Yuan-yuan, Consort Tian turned to her instead and asked bluntly, "Yuan-yuan, would you like to be a consort to the emperor?"

Yuan-yuan was equally cunning. Although she'd love to enter the emperor's intimate circle, she played coy by responding politely, "Your Honor, it is not my decision to make in this matter."

The father tried to pour cold water on the growing flame. "My daughter, have you consulted with His Majesty in this matter?"

"Father, my plan is to surprise His Majesty. I am hoping

that Yuan-yuan will be a catalyst to jolt His Majesty out of his doldrums."

After more sparring between father and daughter, Yuan-yuan was secretly hoping that fate would finally smile on her.

Minister Tian reluctantly acceded to his daughter's wish. Deep down, he prayed that the emperor would reject his daughter's generosity.

Two days after the encounter, Consort Tian, along with two maids as company, escorted Yuan-yuan to Emperor Chung-chen's private chamber.

Emperor Chung-chen's private chamber was opulent in color but sparse in decor. It lacked the dimension and splendor that would become an emperor. Perhaps it represented more of Chung-chen's personal taste for simplicity and austerity. He had never expected to be emperor, let alone wanted to be one. Perhaps for that reason, he was not comfortable living the lifestyle of an emperor.

Consort Tian's entrance to the emperor's private chamber was unannounced because of her intimate relationship with him. The four women entered and quickly kneeled when they found the emperor sitting behind his desk, totally absorbed in reading a document.

"Your Majesty," Consort Tian called out in a velvety voice.

The emperor lifted his head and saw four women kneeling in front of him; he recognized his loving consort and the two maids, but the other woman he did not know. He raised his right hand to allow them to rise from their knees. The women rose.

"Your Majesty, Lily told me that you had been reading all day," Consort Tian said, pointing at one of the two maids standing behind her.

"Oh! There are many urgent messages from the court and the field, and I have to read them all so that I can get up to speed with fast-changing events," the emperor muttered, pointing at a pile of scrolls on top of his table. He then lowered his head once again, peering at the document he was still holding.

The consort detected the emperor's lack of attention or interest, so she spoke in a slightly louder voice. "Your Majesty, I would like to introduce you to Yuan-yuan, a very talented young lady from Soochow. She is a professional singer. Perhaps you would like to have her sing for you."

The emperor raised his head again and leaned forward to gaze at the unfamiliar face. He'd been reading for too long, and his eyesight appeared to have blurred. He rubbed his eyes gently with his sleeve and gazed at Yuan-yuan once more. "She is really quite beautiful," he said to himself. He could not resist a closer inspection of her shapely body. He seemed to be momentarily mesmerized by the exceptionally beautiful woman, one who surpassed even the beauty of his favorite, Consort Tian. On the one hand, he was tempted to accept the offer, but on the other, his mind harkened back to his awesome responsibilities as the head of an empire in these trying times. Indulging in a new female or a sexual liaison was the farthest thing in his mind.

Chung-chen continued to gaze at Yuan-yuan, but he said nothing. Yuan-yuan returned a faint smile, raising her lowered head by a few degrees. She knew that she was not allowed to make eye contact with the emperor unless he gave her permission to do so. But she knew that this was a chance in a lifetime for her to sell herself to the emperor and be freed from bondage, so she boldly stole a glance at him. There was a very prolonged hush in the chamber as Chung-chen and Yuan-yuan exchanged quick glances.

Consort Tian finally broke the silence. "Well, Your Majesty, do you wish to have Yuan-yuan sing for you? To relieve the tension in your mind and body, if temporarily?"

Chung-chen at last took his eyes off Yuan-yuan. He shook his head slowly and said, "Thank you for your kindness, my dear consort. Maybe another time." Then he raised his right hand in a gesture to dismiss the women.

Consort Tian was disappointed by the emperor's behavior, but Yuan-yuan was more disappointed. The consort thought she should make another attempt, so she bravely pleaded, "Your Majesty, if it has to be another time, would you prefer that she comes back to sing for you tomorrow evening?"

The emperor had made up his mind that he really did not have the time and energy to be entertained by another woman, even though he found Yuan-yuan exceptionally desirable. He had already resumed his reading when he raised his right hand once more to direct the women out the door. Consort Tian finally accepted the order, and she led the women out of the emperor's private chamber, full of dejection.

Yuan-yuan was devastated. She had seen a golden opportunity for liberation from the ravages of undesirable men pass by.

The next day, Yuan-yuan was returned to the Tian mansion. The happiest man in the world was the old minister, Tian Wang-yu!

When the emperor felt lonely and wanted to vent his frustrations, he normally called on Consort Tian. But before she entered his court, he was frequently in the company of his youngest daughter, the fifteen-year-old princess named Chang-ping. Emperor Chung-chen had three sons and another daughter, but he favored Chang-ping because she was mature beyond her age, and, more importantly, her liking for reading and gardening reminded him of himself. More peculiar, though, was their shared affinity for willow trees, one ten-foot willow in the imperial garden in particular.

One day, while walking together and enjoying a glorious spring day in that garden, Chang-ping leaned close to her father and said softly, "Father, you look like you have lost some more weight. You must take more time off to rest and enjoy the fun things in life!"

"With the state of affairs in our court so chaotic, I don't have an appetite even for food, let alone the mood for fun things in life," the emperor lamented.

"Father, a lot of events are out of your control, and neglecting your health is definitely not the solution."

"My daughter, you are too young to know how difficult it is to rule a country. The burden is overwhelming!" the emperor said in a bitter tone. "Without much help from my ministers, I am fighting a lonely war!"

The young princess made a logical remark. "You told me the number of ministers in the court has grown by a large number lately, and I would presume that should help to lighten your burden in running the government."

The emperor shook his head and began a monologue. "It's quite the opposite. Let me give you an example of what happened in a recent audience with my high officials."

Chung-chen then proceeded to relate a rare episode of a court audience to his daughter. It was rare because he had dispensed with daily audiences for years, finding them unproductive and depressing. But to renew his test of his court's loyalty and efficiency, he had called an ad hoc audience in a little used Throne Hall, to emphasize the gravity and solemnity of the meeting.

Emperor Chung-chen sat on his throne and announced to the gathering of officials, standing in two lines on each side of his throne, "Our treasury has been depleted to the level where we cannot sustain the operation of our court. Does anyone have a solution to offer that would help to redress the dire conditions under which we are mired?"

No one wanted to speak because no one had any constructive ideas to offer. More importantly, most of them had contributed to the malaise with corruption, inefficiency, and wastefulness. Besides, no one wanted to take the brunt of the emperor's wrath by being the first to speak.

The emperor scanned the ranks and continued in a dejected tone. "Our troops in the field have not gotten sufficient provisions for months, and I was informed they are not getting paid either. Their morale is at the lowest ebb, and the rebels have taken advantage of that to conquer more of our territories. They are pressing closer toward our capital!"

The minister of military affairs felt the need to respond because the emperor had touched upon his area of responsibility. "Your Majesty, it is true that we have received reports from the fronts that are unfavorable, but our commanders in the field are still optimistic that we can prevail, if we give them the support they need."

"That is precisely my point, Minister Lo," the emperor said. "How long can we expect them to hold on if we do not meet their needs sooner and more frequently?"

Minister Lo could not rebuke the emperor, so he turned and looked at his colleague, the minister of taxation, hoping that he could say something constructive. Minister Yang took the hint and cleared his throat. "Your Majesty, the governors in the provinces have vowed that they will step up their tax collections. If their efforts are successful, then we will be able to replenish our treasury and take care of our troops." Minister Yang was overly optimistic; he knew that the tax collection picture had been grim for years. He was also aware of the corruption taking place in the provinces, as in the case of his best friend, Minister Soong, in Nanking.

The emperor was also well aware of the bleak picture. "Minister Yang, the tax-collecting ministers in the provinces have not delivered what they promised for many years. We cannot expect a miracle to happen now."

The ministers maintained an uneasy silence, waiting for the

emperor's other shoe to drop. But, instead, the emperor continued to vent his frustrations. "And yes. the cadre in our court has grown in numbers over the years. Why are our ministries still mired in the morass of dysfunction and inefficiency, even with more staff to do the job?" The emperor directed his gaze at the head of his court, Minister Tian Wang-yu, the father of his favorite consort.

Minister Tian felt the discomfort of the emperor's gaze, so he nudged his friend standing to his immediate left, Minister Feng, the interior minister, hoping that he could bail him out. The interior minister searched for words. "Your Majesty, we all are working very hard to reorganize the ministries. The additional hiring has resulted in higher productivity and efficiency in some departments."

Minister Feng had told a lie. The truth behind the swelling in the ranks of the court was rampant corruption: creating more positions so the high ministers could fill them with family members, relatives, and friends or sell them outright to office seekers and pad their own pockets.

"Minister Feng," the emperor said dejectedly, "if you consider the state of affairs in our court today to be highly productive and efficient, then why is unrest fomenting at such high levels in our provinces?"

Minister Feng had no answer to the emperor's challenge, so he lowered his head, as did most of his colleagues.

Failing to regenerate the energy in his court, the emperor decided on a new course of action. Even though he had previously sent out requests for cash contributions from his ministers, the results were mostly inconsequential, much to his dismay. He told his court that unless they gave their financial support, the army would not be fed or paid, and morale would further deteriorate. In that case, their will to fight would dissipate. Chung-chen also admonished the ministers to cut back on extravagancy, which he himself had done. But his pleas had fallen on deaf ears. With no other alternative, the emperor let the other shoe drop. He renewed a request for cash donations by his ministers to help fund the treasury.

The emperor raised his normally gentle voice by a few octaves and snapped everyone out of the doldrums, especially Tian Wang-yu. "Minister Tian, since you are the senior member in my court, would you like to start a new round of donations to help to save our troops?"

Minister Tian released a soft grunt and an uneasy smile as he bowed low to the emperor. He mumbled, "Ah, Your Majesty, as you know, I was the leading donor for the 'Save our troops' campaigns many times. Perhaps it's someone else's turn to rise to the occasion." He then looked to his right, where his good friend, the minister of taxation, was standing, but the tax minister lowered his head as if to avoid eye contact with him. These two high officers of the court had colluded to defraud the treasury for years, channeling cash secretly into their own pockets and altering the books to cover their misdeeds.

Minister Yang knew he had better respond to the silent plea of his close friend and the demand of the emperor, so he straightened his shoulders and said in a somewhat incoherent but loud voice, "Your Majesty, your humble servant will donate fifty ounces of silver to the campaign!"

Emperor Chung-chen was disappointed by the attitude displayed by the father of his favorite consort, but deep down, he knew that whatever amount his high officials could donate would be inadequate to save the troops—and his empire. It was literally too little and too late, he thought.

But the high ministers of the court harbored secret resentment over the double standard related to the issue of finance that the emperor had employed. He had let his empress and, especially, his father-in-law accumulate substantial wealth clandestinely. And he had not approached or directed them to donate to the national treasury when it had been in dire straits for many years. Worse yet, he had not demanded that they scale down their lavish lifestyles, as he himself had.

Back in the garden, as father and daughter continued to meander, he let out a huge sigh and lamented, "Now you can see why our troops are failing in the battlefield. Our court is occupied by selfish and useless officials!"

Princess Chang-ping imparted some encouraging words for her father. "Father, you have worked hard, and I am sure heaven will reward you for your efforts."

"I am afraid I will soon be the emperor who lost the realm of the Ming dynasty!" Emperor Chung-chen declared as his eyes welled. "How am I to answer to our illustrious ancestors for my failure?"

"Father, I am sure it will not come to that!" The daughter tried to comfort her father, but she did not speak with much conviction. Knowing her father was desperate over the fast decline of the empire, she put on another brave effort and said, "Father, I am sure our illustrious ancestors will forgive you. It's not you who will lose the realm. It's the officials in your court who will lose it!"

The princess's last statement struck a chord in Chung-chen's psyche. He had wrestled with how history would ultimately judge him. His recent frame of mind tended to tilt toward the sentiment expressed by his daughter: to place blame for losing the realm squarely on the shoulders of his ministers. His campaigns to save the troops had been failures, and it was these failures and the ambivalence of his court that were the main reason for the demise of his empire, *not* his failed leadership.

The emperor and the princess prolonged their aimless wandering in the garden, and they ended up at the foot of his favorite willow tree. He slowly sat on a small marble bench under the tree.

He pointed at it and said, "You know, I planted this tree when I first came into this garden fifteen years ago. You and this tree came into this rotten world at about the same time."

The princess looked at the tree and transferred her gaze lovingly back to her father. Then she sat down next to him.

Chung-chen suddenly rose from the bench and looked up forlornly at the tree. He muttered in a low voice, as if he were talking to himself, "Look at the beautiful leaves of this tree. They drape down and spread so evenly, like an umbrella shielding me from a rainstorm or a parasol shading me from the burning sun." He reached up and touched the leaves that were caressing his forehead. He seemed to find peace and tranquility in doing so.

The princess was saddened by her father's statement. Lately she had detected that he was rather fatalistic in his views.

"Look at yourself and this tree," the emperor continued in a cracking voice. "You both have grown up so beautifully ... I love the both of you!" The emperor's love for his daughter was understandable, but his love for a willow tree was most peculiar. There was only one person in whom he had confided about his love of the willow. That was his trusted servant, the eunuch Wang Tung-yin. When the eunuch asked him why he was so dearly in love with the tree, Chung-chen said that only the tree could give him comfort, a covering over his endangered being. When he sat beneath that tree, he confessed that he found safety from all the woes and foes that were converging on him.

When they returned to the imperial residence, the emperor led his daughter directly to the chamber where the altar in honor of his ancestors was located. The altar was hung high on one wall, displaying the names of all fifteen of his predecessors, each with a golden burner in front of it. When he saw them enter, Eunuch Wang and two junior eunuchs greeted the emperor and his daughter, bowing low to them. In the junior eunuchs' hands were bundles of incense sticks brightly lit, ready to be placed in the burners. The emperor took the bundles, one at a time, from the eunuchs. He then got down on his knees and bowed three times to each of his predecessors before placing the incense sticks into the burners from right to left, from the first emperor to his most immediate predecessor. The daughter followed behind her father as the ritual continued while the others in the room stayed prostrate.

Lately, the emperor had performed this ritual frequently. He prayed often to his ancestors in heaven to grant him the strength and wisdom to save the empire. Truth be told, it was more likely that he was begging for his ancestors to forgive him, in case he was to lose the realm.

CHAPTER 9
The Rebels

WHILE THE EMPEROR WAS PRAYING FOR FORGIVENESS AND HELP from his ancestors in heaven, his subjects were praying for heaven to grant them relief from starvation and disease.

Since Chung-chen had been reigning, China had not had a year when people were well fed and free from natural disasters. From 1627, the year he ascended to the throne, north China, especially the provinces of Shansi and Shensi, had endured droughts and famine over a span of a decade. On the outset, the people living south of these two provinces had fared better, but as time went on, they were also swept by the fate that had overtaken their neighbors in the north.

Shensi was hit the hardest by natural disasters, relentless droughts in the summers and snowstorms in the winters, which gave rise to pestilence, disease, and starvation of major proportions. Located at a higher elevation and with more high wind coming from the west, it had received very little rainfall. As a result, the land there was mostly barren. With the central government unable to offer financial aid to build new irrigation systems and repair the old, farming by the natives of Shensi was unsustainable, and famine prevailed for a long time.

Long period of famine bred malcontent, and malcontent bred unrest. Small pockets of unrest began to foment into larger revolts. With the people of Shensi on the forefront of many of these revolts, a rebellion of national proportions was in the making.

There was no lack of rabble-rousers to rise and challenge the status quo. A young man from Shensi named Li Tzu-cheng stood the tallest. He was born on or around 1610. His exact origins and birth date were not recorded in the annals of Chinese history. Traditional Chinese historians and scholars did not consider him worthy of recognition because he was branded as a highwayman, or, more aptly, a rebel. Li was not formally educated, but he had an avid interest in books on history and warfare. The book *The Art of Warfare* by Sun Tze especially interested him. So he would find people who were literate to read him the books.

Li's father left his mother when he and a younger brother were still toddlers. He had to grow up fast, and he worked odd jobs to support himself and his mother and brother. He began his working life as a shepherd for a former provincial official who had become a farmer after being discharged from his position for accepting bribery. Li worked for small pay, and he was beaten constantly by his master for not working hard enough and for stealing fruit from his trees. When the abuse became frequent and harsh, Li decided to walk off the job and return home to his mother and brother.

Traveling on foot, it took him two days to get to his hometown. Along the way, he encountered scenes of people fighting among themselves for food, mostly dead animals and dried-up vegetation. Because he had picked some fruit from his master's trees before he left, he was able to stave off hunger for two days.

When he reached his home, a rickety hut, he pushed the door and entered. To his surprise, he found three men and two women circling a pyre in the corner of the house. His mother and brother were nowhere to be found.

"Who are you?" Li yelled. "What are you doing in my house?" He walked closer to the gathering and kicked one of the men. "Where is my mother? And my brother?"

The man shook off Li's foot, got up, and faced him. "How in hell do I know where the fuck your mother is! Get out of my face!"

Li approached and looked down at the pyre, and he saw what appeared to be ribs from a small human body scattered on the floor. The stench emitted by the fire confirmed his suspicion that the group was eating the remains of a small child. He felt an urge to vomit, and he covered his mouth and dashed out of the house. After taking in a heavy dose of fresh air, Li ran to the nearest house and knocked at the door. When the door finally swung open after much pounding, a skeletal old man appeared.

"Uncle, do you know where my mother is?" Li asked, pointing at his hut.

"Young man, the old woman who lived there was your mother?" the old man asked.

"Yes, you remember me? My mother, my brother, and I lived in that house for many years. We were your neighbors."

"Oh." The old man looked confused, and he mumbled, "The old woman was your mother?" He kept repeating the phrase, glaring at Li.

"Yes—do you know where she is?"

"Your mother, that old woman?"

"Yes. Where did she go? And my brother ... Where—"

Before Li could complete his question, the old man blurted, as if he'd suddenly regained his memory, "She died ... and he was taken away!"

"When? And how?"

"A few months ago."

"How did my mother die?"

"Oh! Very sad! She was very sick for a long time."

"Very sick?"

"Yes, she was moaning every night for a long time. Very sick! Very sick!"

"How long?"

"I don't know. Long time! She died suddenly one day."

"Who took my brother away?"

"People in uniform."

"Where did they take him?"

The old man shook his head and went back into his house. As he tried to shut the door behind him, Li put his hand up and stopped the door from closing. "Uncle, do you have anyone inside your house with you?"

"No! Everybody died! My wife, my daughter ... and my son was taken away!"

"You are by yourself?"

"Yes!"

"What do you live on?"

"I eat rats! After eating all my livestock many months ago, I now eat whatever I can find," the old man lamented. "I can't even find a rat to eat anymore. I must have eaten the last one many months ago. So delicious!"

Li Tzu-cheng lowered his head. He succumbed to total sadness over the plight of the old man and his townsfolk, the death of his mother, and the disappearance of his brother. He turned on his heels and walked away without another word.

After wandering about, homeless and hungry, for some time, Li Tzu-cheng finally decided to join the imperial army, much against his will. But he had to find a way to survive.

In the army, Li Tzu-cheng was assigned to a unit close to his home; his duty was to maintain order in the region near his village. In simple terms, that meant policing the streets and picking up bodies of people who had died from starvation and disease. There was no shortage of dead bodies for Li and his unit to deal with for a long time.

"I am really sick and tired of this shit," Li cried out to two of the soldiers who were working with him as they picked up and carried the body of a young woman and threw it on top of the pile of cadavers on the rickety wagon parked alongside the road.

"You think you are tired of these shit? I have been doing this a lot longer than you have," the older of the two men working with him lamented.

"Yes! There seems to be no end to this," said the other man, who was leaning down again to pick up the body of an older man lying next to three more dead people. He waved at his teammates to help him. After throwing that body into the wagon, they went over to pick up the others. Suddenly a small gust blew, and a stench hit the faces of the three men. They buried their noses under their forearms and let out a yell, almost in unison: "Oh! Shit!"

"It's worse than shit," said Li. "With the hot sun burning down, the smell of the dead bodies gets worse as the day wears on."

As they moved slowly to pick up the next body, a man on a donkey rode by and handed a small basket over to one of the men. "Your rations." He hit the donkey with a stick he was holding and added, "Li, keep moving! There are more bodies down the road. You'd better pick them all up before sundown." He rode on.

Li spat at the donkey's tail and cursed. "That son of a bitch picks on me all the time. If lightning does not strike him first, I will strike him with this!" He picked up a shovel lying on the ground and swung it wildly at an imaginary target.

The man who accepted the basket muttered, "Forget it! He picks on all of us." He sat down on the grass and looked at the basket with disdain. "Same old shit. Boiled rice."

The other man promptly sat down on the ground and picked up his bowl from the basket and said, "Brother, don't complain." He downed his bowl in one motion. "Look over there and feel lucky."

Li slowly picked his bowl up and turned his head. He saw two men and two women fighting over a large scrap of food on the other side of the road. What they were fighting over was not clear, but to these famished people it was obviously something worth fighting for.

Then the other man pointed farther down the road and said, "Look down there—a bunch of people are tearing the bark from that old tree. I am glad I won't get to be like them."

"Brother, it won't be long before we'd all be eating grass and trees like them," answered Li. "I've seen people eating people with my own eyes. It's getting worse by the day!"

"I am not surprised," replied one of the men. "Before too long, people in the whole country will be doing that!"

"When I joined the army, I thought I'd be fed by the emperor," Li lamented.

"You are fed, aren't you?" said one of the men. He let out an uneasy chuckle.

"Yes! Watered-downed rice. You call that food?" the other man grumbled.

"We'd better get back to work before we get punished for falling down on the job," cried Li. "I thought I'd join the army to fight the enemy, but we have become body collectors."

The three men stood and went back to filling the wagon with more bodies. When the sun began to set, they were exhausted, and their wagon was loaded to the maximum. When they brought the wagon back to the compound, they were confronted by the sergeant in charge of the unit. While the three men followed his order to unload the dead, the sergeant was busy counting the bodies. Li was puzzled by the counting, and he muttered to himself, "Are we getting paid by the number of bodies we pick up or what?" When the unloading was done, the sergeant pointed and yelled at Li to pour oil onto the pile and light a fire to burn the bodies. Li hesitated because he had done that too often; he had come to hate being picked on for the dirty work. "I have got to get myself out of this shithole," he muttered to himself. "I joined the army because I wanted to escape another shithole, but the fucking army is a larger shithole than the other one!"

The sergeant slapped him in the face and yelled, "Li, get with it. Light the fire!" The fire finally caught on, and the burning of human remains created a permeating stench that almost suffocated everyone nearby. To Li, the stench was familiar; he had encountered it before.

Li's miserable life in the army did not change drastically, but the conditions in Shensi and the neighboring provinces took a turn for the worse. Famine and disease had overtaken the population south of Peking, and as a result, the discontent of the people was at a fever pitch. With the farmers in Shensi leading the charge, pockets of resistance against the rule of the provincial government began to form. By the late 1620s, these pockets had become formidable local militias and the foundation of a national rebellion.

In an effort to suppress these small uprisings at their roots, the emperor appointed an imperial envoy to take charge of the troubled regions. Unable to calm the natives and rein in the uprisings, the envoy decided on a military alternative: to demonstrate imperial resolve to take control of matters by slaughtering the masses. Over a few fateful days in 1627, tens of thousands of innocent poor people were murdered in broad daylight by the army of the emperor. Because the slaughter took place in the region where his unit was stationed, Li Tzu-cheng had to follow orders and participate in the atrocity.

"Brother, I cannot do this anymore," Li yelled at a fellow soldier who was standing next to him, swinging a sword at some defenseless people in a small farmhouse. His eyes were full of tears, and he could not bear to see the bloodshed and hear the cries of the dying people. While he was frozen with pity and fear, a sergeant came by and slapped him in the face, shouting, "Get moving! We have more killing to do."

Li Tzu-cheng spat at the back of the sergeant and returned to the mayhem, but he pushed most of his victims away from the scene, urging them to hide. On the last day of the mission, while he was going through the motions of killing, he suddenly heard loud noises coming toward him. The noise quickly became louder, and he and his unit were ordered by their commander to stop killing the innocents and take on a group of local militiamen. When he went out to confront the noisy crowd, Li noticed a man at the forefront of the group riding a mule and holding a banner made of a piece of red rag. As the man waved the red banner around and chanted, "Down with the emperor!" the crowd of around two hundred men, wielding large sickles, knives, and clubs, yelled loudly and charged at the army coming toward them. The two forces engaged in hand-to-hand combat for over an hour, and both sides suffered heavy casualties. Even though he fought bravely alongside his fellow soldiers, Li's heart was not in the fight; he fought for his own survival. His heart was really with the poor people and the local militiamen.

The scrimmage was fought to a draw. While the soldiers were licking their wounds, what remained of the militiamen withdrew to their hideouts. For a few weeks, scrimmages took place frequently, and they succeeded only in distracting the army from slaughtering the innocents for the time being.

Li Tzu-cheng endured many sleepless nights, reliving in his dreams the ugly scenes of killing innocent people. The thought of the old and the very young being murdered by their emperor was particularly revolting to him. He vowed to himself that one day he would rise to hold the emperor accountable for these heinous crimes.

As the natives of Shensi continued to suffer atrocities, their neighbors in the nearby provinces would soon begin to feel the pains themselves. The province of Shansi was not much better than the badland known as Shensi, its neighbor. Even though it was able to grow limited amounts of food, most of the harvest was confiscated by the government for military consumption. As the common people began to feel the pinch of famine, the natives truly became restless.

In the build-up to the Drama of 1644, 1629 was a pivotal year, the year when the populace rose from a state of dormant protestation to actively challenging the power of the throne. The provinces of Shansi and Shensi became the linchpins that drove the country to the state of revolution. With the farmers in Shensi taking the lead, province after province started agrarian revolts of their own.

A middle-aged farmer from Taiyuan, the capital of Shansi, led the way by building the first and the largest stronghold of rebels in China. The man and his cousin, known as the Brothers Kang, amassed a force of more than a thousand followers in a short six-month period.

One day, Big Kang, as he was called, said to Little Kang while they were eating a scanty meal consisting of rice soup and vegetables, "Brother, so many of our brothers and sisters are being slaughtered by the governor. We have fought hard and are still not able to slow down the killings. I am so frustrated! Do you have a better idea?"

"Big Brother, I have an idea that might work," Little Kang said after downing his bowl of soup.

Big Kang looked up. "Any idea is better than what we had been doing. We simply cannot face those bastards head on because they are stronger and better fed and have more logistics."

"You are right, Big Brother. We fought them pretty hard the other day and still came up empty. We lost many men and only succeeded in slowing down the slaughter of more innocent people a day or two."

"If you have a better idea for taking them on, spit it out."

"My thought is that if we spread our forces out and confront them on more fronts, that would divide their force and lessen their power," said Little Kang. "Also, scattering our attacks will add elements of surprise they must deal with."

"You might have a point," Big Kang said slowly as he pondered the strategy offered by his cousin. "I don't know if it will work, but it's sure worth trying."

The next day, the Brothers Kang called a meeting with the group leaders of their followers. They divided their force into ten smaller units and assigned them to ten separate locations to begin their offensives. Responding to insurgencies in ten locales, the governor had to divide his force to take on the rebels. Fighting in smaller skirmishes with the element of surprise in their favor, the rebels routed the imperial army on all fronts. Continuing to deploy guerrilla warfare, the rebels were able to sustain and prolong their resistance. Over a period of ten years, rebel forces throughout China adopted this "hit and hide" tactic and succeeded in building a major force against the emperor's army.

Living miserably as a soldier in the imperial army, Li Tzu-cheng began to feel restless and frustrated. Not only was he unhappy over taking part in the murder of his fellow villagers, he was also concerned about the future of the country. He was not educated, but he prided himself on being a man in the true Chinese tradition. He often told his close friends that to be "a man of man," one must be able to swallow the bitterest of the bitter pills of life.

His closest friend in the army was Liu Tsung-min. Liu was a year younger, but he came from a family of some means and was somewhat educated. After his father had lost his small wealth and was killed by the emperor's army, along with his family, Liu was forcibly taken into the army. After going through basic training, he was assigned to the unit where Li had belonged. The two were instantly attracted to each other, even though their education and temperaments were very different. While Li Tzu-cheng was strong-minded, Liu Tsung-min was opportunistic. While Li thrived on hardship, Liu sought the easy life. They did have one thing in common: they hated the status quo.

"Brother Liu, I really cannot take this shit any longer!" Li said to his newfound friend on many occasions when they were alone in their rickety barracks.

"I was thinking the same thing," Liu would answer in an even lower voice. "Do you have a solution to get us out of this shit?"

Li leaned over to his good friend and muttered into his ear; his words jolted Liu out of his cot. "You must be crazy!" Liu yelled.

"Well, do you have a better idea?"

"They will chop our heads off if we get caught doing what you suggest!"

"I'd much rather have my head cut off than to continue with this miserable shit!"

"Well, losing your head is not going to do anyone any good. I thought you had grand designs of saving our countrymen from their miseries."

"What good will come of us being locked in this shitty army? We cannot do anything for ourselves, let alone help save the human race!"

Liu remained apprehensive about his friend's plan. "How are we to accomplish what you said?"

"We will just have to wait for the opportunity to come. Patience might be the better part of valor in this case." Li had suddenly taken on the role of the opportunist, which was usually the forte of his friend. Liu nodded and put the case temporarily to rest.

After the two restless men had spent four miserable years in the army, their opportunity finally came in the spring of 1633. In response to an attack by a rebel force led by Big Kang on the outskirts of a village in Shensi, Li's unit was deployed into action. On a vast expanse of land, the two forces met and engaged in a fierce battle. Li and Liu fought side by side for more than an hour before they eventually separated. While Liu continued to battle on foot, Li forcefully claimed a horse from an enemy officer and took off in the direction of the flying red banner. He had seen that red banner on many occasions, and he knew that it identified where the rebel leader would be. He knew instinctively that to win a battle, one must kill or capture the leader of the enemy.

As he battled his way to where the red banner was, he noticed that the sergeant of his unit was engaging in a fierce fight with the rebel leader. As he was busily fending off enemy soldiers coming at him, Li noticed that the rebel leader had fallen off his mount. When the sergeant was about to plunge his sword into the fallen rebel leader, Li let out a loud yell. "No, you bastard!" He raised his sword and pierced the heart of the sergeant. As the sergeant fell to the ground, Li raised his sword triumphantly and yelled, "Down with the emperor!" He turned himself around and started to engage soldiers instead of rebels. With the help of his men, Big Kang escaped to safety.

After seeing his good friend ride off in a horse, Liu Tsung-min followed his lead and pilfered a horse of his own. He found his friend just as Li was engaging the soldiers. Liu knew it was time to also change his allegiance. So the two fought alongside one another again, which Big Kang observed with total delight and wonder. At the end, the imperial army was soundly defeated, and many soldiers deserted or surrendered to the rebels.

Big Kang was grateful for the heroic action of Li Tzu-cheng. He immediately ordered his lieutenants to track down the young soldier who had saved his life. The effort to locate his benefactor did not take long. Li Tzu-cheng and Liu Tsung-min had led a contingent of a hundred or so soldiers to the temporary camp of the rebel leader, about two hundred yards away from the battlefield.

Big Kang got down on his knees as soon as he saw Li Tzu-cheng approach. "My benefactor, I'd like to thank you for saving my humble life!" He knocked his head on the ground nine times to pay respect to the surprised deserter.

Li quickly dismounted, as did Liu. They both bent down and helped Big Kang off his knees and simultaneously prostrated themselves in front of the rebel leader. "Sir, we'd like to pledge our allegiance to your cause. I am sure the brothers who came with us will do the same."

Before Big Kang could utter a word, the soldiers who had come with Li and Liu shouted almost in unison, "Sir, we are here to fight for you! Down with the emperor!"

CHAPTER 10

The Manchus

WITH THE PEOPLE IN THE NORTHERN PROVINCES OF SHENSI and Shansi leading the charge, the other provinces answered the call to take arms against their oppressive emperor. By the late 1630s, barely eight years into the insurgency, the rebels had won major battles in many provinces and occupied more than half of the territories that had been under the control of the Ming government. While the emperor and his court were preoccupied with the growing menace of a full-scale agrarian revolt, the threat looming to the northeast of the capital intensified.

Northeast of Peking lay a vast landmass with dense forests known as Manchuria. The people in that region had risen to political prominence in the twelfth century. Around 1110, a Tungus people called the Jurchens had founded a small but powerful kingdom in that territory. They called it the Chin dynasty: the golden dynasty. While the Sung dynasty, of Han Chinese origin, in the south was in chaos, the Chin ruler took the opportunity and invaded their capital and captured two reigning emperors. Unable to resist, the Sung regime moved its capital to Hangchow in the south. For two hundred years thereafter, the Sung dynasty coexisted with the Jurchens.

With the Mongols rising to power under their charismatic leader Kublai Khan in the thirteenth century, China was united again. Both the Sung and the Chin empires collapsed, and the Jurchen people scattered to the four winds. However, when the Mongol rule in China came to an end less than a hundred years later, the Jurchens rose again to fill the power vacuum in the northern region of China.

For three hundred years after the demise of the Chin dynasty, the Jurchens did not play a significant role in the geopolitical history of China. They divided into many clans and lived with one another, sharing the forest clearings in northeastern Asia. Unlike the Mongols, who had lived in the steppes and excelled on horseback, the Jurchens, who became known as Manchurians, or simply as Manchus, were basically hunters. At the beginning of the seventeenth century, a star was born to the Jurchen race, and the historical landscape of China was forever changed.

Nurhaci was born in 1559 into a family belonging to the Aisingioro clan, the highest ranking of the more than ten clans in the Jurchen race. It was said that at his birth, bright lights glowed in the northern skies and lit up the horizon for a long time. As he grew up, Nurhaci came to a firm belief that heaven had bestowed on him a destiny for greatness. With an imposing physique and a daring personality, he commanded respect and inspired awe among his contemporaries. Unfortunately, he was neglected by his father, a strongman in his clan, and scorned by his stepmother. His mother had died young, leaving him and two younger brothers unloved and unattended to. The father favored his second wife and the two sons she gave him. Living a lonely life in his adolescence, Nurhaci cultivated a strong will to survive and succeed. He spent much of his time living in the forest, hunting big game and honing his skills in horseback riding and archery. With the passing of his father, Nurhaci took charge of the clan. He faced bitter opposition, but with the help of his brothers and some loyal followers, he was finally able to consolidate his power.

Nurhaci's overarching ambition was to conquer China. But, as a realist, he knew that he must first unite his race. After thirty years of tireless efforts, he finally succeeded in forging a kingdom from a loose alliance among the Jurchen tribes.

He frequently called on senior tribal leaders to discuss options for improving the administration of the kingdom. Included in the group were three princelings, called senior *beiles* by the Manchus. Nurhaci had one wife, two titled consorts, and many concubines. He had sixteen sons from his wife and the two titled consorts, the wife giving birth to three. These three were given the title senior beiles. The first-born's temperament did not endear him to Nurhaci because of his penchant for books rather than horse skills. So Nurhaci favored Abahai, his second son, who was very much like him in personality. According to the law of succession embraced by the Manchus, Nurhaci had to anoint the eldest son as the crown prince. However, he persisted in calling on Abahai in official matters and appointed him a de facto crown prince, over the objection of many tribal leaders.

The close relationship between Nurhaci and Abahai did not please his stepbrothers and the first titled consort, named Diada. But Nurhaci was still in charge; there was little or nothing anyone could do to alter that strong tie. Abahai, also known as "Hung Taiji" in history, had visions for the Jurchens far greater than those held by his father. In the many moments Abahai and his father had shared while hunting in the lush Manchurian forests or fishing in the beautiful rivers, the young beile expounded on his visions for his race to his father.

"Father," he would boast after shooting down a deer from fifty yards away while perched in the saddle of a Mongolian horse, "dead on! Can you match that?"

The father, sitting on a stallion of his own, clapped his hands and said, "My son, if you can be as accurate in killing our enemies, then I will applaud you again and again!" Nurhaci then took a bow and an arrow from one of the escorts near him and unleashed a shot of his own at a deer about fifty yards away, but he missed the target. "My son," he acceded, "you have won this round."

The father and son let out hearty laughs and galloped off to a house on the shore of the beautiful Liao River, where the summer palace of the Manchu kingdom was situated, and enjoyed a lunch that awaited them. Sitting side by side, Nurhaci put his hand on the son's shoulder and said softly, "My son, your father is getting older by the day. Even though it has been a rewarding life, I still have one regret." He gazed forlornly at the slow-flowing green water in the river, shaking his head slowly.

Sensing that his father would have preferred the power of the kingdom be passed to him rather than his elder brother, contrary to the law of succession, Abahai cut in. "Father, you have done well for yourself, the family, and, most importantly, our people. What regret do you still have?"

"Time is flowing like the water in this beautiful river, and I still have not been able to conquer China!" Nurhaci sighed. "I am afraid I am running out of time to achieve that goal."

Abahai tried to comfort and reassure the father. "Father, there is still time left for you to do greater things."

Nurhaci shook his head slightly. "I am afraid your brother will not have the ability or the temperament to carry on with my dream."

"Father, I think you can realize that dream yourself soon."

"If I did not suffer that defeat in Shan-hai-kuan, my dream of conquering Peking would have been within my grasp," Nurhaci lamented. "That up-and-coming young warrior in the Ming army put up a good fight!"

"Wu San-kuei!" Abahai said quickly, with a trace of contempt in his voice. "I will take care of him one day!"

"If I had taken that fortress, our march to Peking would have been easy. But that young warrior's ability to defend his fort really took me by surprise!

The son stood up, about to speak, but his father cut him off.

"I have fought hundreds of battles since reuniting our race ten years ago. I have not experienced such a bitter taste of defeat! We must take Shan-hai-kuan!"

"Father, not a problem," vowed the son. "Your wish is my will!"

"My son, I know that you will avenge my humiliation by that Ming general one day. However, I am somewhat concerned that with my departure from earth you will be faced with a divided family and a court in disarray."

"Father, don't worry! You have many more years to live. If and when the day arrives, I have confidence that I will rise to the occasion and not let our empire come apart."

"I have gone against the advice of many of my senior advisers to call on you more than your elder brother for official business. They advocated a council to run the kingdom at my death and assist your brother. The council is to be manned by four senior beiles, and you will be one of the councilmen. But, as you know, your elder brother is a weak man who has no interest in military affairs."

"Father, I understand!" Abahai said confidently. "I will see to it that your dream of ruling China becomes a reality!"

Nurhaci smiled. Deep down, he knew that Abahai will carry on with his will, regardless how difficult his path to power would be.

Nurhaci decided to mount an offensive action against the Ming empire. He marched south and took the Liao-tung region with little resistance. Capturing two cities with large Chinese populations, Fu-shun and Shen-yang, he chose the latter as his capital and proclaimed himself the first khan of a new dynasty: the Latter Chin dynasty. He chose that name to remind the world of the glory days of the late, great Chin dynasty, founded by his illustrious ancestors many centuries before.

Nurhaci ruled the new territory with zeal and an iron fist. He established strict discipline in his troops, forbidding them from looting or raping the Chinese people. He also demanded total subservience from the Chinese: to obey Manchu rules, even to the extent of ordering them to queue their hair and shave their foreheads, as was Manchu custom. He took the Ming officials who had surrendered to him into his government, but he kept them on the lower rungs of the political ladder. His hope was to commence an all-out assault at Shan-hai-kuan as soon as he could stabilize the new territory he had conquered. But Nurhaci did not get to accomplish that goal; he died within a short time, in 1627, at age sixty-eight. He had lived an adventurous and fruitful life and brought a minority race in Asia back to the forefront of Chinese history.

Within days of his father's burial, Abahai took up the matter of succession in a meeting with the senior beiles and key officials of the court.

"My brother, shortly before his passing our father asked me to take the reins of our kingdom," Abahai said boldly to his elder brother, the crown prince.

"Your Honor," volunteered one of the senior officials in attendance, "the law of the land dictates that the eldest son, your brother, will take the throne upon the passing of the khan."

"The khan intimated to me that he wished to conquer China without delay," said Abahai, "and he designated me as the leader for that task. Unless I take over the kingdom, the late khan's wish will not be fulfilled. For that reason, I submit that the wish of the late khan will supersede the law of the land."

The debate went on for a long time until the crown prince finally raised his hand to halt the barrage. "I believe my brother is right. I do not possess the character and ability to carry out the late khan's wish."

Everyone in the meeting was surprised by the crown prince's statement, especially Amin, a cousin, and two of the crown prince's half-brothers. Amin was particularly upset, but he held back his urge to air his opposition. Abahai was glad to hear the concession made by his elder brother. Sensing that the crown prince would not stop him from taking the throne, Abahai called the meeting to an end, While the crown prince and his contingent left quietly, Amin and the two half-brothers were highly agitated.

Within a few days, Abahai installed himself as the new khan with much fanfare and festivities. The ceremonies and the afterglow further irritated Amin, so he spun into action by calling on Daisan, one of the half-brothers, and his mother, Diada. Daisan, the most ambitious of the three sons borne by Diada, was only nineteen years old. With Amin's encouragement and his mother's support, Daisan began a scheme to try to usurp the throne. The three met to work on a plan to undermine Abahai.

"Mother, I'd like to invite the new khan to our chambers to celebrate his ascension. Do you think he will accept?" Daisan asked.

"I don't see how he can decline your invitation, especially if he wants to rule the kingdom peacefully," Diada replied matter-of-factly.

"Good! Then I will issue the invitation."

"Wait! I have an idea." Amin pulled Daisan close and whispered at length into his ear. At the end, Daisan wore a look of disbelief.

As the cousin's words finally sank in, Daisan reacted. "Are you sure that's a good idea? Abahai has a network of loyal followers."

"What choice do we have? We will be miserable under him!" said Amin.

The mother was curious about what Amin had whispered into the ear of her son, so she gave Daisan a puzzled look. Sensing his mother's curiosity, Daisan mumbled to her what Amin had proposed. After hearing Amin's plan, the mother nodded in agreement but said nothing.

"Let's not issue the invitation to him yet," Daisan said suddenly.

The mother and Amin were surprised at Daisan's comment.

"There is one person I must see before putting our plan into action," Daisan added. He called the meeting to an end and declared, "I will get back to you when I'm ready."

Amin left, and Daisan withdrew from his mother and went directly to see his youngest brother, Dorgon.

Dorgon was a mature young man. At seventeen, he was full of energy and confidence. He had read many Chinese classics and books on the history of China, and he was well aware of the station occupied by his race in Chinese society. He was proud of his ancestral roots, especially the greatness of the Chin dynasty. Like his half-brother Abahai, he believed in the supremacy of the Jurchens and in the prospect that his race would one day rule China again. He wanted to play a major role in that event if it were to become a reality. When Daisan came calling and asked for his advice on Amin's plan, Dorgon expressed his ambivalence.

"I am not too sure it's a good idea to do what you are planning to do," Dorgon said. "Even if it did work, we'd still have to deal with the loyal followers in Abahai's camp. That's not an easy task!"

Daisan was somewhat taken aback by Dorgon's timid response, so he retorted, "I thought you'd be the strongest in our family. Can you really live with Abahai?"

"Not that I cherish an Abahai rule, but many things are out of our control. For instance, he controls the army," Dorgon responded icily. Even though he pretended to despise an Abahai rule, Dorgon harbored no animosity toward his half-brother. As a matter of fact, he had always looked up to Abahai and admired him for his bold visions. The dream of conquering China especially appealed to him.

Dorgon, like Abahai, was one of those rare men who appeared from time to time on the Chinese political stage. He was born not to the Han Chinese race but to a minor race, very much like Kublai and Genghis Khan of the Mongols. Unlike either of those military geniuses, Dorgon was a scholar and historian. But he held a firm belief that to rule China, his people must be equal to the Chinese in many aspects, especially in law and culture. In his mind, the existing culture and rules of his own race would not be sufficient to sustain rule, even if they were militarily superior to the Chinese. So he diligently and methodically studied the systems used by the Ming dynasty and many successful past dynasties. Deep down, he also knew that only Abahai could bring the Jurchens back to the heights of glory; no one else would be up to that task, especially not Daisan.

"If he is eliminated, the army will support me," said Daisan, bringing Dorgon back to reality, "because I will be the khan!"

"Don't be so sure," Dorgon shot back.

"I don't know about you," Daisan asserted, giving Dorgon an antagonistic look, as he stormed out of the chamber. Ultimately, Dorgon did not commit to take part in the plan, but he did not ask to be excused from taking part in the event either.

Within a fortnight, an invitation was officially issued to Abahai when preparations for the event were completed.

One beautifully moonlit evening, the celebration for the new khan was held in Daisan's palace. The hall was highly decorated and brightly lit with many large candles. In the center of the hall was a huge round table placed on top of a raised platform. Surrounding the platform were ten tables; the higher-ranking tribal chiefs sat front and center, the lower-ranking ones around the sides. The khan's seat was higher and larger than those surrounding him at the head table. Seats beside him were reserved for Daisan, on the right, and Dorgon, on the left. To the right of Daisan was Amin, and to the left of Dorgon was the deposed crown prince.

The event began with dancing performed by ten young and beautiful women dressed in colorful Manchu banner costumes, accompanied by five pipers. At the end of the first performance, rounds of toasts to heaven and to Nurhaci and the ancestors of the Jurchens began. At the end of the toasts, Abahai made a brief speech, expressions of gratitude to heaven and to the ancestral temple and a plea for their blessings for a peaceful and successful reign. At the conclusion of the khan's remarks, everyone stood and sang out in unison, "Long live the khan! Long live the khan!"

The evening went on cheerfully as another group of beautifully attired young females performed more native songs and dances. When midnight approached, Daisan rose, reaching for a new bottle of wine. Dorgon responded by also reaching for the bottle, which was placed near him. He opened the bottle and handed it over to his brother. Daisan took the bottle and promptly filled a new chalice and offered it, with two hands, to the khan. Abahai accepted the chalice with a broad smile. He lifted it to show the crowd and drank it in one swift motion. He tipped the chalice over to show that it was empty, and everyone picked up a glass and sang almost in unison, "Ten thousand years to Your Majesty, the new khan! Ten thousand years to the great Latter Chin dynasty!" They all emptied their glasses.

As the festivities wound down, the khan rose to depart. The crown prince also rose, but his knees suddenly buckled under him, and he fell to the floor. His escorts quickly came forward and assisted him off the platform to a nearby chair. Moments later, after the khan had departed, he regained his senses and was carried from the scene.

After the guests had dispersed, Daisan and Amin cornered Dorgon and gave him a bewildered look, wondering why the crown prince had been drugged instead of Abahai. Dorgon looked away, turned on his heels, and left without uttering a word.

Two days after the event, the crown prince died suddenly. The diagnosis was that he had ingested a dose of poison and suffered a slow and agonizing death. The khan ordered an investigation and discovered that the poisoned wine had been intended for him. Apparently, Dorgon had saved his life by adroitly switching the bottles, handing the clean one to Daisan. The crown prince had taken a drink from the poisoned bottle. Since Abahai lost no love for his elder brother, his grief over the loss was short. However, when he discovered that the plan to poison him was instigated by Daisan and Amin, with the help of his stepmother, he had them promptly executed for treason. The next day, Abahai summoned Dorgon to his palace for a meeting.

Kneeling in front of his half-brother, Dorgon paid verbal respects to him. "Your Majesty, I am saddened by the passing of your elder brother. I am pleased that Your Majesty is safe and secure!"

"Rise!" Abahai reached down to help Dorgon off his knees. "My brother, thank you for your quick wits. By the grace of our ancestors, I am alive and well!"

"Your Majesty, our country needs you! I hope my action helped ensure the greatness that will come from a long and illustrious reign by Your Majesty."

"I hope you understand that the execution of your elder brother and mother could not be avoided, in the fair administration of the law," said the khan. "I am not asking for your forgiveness but for your understanding of the rule of law."

"Your Majesty, I understand," Dorgon answered in a lowered

voice. "I am saddened by the death of my mother and brother. But they brought their demise on by themselves, even though I warned them against such treachery. If I were in your position, I would have done the same, in the name of justice!"

Abahai was impressed by his half-brother's maturity. As time went on, the khan and Dorgon became closer and saw each other regularly. The khan was impressed with Dorgon's knowledge of government, so he decided to further test his mettle and loyalty. "I heard that you are not only a devout pupil of Chinese classics but also an ardent student of the art of war."

"Yes, Your Majesty, I enjoy reading Chinese classics and history. I also like to hunt and practice archery. I especially like playing a Chinese chess game that imitates war games."

"Interesting!" The khan was amused. "Are you a good equestrian?"

"I have ridden enough to be an average equestrian. I am sure I still have a lot to learn to be equal to Your Majesty," said Dorgon respectfully. "I heard that you and Father rode together frequently in his later years."

"Yes!" the khan said, a touch of emotion revealed in his voice. "Our father was quite a great man. Too bad you were so young when he died and did not have more time with him. If he knew you as well as I do, he'd really have enjoyed and loved your company!"

In the next ten years of his reign, Abahai embarked on many successful military campaigns against China. As a result, his empire expanded across the Gulf of Liaotung into a territory called Liaohsi, west of Liao River. With Dorgon's help, he also set up rules and laws similar to those of the Ming government, to make the Chinese people's assimilation into the Jurchen societies more comfortable and easier. Unlike his father, Nurhaci, who had placed the Ming officials who surrendered to him in the lowest ranks, Abahai and Dorgon took them in and gave them equivalent ranks to those they had held in the Ming hierarchy. Such benevolent acts had paid large dividends in running a smooth and efficient government.

On the military front, Abahai was eager to step up his assault on Shan-hai-kuan and ultimately Peking. He was an impatient man; he realized that time was passing him quickly by and he still had not made major progress in conquering China.

"General Wu San-kuei is a pain in my gut," the khan often lamented to his generals and to Dorgon in particular.

"Your Majesty," Dorgon would counsel him, "yes, he is a pain in the scheme of things, but we can deal with him! It's a matter of time."

"We cannot wait much longer," the khan insisted. "I made a vow to Father that I would conquer China quickly." He paused. "It has been more than ten years since our father died."

"Your Majesty, we are not ready to take the big steps in our plan to enter China," Dorgon said, trying to calm the khan's anxiety.

"How much longer do you think it will take to get us to be ready for that first big step?"

"Your Majesty, the Ming army has a powerful new weapon at their disposal. They have so-called cannons that can mow down hundreds of horses and foot soldiers at a time." Dorgon had learned from his intelligence sources about the Ming defenses on the Great Wall.

With his military at Shan-hai-kuan being held at bay by Wu San-kuei, Dorgon advised the khan to use the lull to build up his treasury and the army. Abahai reluctantly agreed to bide his time.

In 1636, strange streaks of lights appeared in the northern skies in Manchuria, much like the events that had taken place in 1559. Watching the strange phenomenon with Dorgon and some close advisers, Abahai was in awe of the spectacle. He mused to them that perhaps the lights were positive omens being sent from heaven. He told them that he wished to abandon his title as khan and take on the title of emperor. Dorgon echoed the khan's sentiment, and he told him that he too read positive signs into the appearance of the Northern Lights. He further reminded the khan that at the birth of their father, Nurhaci, strange lights had also appeared in the northern skies. It would be natural for the khan to take on the titles son of heaven and emperor of his people.

Abahai was delighted to hear Dorgon's interpretation of the lights in the skies, so he converted his kingdom into an empire, in the traditional Chinese fashion. He proclaimed his empire the Great Ching dynasty. This action, he thought, would strike fear into the hearts of the Han Chinese population, signifying that he had received the blessing from heaven to rule them as an absolute monarch. He also wanted to imitate the great Kublai Khan of the Mongols, who had conquered and united China after taking over the reign from the great Genghis Khan.

Unlike his father, Abahai succeeded in adopting the Chinese form of government by shredding the barbaric methodology of the Jurchen people. Dorgon recruited many high-level Chinese scholars by promising high positions to those who would agree to join the new Manchu regime. As a result, many Chinese officials and generals turned their backs on their emperor and surrendered to the Manchu empire.

Within a decade, Abahai succeeded in building a stronger military force and an efficient civil administration. He poised menacingly, north of the Great Wall, waiting for the time to come when he could challenge Ming rule in Peking.

CHAPTER 11

The Dashing Prince

AFTER THEIR DESERTION FROM THE MING ARMY, LI TZU-cheng and Liu Tsung-min fought hard alongside the Brothers Kang. Over a ten-year period, they waged many battles against the Ming army and took over many villages and towns in northwestern China. In one bloody battle in the spring of 1635, Little Kang sustained a major wound that took his life. In need of leadership on the frontlines, Big Kang called Li Tzu-cheng into his camp.

"Brother Li!" Big Kang greeted Li with a wide grin when he saw Li arrive at the large tent in a small village in southern Shensi province. "I'd like you to assume the command of the southern region and take the city of Loyang."

Li was thrilled to learn of the promotion, but he suppressed his excitement and said, "Big Brother, I am most humbled by your trust in me." He bowed low. "But why Loyang again? We've captured most of that region already. We should concentrate our forces on a push northward to Peking!"

"You are right, Brother," said Big Kang. "Unfortunately because we lost our younger brother, the Ming army has recaptured some of the areas in that region. We not only have to reclaim the lost land, but we must also blunt the resurgence of the enemy forces."

"I understand, but why Loyang in particular?"

"I learned recently that Loyang has a large cache of treasure stored there. We need to take those resources in order to make our push to the north easier."

"I hope I am up to the task, sir!"

"I am sure you will be. You are highly recommended by my senior advisers, and, to a man, they think that you are prime to take on more responsibility. So go and get it done, Brother!" Big Kang got up from behind his wooden table and put a hand on Li's shoulder to give his parting comment. "Good luck! Oh yes, take Liu Tsung-min with you. I understand that he is a capable leader of men, like you, and the two of you work together well."

"Yes, sir." Li bowed to Kang and said, "I shall proceed without delay!"

Back in his camp, Li immediately hunted down Liu and told him of their new orders. The next day, they proceeded south to assume command of the rebel's southern regiment.

"Brother Liu, the opportunity has come for us to shine!" Li said with enthusiasm after arriving in the southern rebel headquarters.

"Brother, it's a tribute to your ability," Liu said with a big smile, and he patted his good friend on the back. "As you rise in rank, do not leave this good friend behind!"

Li, pointing a finger at the sky, said, "Heaven will be our witness—we will share the good times as well as the bad times together. Forever!"

"Thank you, brother. Let's march together to Peking! We will share the spoils!"

"We will," said Li, "but not so fast." He paused momentarily. "Big Kang ordered us to take Loyang. Remember?"

"That means we are retreating from our current position. Why waste resources going backward? We should direct all of our energy and forces at Peking!"

"Brother, that's what I said to Big Brother. But he said he wanted to conquer Loyang first because the emperor's uncle lives there and has a large cache of treasure worth a tremendous sum."

Liu's eyes opened wide when he heard the news of the treasure, and he was momentarily lost for words. However, he was secretly delighted; he could not wait to get his hands on some of those precious treasure.

"Big Kang ordered us to take Loyang and the territories we have given back to the emperor since of the death of his cousin. Go and prepare to attack the city immediately." Li issued the order without hesitation.

Within a few days, Li Tzu-cheng and Liu Tsung-min took five thousand of the best trained soldiers and proceeded farther southwest toward Honan Province, where Loyang was located. Li was a strict disciplinarian in the true military sense, even though he was not educated and was basically a peasant by origin. The whole rebel force was a ragtag bunch because it was poor and led by a peasant, Big Kang. Li, however, molded his unit in accordance with his beliefs: only well-disciplined soldiers could win battles, and discipline began with obeying orders and presenting a good appearance. So he demanded that his soldiers be outfitted with uniforms, even though it was difficult to achieve his desired goal due to the shortage of monetary resources. But he did his best in very trying circumstances. He would dress in a neatly tailored short green robe with black trousers. Instead of a small military cap, like those worn by all his subordinates, he opted for a green Stetson so that when he was perched on his horse, his troops could see him easily from all sides of the battlefield.

Within a fortnight, Li's regiment had recaptured almost all the land lost to the imperial army. The rebels encountered scant resistance. The imperial troops had run out of provisions; most deserted, and some surrendered without a fight. Li's troops were poised near the east gate to Loyang when they encountered cannon fire, much to Li's surprise. Li had never experienced firepower like the salvos that were hurled at them from the tower at Loyang. So instead of ordering his men to storm the gate, Li gathered his senior officers to decide on a strategy to handle the emergency.

In the meantime, inside the city gates of Loyang in his opulent mansion, Prince Fu called an emergency meeting of his own to deal with the imminent attack by the rebels. The mansion was located in a huge square in the center of Loyang, surrounded by three smaller halls. Loyang had been a capital to a few Chinese dynasties in the past, and it was a highly civilized hub on the western rim of the rich Central Plain of China.

Prince Fu was one of Emperor Chung-chen's uncles, the favorite son of Emperor Wan-li, who was Chung-chen's grandfather. The prince was in his midforties, an extremely obese man who had, literally, enjoyed the fat of the land to the extreme. Sitting in a chair specially built to accommodate his bulk, he vented his fear and frustration at the men gathered around him. "The rebels are at our doorsteps! Can our firepower hold them back?"

"We have the best firepower in China. I submit that it should do the job!" said his most-trusted lieutenant.

The firepower being discussed was the cannons the prince had purchased from the Portuguese through a middleman named Cheng Chih-lung. Cheng, who had grown up in Macao and lived in Manila, had become a fisherman and, ultimately, a pirate on the China Sea. By virtue of his association with the Portuguese, he ventured back to China to peddle arms, which he did with modest success. He tried to sell the cannons to Peking, but the government was poor, and his efforts met with dismal failure. However, through his tenacity, he did succeed in peddling some smaller cannons to Wu San-kuei for his defense of Shan-hai-kuan. Cheng, in his later years, had gained some notoriety because of his enterprising nature and accumulation of small wealth. But, unfortunately, most of his fame was achieved in Nanking, after the collapse of the Ming dynasty. He did not play a major role in the Drama of 1644, and he'd dearly have loved to be at its center. It was his son, Cheng Chung-kung, also known as Koxinga in the west, who gained historical acclaim because of his heroic endeavors in trying to restore the defunct Ming dynasty. But even his persistent efforts had gone for naught. In the end, it was the descendants of Koxinga who extended the saga when they founded a Chinese kingdom in Formosa in the late seventeenth century.

Desperate to protect his domain and substantial ill-gotten wealth, Prince Fu paid a large sum to buy the cannons. It was said that when his nephew, the emperor, came calling for financial support to save the empire, Prince Fu donated a small sum of five thousand ounces of silver. According to most estimates, in twenty-plus years of profiteering the prince had accumulated more than two million ounces of silver and a large number of jewels and other treasures. He opted for self-defense by spending hundreds of thousands to buy and transport the cannons rather than helping to save his family's empire. In reality, from a lack of technical knowhow and properly trained personnel, the cannons had become nothing more than showpieces. And the supply of cannonballs was insufficient to do the job at hand.

Feeling insecure, the prince prepared for an evacuation. He had a plan drawn up to help him escape from Loyang. But the logistics of an ideal relocation were difficult, to say the least, because he had little or no time. "To save myself is easy," he would lament to his subordinates, "but to take the treasures and the amenities of the lifestyle I am accustomed to will be impossible!" He was not willing to give up the sumptuous and comfortable lifestyle that he had enjoyed for more than twenty years, so he ordered a massive evacuation.

"Your Excellency, we have put together twenty wagons of your valuable possessions," volunteered one of his assistants, "but we had better begin to identify what we'd like to move with us."

"First and foremost will be my women," the prince said unabashedly. His "harem" had more than thirty young women, varying in ages from fifteen to twenty-five. "Next, we must have food to last us for a month on the road, until we find a safe place to settle." He was not about to forgo the quality and the quantity of the food and sex he would need to fulfill his insatiable appetites, even in a time of crisis.

"Your Excellency, the commander of the police unit that is charged with guarding the gates said that he cannot hold for more than a few days," said his chief lieutenant urgently. After pausing momentarily, he continued. "Sir, we must prepare to depart before the rebels break through the east gate."

"Our cannons should be able to deter that eventuality a little longer, should they not?" the prince asked his lieutenants, scanning their faces, anticipating a positive response.

No one dared speculate how long the cannons would hold off the enemy assaults, so there was no quick response. Finally, the chief lieutenant again broke the silence. "Your Excellency, the police chief said his men are not adequately trained to work the cannons, and there seems to be a short supply of cannonballs. We might not be able to hold the fort for more than a few days."

Prince Fu shuffled his fat body uneasily on his chair. Suddenly he realized the danger he must face was imminent. So he blurted out, "Let's prepare for our journey out of here quickly. Issue the order to the police chief to do his best and to inform me if things take a turn for the worse!"

Li Tzu-cheng ordered his unit leaders to scatter his men into ten groups, creating a frontal attack the width of the city wall. Some men would scale the wall, and some would storm the gates. The units would begin their attacks at intervals of one hundred drumbeats. Then the defenders of the gates would have to deal with ten fronts rather than concentrating the firepower in one direction. The strategy worked; most cannon salvos landed in empty spaces, and the rebel troops suffered minimal casualties.

Within two days, the rebels succeeded in penetrating the city walls, even though they were unable to force open the east gate. The police chief could sense the rapid falling of the city, so he hurriedly dispatched a messenger to inform the prince of the imminent danger.

Hearing the bad news, Prince Fu swiftly gathered his entourage, consisting mainly of his women and trusted servants, and ordered his men to load all his treasures in the wagons. The next day, with the sun barely risen, he ran out of his mansion to direct the exodus toward the west gate, away from the approaching rebels. Suddenly, he shouted frantically, "Hold on! I have to find my lucky charm—where did I put it?" He checked his neck and his pockets for the charm: a large piece of jade dangling on a gold chain that was bestowed on him by his father, the Emperor Wan-li. He waddled back into the mansion and reappeared with his jewel within a few moments. With the help of two of his manservants, he climbed into his sedan, which was a large horse-drawn wagon equipped with a comfortable bed within. As his wagon began to move, suddenly a heavy rain fell. With his wagon leading the way, the caravan of twenty horse-drawn wagons weaved through the narrow streets of Loyang toward the west gate, directly opposite from the advancing rebel soldiers.

By midday, the rebel troops broke open the east gate, and Li Tzu-cheng entered Loyang triumphantly, Liu Tsung-min riding behind him. While settling themselves in the posh Fu mansion, Li ordered a posse of twenty soldiers to hunt down the escaping caravan. It did not take long for the rebel posse to catch up with the caravan, as the huge downpour had wreaked havoc for the escapees. The wagon was mired in a muddy road because of Prince Fu's excessive bulk. The rebel soldiers caught up with him and redirected the caravan back to the Fu mansion.

While Li Tzu-cheng was busy tending to military affairs, Liu Tsung-min was more concerned with finding the treasure. When Prince Fu and the caravan were brought back to the mansion, Li singlehandedly sat in judgment of the prince. Seating in the throne belonging to Prince Fu, Li acted like a man who had finally made it to the top of the world. The prince was brought in by two of Li's private guards, who pushed the obese man to his knees in front of Li.

"Prince Fu?" Li said, not believing his eyes: he was looking at an extremely fat man, unshaven and disheveled. "Do you have an apology for the people of Loyang for the extreme hardship that you have put them through all these years?"

Prince Fu's initial reaction was defiance. However, he quickly came to the realization that he no longer controlled his own destiny, so he lowered his voice and responded contritely. "I have nothing to be apologetic about. My wealth was bequeathed to me by my father, the Emperor Wan-li."

"As the head of this fiefdom, you must take care of your subjects and ensure they are fed and have a place to live."

"That is the charge of the emperor, not mine."

"You have enjoyed the generosity of the country for many

years, and I know that you have accumulated substantial wealth. It's your duty to share that with the people of the land."

The prince hung his head low and knew that whatever response he could offer would not extricate him from the guilt that Li was about to place on him. He tried to beg for clemency. "My life is in your hands. Give me a second chance, and I will make good to my people."

Li was not interested in the prince's promise. Rather, he preferred to use him as an example to show the ultimate price one must pay for turning his back on his people. So he declared, "Prince Fu, you have violated a cardinal rule for one who governs: take care of the people you govern. You have not done that, and your people have suffered for a long time."

The prince began to realize that he was a doomed man, and he barked, "It Is not my duty to take care of the people of Loyang. The governor and the emperor should pay the price for the suffering of the people!"

"I believe the emperor will ultimately pay his price," said Li Tzu-cheng confidently. "For now, it is you who must pay that price!" He paused for a moment and continued in a deliberate voice. "Take ... him ... down!"

The two guards who had brought the prince in helped him up from his knees with some difficulty because of the weight of the obese man. When he was finally on his feet, the guards pulled him out of the hall. Before sunset, Prince Fu was put to death by hanging from the portico of his opulent mansion, to demonstrate to the people the fairness of the new master of Loyang.

The next day, Li gathered his lieutenants, with Liu Tsung-min in attendance, and lectured them on his newfound philosophy of military justice and discipline. "As you can see, under my command, justice is equal for all, regardless of rank and position. When a soldier violates my order, he will be punished without delay.

My first order is this: the people of Loyang shall be left to live peacefully. Those who commit looting or rape the citizens will be executed at sundown, as I have done to the prince who mistreated his people."

Those in attendance were dumbfounded by the pronouncement. They looked at one another in disbelief. Before, the soldiers who had committed looting and rape were not punished. They thought that to punish transgressors with light sentences might be justifiable, but punishment by death appeared excessively harsh.

Li broke the silence and continued to expound on his philosophy of governance. "Conquering Loyang is a major victory for us! I am confident that we will conquer more cities and more people in the near future. We must impose stricter discipline in our soldiers in order to shed our labels as rebels and brigands!"

Liu Tsung-min rose from his seat, put his hands together, and spoke in a loud voice. "Here, here! Hail to the new prince: the prince of Loyang!"

Everyone got off his seat quickly and applauded. "Hail to the new prince! The Prince of Loyang! Our dashing prince!"

From that day on, "the dashing prince" became synonymous with Li Tzu-cheng.

Accepting the accolade, Li said with a wide smile, "Thank you, brothers! Our job is far from accomplished." Turning his face toward his good friend, he continued, "Have you taken inventory of the money and treasures that Prince Fu had stored away?"

"My staff is working on that feverishly. I will have a report for you shortly, dear prince." Liu reported. Actually, he already knew that Prince Fu's wealth was in the millions. While Li was busily tending to the affairs of the army and the city, Liu was busy planning for his own financial gains and having orgies with the newly found harem left behind by Prince Fu.

"I want to use some of the money to outfit our troops," Li ordered Liu.

"To outfit our whole army with new uniforms would cost a massive amount," Liu said. "I submit that building up our arms and provisions might be of a higher priority." But deep down in Liu's mind, the first priority for the treasure was his own enrichment.

"We should, at a minimum, procure new uniforms for the five thousand troops under our command now. I want to boost the morale of the men and show the world that we have gained legitimacy." The dashing prince dismissed the group with this final instruction: "I have a design for the new uniform for you to reproduce within a few days."

By taking back Loyang and the province of Honan, Li found himself in a territorial conflict with another rebel force, which had conquered and now occupied a neighboring province. Chang Hsien-chung, the leader of the rival group, had built a force to be reckoned with by the Brothers Kang, as well as the emperor. Chang, much like Li, was a peasant, but he was less educated and more ruthless. He was a smart field tactician, nevertheless, and for that reason able to win many battles. He controlled a vast western region near the major city of Sian. Now, with Li's force expanding westward while Chang was moving in the opposite direction, the two forces crossed paths. Since they were not adversaries and had a common goal to conquer Peking, Li took the initiative to make peace with his formidable neighbor.

Accepting Li's invitation, Chang traveled to Loyang and met with him. Li staged a sumptuous reception in the Fu mansion, and the two rebel leaders ate, drank, and struck a deal.

Chang Hsien-chung got right to the point, knowing that Li was not yet the ultimate authority in his camp. "Brother, I like your idea, but will your leader up north agree with your proposal to make peace with me?"

"Big Kang will not go against my advice, especially if it is beneficial to our common goal." Li knew that he was the man of the hour, and Big Kang would not be an obstacle in his path to glory. "If you agree with my suggestion, Big Kang will buy into our pact."

"As I understand, our deal is that we will maintain our independence in territorial and in military matters. We will march to Peking separately, take it, and share the spoils?" Chang sought the reassurance of his new ally.

"My word is our bond!" Li raised his glass and emptied it with a big smile. Chang had his glass refilled, and he downed it in one motion.

The night ended after many beautiful young women had performed their songs and dances. The next morning, Chang Hsien-chung led his contingent back to Sian. Li Tzu-cheng planned his return north to the Kang headquarters. Calling Liu to his chamber, Li spelled out his plan to his good friend.

"As you know, I have just forged a pact with Chang Hsien-chung. We have neutralized his threat from the west," Li said to Liu. "With the emperor's army in such disarray, I believe that we have some time to regroup and prepare for our northern expedition."

"My dear prince," Liu said admirably, "you've done well for yourself, and for our cause. We are most proud of you and honored to serve under you."

"Brother, I plan to return soon to the northern headquarters and help Big Brother plan our march to Peking, I'd like to have you stay behind and watch over the treasures here until we are ready to take the northern march."

Li's words were music to Liu's ears. With Li gone, he'd have total say in Loyang as the guardian of a massive trove of treasure and a harem full of young and beautiful women. "I will do my best to guard our treasures," Liu said with confidence.

"I will take three thousand men back up north with me, leaving you with two thousand. With few or no threats looming, that should be sufficient for you to defend this city. Besides, we still have the police force with a few hundred men to reinforce your army should the need arise."

"Don't worry! With me in control, things are in good hands!"

A few days later, the dashing prince took three thousand men and left Loyang for the journey up north. Liu Tsung-min was a liberated man, and he spent most nights in the company of beautiful young women.

The dashing prince's trek up north was uneventful. He encountered minor resistance from some dispirited imperial army units, but they were put down with little difficulty. Upon reaching the Kang headquarters after about five days of travel, Li promptly visited with his superior. Entering Kang's camp, Li was surprised to find his superior looking tired and pale. As Li bowed to pay respect, Big Kang reached over from his chair to shake Li's hand, and he found it difficult to do so.

"You look well," Kang said slowly. "I understand that you have become a prince." He looked at Li again. "You sure look like a prince!"

"It's a bogus title my subordinates pin on me because I deposed a Ming prince. I don't deserve to be a prince, but I suppose the name just got stuck to me," Li said contritely.

Big Kang smiled and said, "You deserve it! You did a great job taking Loyang. The treasure trove there will help our cause immensely."

"Big Brother, you have lost a lot of weight since I last saw you," Li muttered in a concerned voice. "Are you not feeling well?"

"To be honest with you, Brother Li, I think my days are numbered," Big Kang lamented. "The doctor told me I have contracted an incurable disease. He confessed that he does not know how to cure my ailment."

Li offered hollow words to comfort Kang. "With some rest, time will heal you!"

Big Kang shook his head repeatedly. "Brother Li, the torch will be passed to you soon. The task of completing our revolution belongs rightfully to you. You have saved my life, and now you will have to save the cause that most of the people in China believe in!" The eyes of Big Kang began to well.

"Please do not talk that way," pleaded Li. He looked at Big Kang again, and an ominous feeling overcame him. As he was searching for words suitable to the moment, Big Kang rose from his chair.

Leaning on the table next to where he was sitting, Big Kang raised his right hand and said loudly to an assistant standing nearby, "Issue an order. In the event of my death, Li Tzu-cheng will be the supreme leader of our band!"

Within a fortnight of the order, Big Kang died in his sleep. To minimize confusion in the ranks and avoid a power struggle, the dashing prince took control of the rebel force quickly by placing his most-trusted lieutenants in all command positions. He ordered that a strict ban on looting and raping be enforced, violators to be punished by death, without clemency. A program to provide uniforms to the soldiers would begin as soon as funds were made available. Most importantly, all unit commanders would step up the training of their men in preparation for a northern expedition.

Two years after Li assumed command, his rebel forces were primed for the northern campaign. He ordered Liu Tsung-min to mobilize his unit back north to join the expedition. Liu was reluctant to leave behind the posh life in Loyang that he had become accustomed to, but knowing his friend was a strict disciplinarian, he accepted the order without delay. He left Loyang in the charge of his chief deputy and brought his troops and many wagons loaded with money and treasure back to northern headquarters.

In the spring of 1642, the dashing prince led his forces out of his stronghold and headed northeast toward the Ming capital. With a force led by Chang Hsien-chung mounting a simultaneous march from the west, the emperor's army suffered irreversible setbacks on many fronts. The invasion from the southwest of Peking was not to be stopped.

CHAPTER 12

The Panic

By the summer of 1643, panic began to set in in Peking.

The rebel army led by Li Tzu-cheng had advanced to within three hundred miles south of the capital. Chang Hsien-chung's army, coming farther from the west and encountering heavier resistance, was not far behind. For the emperor, the prospect of an imminent occupation of the Forbidden City by the rebels was rapidly becoming a reality.

Reports from the field flooded the emperor's palace, bleaker by the day. Emperor Chung-chen had exhausted his ability to rally his troops, and his ministers were unable, and in many cases unwilling, to help him. Finding himself helpless and isolated, he could place his trust and reliance in only one person, and that person was his attending eunuch, Wang Tung-yin.

"Tung-yin," the emperor said while he was reading urgent reports from the front, "the rebels are getting stronger by the day." The eunuch hung his head low and shook it slowly as Chung-chen continued. "According to our field commanders, our soldiers have lost their will to fight, and many have surrendered to the enemies."

Trying to put a positive spin on things, the eunuch said, "Your Majesty, you have done your best. I am sure heaven will reward you for your efforts."

"What good will that do? Our treasury is bankrupt! My many efforts to raise funds by seeking donations from my ministers have gone for naught. Without financial help, we simply cannot continue to defend ourselves against the enemies."

"Your Majesty, not all is lost yet!" the eunuch said, jolting the emperor out of his melancholy mood.

"I do not share your optimism. I am ready to go on my doomsday program."

Even though the emperor had not divulged to him what his doomsday program was, the eunuch had a notion that his master was prepared for the worst for him and his family.

"Your Majesty, since our ministers have not been able or willing to come up with money to help us, why not ...?" The eunuch stopped short, unsure how the emperor might react to his idea. The emperor darted a quizzical look at him, expecting to hear a solution that would work. The eunuch finally completed his suggestion. "Sir, should you not ask your ... relatives for help?"

The emperor shook his head sadly and muttered, "Which relative do you suppose could be helpful to me?"

"The imperial father-in-law!" the eunuch said without hesitation.

"The father of my ... wife, the empress?"

"Yes, Your Majesty. He is the wealthiest man in our country, according to some sources."

"He could be," the emperor said. He was, in fact, ashamed that his wife's father had laid claim to such a dubious honor. "But I'd be afraid to approach him. Empress Chou might not approve of the idea."

"Your Majesty, in times of crisis, such as now, you cannot let personal feelings transcend official matters," the eunuch said boldly. "Sir, I hope you will forgive me for speaking out."

Emperor Chung-chen hung his head low. Deep down, he could not disagree with the eunuch's comments. "I suppose you are right. Call Minister Chou to my chamber at once."

Answering the emperor's summons, Minister Chou appeared in front of his son-in-law, full of trepidation and anxiety because the emperor had never called on him for any matter, personal or official. He knelt and paid respects to his son-in-law in a very nervous manner. "Your Majesty, ten thousand years to you!"

"Minister, rise!" The emperor pointed at a chair across from where he was sitting. Minister Chou sat himself down quite erectly, clearly uncomfortable.

"Your Majesty, I overheard reports that our capital is in a very precarious situation. Does Your Majesty have any contingency plans in the works?"

"Minister, that is the reason why I asked you to be here. I want to hear the views of all my venerable ministers about how we can avert the certain disaster that looms over us. You are respected by many as one of the most venerable members of our court. Can you tell me how we can save this sinking ship?"

The old minister blushed. He had an inkling that nothing good, at least for him, would come of this meeting. So he said, "Your Majesty, you well know that I am a novice when it comes to politics. And in matters relating to military tactics, such as how to win a battle, I'm the last person you should consult."

"Minister, I understand!" The emperor paused to calm his nerves before continuing. "You have lived a luxurious life and received large stipends for many years. You owed that to the grace of our ancestors. Don't you think that this is the time for you to repay them?"

The minister was shocked by the emperor's candor and curtness, and he became more nervous as he waited for the other shoe to drop. In the meantime, he could only murmur, "Err!" in reaction to the emperor's comment.

The emperor finally got to the point. "I'd like you to donate one hundred thousand ounces of silver to help provide for our troops. We've got to have the money in short order. Our situation is desperate!"

Minister Chou knew that he could not dodge his son-in-law's request, but he was very reluctant to part with such a large sum of money, even though it was widely known he had amassed over a million ounces of silver and many more items of value over a long period of time.

Hearing no reply from his father-in-law, the emperor persisted. "Minister Chou, I will have Eunuch Wang come to your mansion to pick up the silver tomorrow morning." The emperor motioned to dismiss the old minister.

The minister rose from his seat, bowing to his son-in-law, begging for a reduction in the levy. "Your Majesty, your humble servant does not have one hundred thousand ounces of silver at his disposal. I will … donate five thousand without delay and work on the other rest in the near future."

The emperor turned in a huff and entered his bedchamber without uttering another word.

The next day, Wang Tung-yin, along with his assistant, descended on Minister Chou's huge mansion. After much wrangling with the minister and his secretary, the eunuchs brought back only ten thousand ounces of silver. As measly as this sum was, though, it was by far the largest amount given by a minister to help save the falling empire.

By the autumn of 1643, the rebels had come within striking distance of the capital. Emperor Chung-chen called an emergency meeting with his high ministers; none answered the call. Saddened by this event, the emperor called on Tian Wang-yu, the father of his beloved consort and ostensibly the chief minister of his court, for an urgent consultation. The minister did not ignore the call, unlike his fellow ministers.

The minister knelt and said, "Your Majesty, may peace be with you!" to the emperor, after entering his private chamber and seeing him sitting behind his desk, which was piled high with documents.

"Rise! Thank you for your prayer. But peace deserted me a long time ago," the emperor said dejectedly. "Look at this pile." He pointed at the pile on his desk. "These are urgent calls for help by our field commanders. But we are broke, to put it crudely." He paused. "Our soldiers have lost their will to fight because we cannot take care of them. The field commanders have informed me that many of their men deserted their units or simply threw up their hands and surrendered to the enemies."

Minister Tian rose from knees and slowly sat in a chair the emperor pointed at. He then mumbled, "I am saddened by our inability to come to the help of our fighting men. Perhaps Your Majesty should call on our ministers for another round of donations."

"What's the use?" the emperor observed in a bitter tone. "The imperial army unit that guards our capital is decimated to the point of almost nonexistence. As you know, we now have to rely on the palace guards and eunuchs to defend the Forbidden City."

"Yes, Your Majesty," Minister Tian muttered. "Eunuch Wang is doing a good job of turning the guards into soldiers."

"Yes, Eunuch Wang is doing more than a good job." The emperor had had little choice but to place Wang Tung-yin, a eunuch, in charge of the guards. But, in reality, the eunuch had little or no knowledge of commanding men, let alone fighting battles. "I had no one to turn to, so I volunteered him for that difficult job. What makes it more difficult is that almost all of the men under him are either youngsters or old men."

The minister asked an inane question. "Your Majesty, can we not recruit some fresh blood?" The answer to his question was obvious: the imperial treasury had no money.

The emperor did not respond to the question. Instead, he turned the question around. "Minister Tian, do you have one last trick up your sleeve?" The emperor knew Tian was a resourceful man who had a unique ability to deal with unusual situations. The emperor had not forgotten that it was Minister Tian who had brought down Chief Minister Wei and his formidable Eastern Factory almost singlehandedly. Besides, other than his personal eunuch, the emperor had no one else to turn to for advice.

Minister Tian found himself in an untenable position. He was a big part of the problem that had contributed to the failure of the government; he'd refused to part with his substantial wealth to help save the troops when called on by the emperor. Further, he was corrupt, and he set a bad example for his fellow ministers.

"Your Majesty," the old minister suddenly yelled, as though he'd been struck by a bolt of lightning. "Wu San-kuei! Yes, Wu San-kuei!" He slapped himself on the right thigh and jumped up from his chair.

The emperor was jolted by the same lightning, it seemed; he also yelled, "Yes, Wu San-kuei! Do you think he can be helpful?"

"He might be our last hope!" said the old minister.

"He has an army of more than thirty thousand up there, is that correct?"

"I believe he has more than thirty thousand, Your Majesty."

"But what good is that to us? He is so far away, and I also understand from his reports that he needs every one of his men there to thwart the Manchu threats!" the emperor said in a dejected tone.

"Your Majesty, your observation is correct," said Minister Tian, "but we do not need thirty thousand men here to defend the Forbidden City. A few thousand able soldiers would be more than helpful!"

"I suppose you are right, Minister Tian." The emperor's mood at last lightened at the thought that Wu San-kuei might be his savior. He said resolutely, "Send a message to Shan-hai-kuan. Summon General Wu here for an audience with me. At once!"

Minister Tian's mood also seemed lighter now that he was off the hook for the time being. He bowed to the emperor and said, "Yes, Your Majesty!" He promptly left the emperor's chamber to issue the summons for General Wu.

The people of Peking were deeply concerned and frightened as rumors of an impending rebel invasion spread like wildfire. Rumors also abounded that the imperial family was preparing to relocate the capital to the southern region.

To citizens with means or high social standing, leaving the capital was a viable solution. But for the average citizens of Peking, life was hell. For them to escape from the brewing political storm was unthinkable because most towns and villages in northern China, especially those surrounding Peking, were in turmoil, much like the capital. Most of those unfortunate people simply had to hunker down and wait for the blow to land. Peking quickly became a ghost town, with daily public activities reduced to a minimum as most businesses and markets were closed. Those who could afford to buy food and supplies found them to be scarce. But most simply did not have money to spend. Rampant looting by soldiers who had deserted from the imperial army added to the bleak environment.

During this social and economic chaos, one line of business flourished: selling and tailoring clothing. Sensing that being associated with the emperor was detrimental to their safety and

well-being, many officials of the Ming court flocked to tailors
to outfit themselves with civilian clothes. They thought discard-
ing their official garments would disguise their privileged status.
These officials were among the hordes of refugees leaving the
capital, leaving the scene with many wagonloads of their ill-gotten
treasures.

Emperor Chung-chen was left literally alone to face the rebels.

CHAPTER 13
The Meeting

IN LIAO-HSI, OPPOSITE THE LIAOTUNG PENINSULA, GENERAL Wu San-kuei continued to defend his fortress zealously from sporadic attacks by the Manchus. Time and again, he fended them off, much to the dismay of Abahai, the emperor of the newly founded Ching dynasty. But with the rebels poised to take the Ming capital, Abahai sensed that his opportunity to conquer Peking was fast approaching. So he continued his harassment of Wu's garrison in Shan-hai-kuan.

Wu, however, with his ability to command troops and manage resources, was up to the task of handling these Manchu forays. Although Peking was drowning in a sea of debt, due to extremely lavish lifestyles and the corruption perpetrated by the imperial family and the ministers, Wu was able to maintain the battle-ready status of the more than thirty thousand troops at Shan-hai-kuan.

In the spring of 1643, Abahai died, and his six-year-old son, Fu-lin, inherited the throne. Because of Fu-lin's tender age, his uncle Dorgon stepped in and took on the role and title of prince regent. There was some opposition to Dorgon's ascension, but he gained control of the court with ease because he had built a power base behind the throne for more than sixteen years.

Dorgon, like his half-brother, embraced the belief that his people would one day succeed in conquering Peking to rule China. With his new power, he increased the pressure on Wu San-kuei by bringing his troops to Ningyuan, a garrison town a short distance from Shan-hai-kuan. Knowing that Wu had in his arsenal weapons that hurled fireballs at his soldiers, Dorgon was patient and deliberate in attacking the fort. Frequently, he attacked the fort from multiple fronts late at night. He managed to take the defenders by surprise and succeeded in disturbing their peace, but inflicting only minor damage. These forays, which had become an annoyance rather than a threat to Wu San-kuei, went on for stretches of time.

"General!" the young aide-de-camp of General Wu called as he ran into his office. "The imperial messenger is here to see you."

"Bring him in," commanded the general, rising from behind his desk quickly.

The messenger entered the chamber and stood erect in front of the general. "General Wu San-kuei, you are to receive an imperial order!" he announced sternly.

Wu San-kuei promptly got down on one knee to receive a large envelope from the messenger with both hands. The messenger bowed and left the room without another word.

Wu rose and opened the envelope. After reading the message, his face tightened before he cracked a thin smile. The emperor's summons had finally arrived, and he received it with mixed emotions. While he would dearly have loved to go to Peking to see his woman, he was concerned about the Manchu threat lurking near his fortress.

"Summon my command staff at once," Wu barked at his aide-de-camp.

"Yes, sir," the aide answered. He made an about-face and rushed out of the room.

While waiting for his command staff to gather, Wu San-kuei fidgeted and appeared sunk in deep thoughts. He had longed to visit Peking to claim his prized possession, the most beautiful woman in China. But he could not visit the capital unless he was given permission to do so. Now that he had received permission from the emperor, he could not wait to depart on his journey. But the thought of leaving his fortress while it was under siege by the Manchus haunted him. He was in a deep dilemma. What was he to do?

Four high-ranking officers who made up his command staff stood erect in front of Wu and called out, "General" in unison.

"Take your seats," Wu ordered, and the men sat themselves in their usual assigned seats around a long table. General Wu took the seat at the head of the table.

"His Majesty has summoned me to Peking," Wu blurted out, waving the message in his hand. "He said that it is most urgent that I meet with him."

"Sir, our surveillance team reported the capital is under siege by the rebels," offered the colonel, the senior member of the staff, who sat to the right of Wu. "I would venture to guess that the emperor is asking for troop reinforcements."

"Sir, we cannot afford to move our troops from here! The Manchu army has been quite active in assaulting our fort," said the staffer who sat next to the colonel.

"I suppose you both are right," replied Wu, "but I cannot defy the order of His Majesty. I must leave for Peking at once!"

"General, how many men do you wish to take with you?" asked another staff officer.

"I am quite concerned that, in my absence, the Manchu might mount a major attack on us." The general was more concerned

about the Manchus than the number of men he would take south
with him.

"Sir, if we keep your absence a top secret, we might be able to
keep them calm for a while," the colonel muttered.

"How do you suppose we do that?" Wu asked matter-of-factly.

"I suppose you can leave in incognito, with a small escort, in
the middle of the night," one staffer suggested.

"Good idea," echoed another officer. "I suggest that you travel
in civilian clothes and take no more than ten men with you, sir."

Wu San-kuei acceded to the recommendations of his advisers.
He called the meeting to an end and ordered preparations for his
departure at midnight; he was to take six highly proficient soldiers
with him as escorts.

Midnight came. Wu and the six escorts dressed in civilian
clothes and quietly left Shan-hai-kuan, carrying a minimal amount
of arms and provisions. They traveled by horseback and made few
stops, arriving in Peking in good time. After entering the capital,
Wu San-kuei reported directly to his father's house.

Wu Shang greeted him with open arms and said, "My son, it's
good to see you!"

"Father, His Majesty has summoned me to the capital. Do you
have any inkling what he has in mind?"

"I suppose that he is concerned about the rebels pressing close
to Peking. With the capital garrison gone, we are relying on the
palace guards and eunuchs to defend the Forbidden City," lamented
the father. "Worse yet, the chief eunuch is acting as commander."

Wu shook his head and muttered, "Are things really that bad?"

"His Majesty is fighting a lonely war! It seems that no one is
able or willing to help him."

"What about Tian Wang-yu, his favorite consort's father?" Wu
was very interested in hearing what the old minister had been up
to, especially relating to Yuan-yuan.

"He is happily living his good life, to the neglect of his duty and the well-being of the emperor and the country."

"Tell me, Father," Wu pressed on, "is Chen Yuan-yuan still living in his mansion?" Wu was hoping that his father could shed more light on the woman's current situation, even though his intel reports had been keeping him rather up to date.

"Do you know Chen Yuan-yuan?" the father asked, curious why his son was so interested in the woman.

"Er ..." Wu was caught off guard by his father's question, so he mumbled, "Oh yes ... I met her once. I really admired her singing!"

The father sent a puzzled look at his son before he turned his attention to another matter. "Your mother is waiting anxiously to see you."

Wu took the opportunity to dodge the subject of Yuan-yuan and hurried to the back of the house to visit with his mother. The next day, Wu rose early and put on his military outfit, with highly polished brass and medals. He headed directly to the emperor's palace.

The emperor greeted Wu San-kuei not at his small palace but in Throne Hall, where he normally held daily audiences. Since no daily audience had been held for more than two years, Emperor Chung-chen thought it would be appropriate to use that location to meet the young general. He had wanted to put on a sumptuous dinner for the occasion, but since he had put the court on an austere status, he decided against that idea. He decided to meet formally, in a solemn audience. He ordered twelve of his high ministers to attend the function, perhaps to stress the point that patriotism should be given the highest respect and honor.

Wu San-kuei was escorted by the emperor's chief eunuch to the throne, which was high on a platform, front and center of the palace. The high ministers were lined up on both sides of the throne. When Wu approached the platform, he saw a thin and frail emperor sitting on the front edge of the throne. He had not met Chung-chen before, and he was surprised the emperor did not project the venerable and solemn appearance he expected to see. Nevertheless, he quickly got to his knees and pressed his head to the floor. He sang out his praises: "Ten thousand years to Your Majesty! Long live the Ming dynasty!"

"Rise, General Wu," the emperor ordered. Chung-chen was surprised to see a handsome young man in front of him. His vision of Wu San-kuei was of an older-looking man with a battle-weary countenance. Instead, the general was a slender man with a middling body and a rather handsome face. "General Wu, I have heard much of your gallantry in battle. I am grateful for your loyalty and dedication in the defense of our empire. You are truly a patriot!"

Wu San-kuei rose and stood ramrod straight, his head low. "Your Majesty, it is my solemn duty to defend our country. I will gladly give my life to serve Your Majesty and the empire. I'd like to repay the throne for all it has bestowed on me and my family!"

"I truly regret that we are not blessed with more patriots like you, especially in times like these." The emperor's remark was intended for the high ministers in attendance rather than Wu alone. The ministers all hung their heads lower, as though they felt the shame the emperor had bestowed on them.

"Your Majesty, I understand the situation in our capital has become precarious. Are our armed forces up to the task of defense against the rebels?" Wu understood the bleakness of the situation in Peking, but he wanted to find out quickly what the emperor expected of him.

"General, I am afraid our armed forces have been decimated to the point of nonexistence. We rely on a small contingent of palace guards, and we will not be able to stop the rebels when they decide to march into our capital. I fear that day will come soon!"

"Your Majesty, you know that the Manchus in the Northeast are rattling their sabers outside Shan-hai-kuan. If they succeed in breaking through our fortress defenses there, we'll be faced with a major disaster." Wu San-kuei was sounding a sensible alarm, as well as dropping a hint to the emperor that he could not rely heavily on him when it came to defending the capital.

"We need at least ten thousand of your soldiers deployed to the capital quickly, General," said the emperor, confirming Wu's fear.

"I beg your forgiveness, Your Majesty. I'd have to reassess my need in the north before I could commit to such a huge deployment of troops." Wu then quickly pinched himself for making a rather defiant remark to the throne.

"We need to come to a decision on that very quickly, General," the emperor said resolutely. "I am afraid an invasion of the capital by the rebels is imminent and real!"

"Your Majesty, I fear the threat of the Manchu invasion is equally imminent and real!" Wu tried to buffer his defiant remark by adding, "In my humble opinion, Your Majesty, the Manchus are a bigger threat than the hodge-podge rebels."

"General, I understand your position, but my situation here will be unthinkable if you do not bring troop reinforcements here soon!"

"When my duties are completed here, I will return to Shan-hai-kuan at once," said Wu in a subdued tone. "Your Majesty can be assured that I will do my utmost to help with the threat faced by the capital."

"I understand, General. I trust you implicitly in these important tactical matters. I am sure you will not let me, and our empire, down!"

"Thank you for your trust, Your Majesty!" Wu San-kuei got down on his knees once again.

The emperor rose from his throne and waved at his eunuch.

"Tung-yin, bring me the medal." Eunuch Wang reached into his pocket and handed a medal over to the emperor. The emperor then walked down from the throne closer to the general and hung the medal around his neck. He loudly pronounced, "General Wu San-kuei, I honor you for your devotion and loyalty to me—and to our empire."

Wu knocked his forehead on the floor three times, and the emperor extended his right hand to help him off his knees. The two men walked slowly down the few steps from the platform to the palace floor; the general trailed two paces behind the emperor. The emperor then signaled to Eunuch Wang to bring drinks for everyone. Three eunuchs handed glasses of wine to the gathered ministers. Eunuch Wang and another eunuch handed a glass each to the emperor and the general.

Emperor Chung-chen raised his glass and declared, "Long live the Ming dynasty! Let's also drink to our ultimate victory over the Manchus and the rebels!" Everyone raised his glass and echoed, "Long live the Ming dynasty! Ten thousand years to Your Majesty!" But no one harbored any conviction that either declaration would come true.

The emperor was ready to leave the hall at the end of the toasts. The general and the ministers all got down on their knees to see him off. After the emperor departed, everyone stood and converged on Wu San-kuei, offering congratulatory remarks. Tian Wang-yu quickly confronted the general and gently nudged him, urging him to step aside. The general had not met Tian before, so he surmised he must be the man he wished to meet. Wu bowed courteously to the ministers gathered around him and stepped out of the circle.

Tian said, "General, I am Minister Tian Wang-yu. I would like to offer my congratulations to you for the honor His Majesty has bestowed on you!"

"Thank you, Your Excellency," Wu said, his mind trying to picture how Yuan-yuan could have lived with such an old man for so long.

"General, it would be an honor if you'd accept my invitation for a visit before you leave the capital," said the minister. He paused. Not hearing a response from the general, he continued, "My sedan will be waiting for you in front of your father's mansion tomorrow at noon."

Wu San-kuei was dumbfounded, as if he were hit by a lightning bolt; he could not utter a word. He was secretly delighted that the old minister had presented him with a gift from heaven. Wu muttered to himself, "If the reports from my sources were accurate, then I will finally get to see the most beautiful woman in China, my Chen Yuan-yuan!" He returned to reality and released these words from his lips: "Minister Tian, it is my deep honor to accept your invitation."

"I shall see you tomorrow, General," Tian said softly.

The two men exchanged bows and walked out of the hall, and the others followed them out.

Wu San-kuei spent a sleepless night in his father's mansion. He could not wait for the moment to come when he would finally get to see the woman of his dreams in real life. At the crack of dawn, he rose and spent hours polishing his appearance. A servant offered him an early meal, but he was not in the mood for food. His mind was already racing ahead to noon. He paced his room in circles, anxiously awaiting the arrival of the sedan. He kept thinking about different scenarios for how he could wrest the woman from the old minister. What if this adventure became a misadventure? If so, how could he live the rest of his life? The thought kept playing in his mind.

Noon came. When Wu San-kuei finally arrived on the doorstep of the elegant Tian mansion, the minister was already standing in front with a small welcoming party. Among those in the party were four manservants and six young mistresses. The general walked up the steps at a slow gait, trying to hide his eagerness. When he reached the top, he bowed to the minister and grinned widely.

"Welcome, General, to my humble residence," Minister Tian said, returning a big smile.

"Your Excellency, the pleasure is all mine," Wu said as he quickly scanned the young women standing behind his host. Without exception, the ladies were all beautiful, but he was certain that the one he most wanted to see was not among them.

After the two men had walked inside to an elegantly decorated chamber, Tian pointed to a chair at one end of a highly polished round table. The general took the seat. The minister took the seat facing him. While the manservants were busily carrying food to the table, the ladies dispersed into two groups of three to stand behind the general and the minister and serve them wine and tea.

Wu San-kuei sipped a glass of wine and turned his head to survey the opulent hall. He was not very interested in the ambience of the surroundings; he was focusing on the entrance where he thought his love was to appear.

"General, have some cuisine," said Minister Tian, offering a heaping spoonful of food to the general.

Only as a courtesy, Wu San-kuei accepted a small portion.

"General, your reputation is well placed." The minister began to tip his hand toward the reason for his invitation. "The emperor and the court are grateful for your efforts in defending the northeastern front for these many years." He raised the glass to toast Wu.

Wu's mind was not tuned to triumphs and battles; he was still wondering if the woman he had come to see would appear soon. Seeing the host raising his glass, Wu nonchalantly raised his. They both took sips from their glasses.

"General, what is your assessment of the situation in the capital?"

"Oh! ... My assessment?"

"Yes. I mean, if the Manchus were to break through Shan-hai-kuan and threaten Peking, can we repel them?"

"With me, Wu San-kuei, as the defender, Shan-hai-kuan will be safe. The Manchus do not stand a chance." The minister frayed the young general's nerves.

"I fear that if the rebels from the south and the west succeed in their march toward the capital simultaneously with a Manchu attack at Shan-hai-kuan, our military will not be able to win on both fronts." The minister's prognostication did not seem far-fetched.

The general did not answer quickly. He was annoyed at his host for intruding into military matters. "Well, let's hope that it will not come to that."

"General, I will be honest with you," said Tian contritely. "I am very concerned about my family's safety if my observations become reality." Over the past ten years, the minister had accumulated huge amounts of wealth, including gold, money, and jewels, and he was mainly concerned that if the capital fell, he would stand to lose the large cache of treasure.

"Sir, I am sure the palace guards will be up to the task of defending His Majesty and the Forbidden City," Wu replied unconvincingly. He had learned since he'd arrived at the capital that eunuchs and old men had become the palace guards, and none of them had had military background or experience. He knew that without his troop reinforcement, the capital was doomed.

The minister came directly to the point. "General, do you think that it is possible for high ministers to have the protection of soldiers in case of an attack in the capital?"

General Wu was taken by surprise by Tian's question. He murmured, "I don't know how that could be done. You heard His

Majesty lamenting the disintegration of the army and seeking help from my garrison."

"I suppose that one can buy the services of an armed unit, if he is willing to pay the price." The old minister was probing the possibility of hiring his own guards.

"I suppose one can hire his own protection, such as having private guards," the general said. He paused and continued. "I believe your question can best be answered by the minister of military affairs." Wu tried to deflect the subject from himself.

Minister Tian paused, and then he smiled at the general with a sudden change of mood. He clapped his hands twice at the head servant standing nearby. The head servant accepted the signal and waved to a small group of ladies waiting outside the hall. Wu turned and watched the group as it entered. He saw four women, each carrying a musical instrument; the last to enter held a fan in one hand, partially covering her face. The general was immediately smitten by the extraordinary beauty of the last woman to enter. "She must be the one I have dreamed about meeting for these many years," Wu said to himself.

Once the women reached the hall, the woman with the fan took center stage as the others lined up behind her. Soon the instruments began to spin out soft music. The woman with the fan started to sing. Her voice was melodic, but Wu San-kuei was more mesmerized by her beauty.

At the conclusion of the song, Minister Tian waved at the singer and beckoned her to a seat between Wu and himself. The woman curtsied and placed herself on the seat.

"This is General Wu San-kuei, the most decorated general of our country," Tian said, facing the young woman.

"General, I have heard of your great name for a long time." The woman spoke softly and looked at the general with her head bowed slightly. But she could not resist her desire to inspect the

handsome young general more deliberately. She had wanted to
meet Wu because he was worthy of admiration, unlike the men
she had encountered so far in her young life.

"The pleasure is, truly, all mine!" Wu muttered, his eyes fix-
ated on that beautiful face. "Er, you are ...?"

There was a moment of silence. The minister finally broke the
ice by saying, "Oh, yes, General, may I introduce you to my sixth
concubine ... Yuan-yuan!"

Hearing the words "Yuan-yuan," Wu San-kuei was excited.
Here she was, the subject of his fantasies and obsessions, finally
sitting next to him. *I should not let this golden opportunity go by*, he
thought. His desire to possess her knew no bounds, but, in reality,
Yuan-yuan was the minister's property. Under the feudal laws of
China, he owned her absolutely. What would it take to free her
from him, a man almost three times her age? If he let this opportunity pass by, Wu knew that there would not be another chance;
time was running against him. He simply had to force the issue
if he were to get Yuan-yuan. He really could not bear to go on
without her.

The afternoon wore on. Minister Tian awkwardly observed the
two young people exchanging glances and smiles. Tian finally rose
with two glasses in his hands and offered one to Wu.

The general accepted the glass and said, "Minister Tian, I drink
to the health of His Majesty and to you!" As he was about to tip his
glass toward his lips, he remarked, "Oh yes. Also to the everlasting
beauty of your dear concubine, Yuan-yuan!"

Minister Tian also tipped his glass, smiling awkwardly. "The
best of luck to you, General!"

Both men emptied their glasses, and Wu took a side glance
at Yuan-yuan once more. All the while, Yuan-yuan's eyes were
focused on the young general. She admired his face, even though
there was a scar to the left side of his nose that detracted from a

perfect contour. More importantly, she admired his aura. Even though he did not possess a tall, erect, strong military countenance, Wu San-kuei's handsome presence, though of middling height, was truly exceptional to behold.

As the host was about to bid his guest farewell, Wu San-kuei suddenly pulled the minister to the side, away from everyone. The minister pointed to an antechamber, where they went. The general said resolutely in a normal tone, "Minister Tian, I want to thank you for inviting me. I must leave now for my post without delay. But before I leave, I must ask you for a favor."

Tian Wang-yu seemed to have a clue of what his guest had in his mind. "General Wu, I, too, have a favor to ask of you!"

The two men smiled at each other, each waiting for the other to speak first. They both harbored selfish motives, and the stakes involved would be high in either case. Wu finally broke the ice. "Minister Tian, I am embarrassed! But I must be honest with you, and myself." He hesitated once more as he summoned the courage to go on. He was someone who had gone through so many battles, but Wu suddenly found himself lacking the courage to confront an old minister. At last, he said, "I would do whatever you ask of me if you will let me have Yuan-yuan! I'd like to have her as my lifetime companion."

Minister Tian was not surprised by his guest's demand, as he had heard rumors that Wu San-kuei wanted Yuan-yuan as his concubine. He was taken aback, however, by Wu's audacity in making the demand so blatantly. For someone as powerful and influential as he was, Tian rationalized, giving up a woman was a small price to pay. Especially if Wu would give him what he wanted in return. So he said, "General, you are welcome to take Yuan-yuan with you."

Wu San-kuei could hardly believe his ears. He responded quickly. "Minister, I'd like to thank you for your generosity. How can I ever repay you?"

Tian Wang-yu walked closer to Wu and whispered that he wished to have a platoon of soldiers for his own protection, in case the rebels did enter the capital. He fidgeted and let out a sheepish smile, waiting for a reaction from the general. He did not have to wait long.

The general simply said, "Consider it done!"

The old minister let out a sigh of relief. He took Wu's hand and walked with him to the main hall. As soon as the minister released his hand, Wu bowed and bade him farewell. "As soon as I get back to my post, I will dispatch a platoon here for your protection." Wu San-kuei did not hesitate to exchange a platoon of soldiers for a woman, while he'd balked at offering help to the emperor when his empire was teetering on the brink of its demise.

"Do you wish to have Yuan-yuan accompany you, General?"

Yuan-yuan's heart pumped rapidly when she heard the old minister's comment. She smiled at the general and hoped that he would take her with him without delay. But Wu was not logistically prepared to take Yuan-yuan back to Shan-hai-kuan. After thinking for a moment, he said, "I will come and get her later this evening."

"I will have her delivered to your father's mansion this evening. Would that be acceptable to you, General?"

"Perfect!" Wu San-kuei answered with pleasure. He took another look at Yuan-yuan, bowed to Tian Wang-yu, and left for his father's home.

Shortly after the sun had set, a sedan carrying Yuan-yuan stopped at the doorsteps of Wu Shang's house. A servant announced the woman's arrival to the general, and he rushed to the front portico, two female servants following him. As the female servants assisted Yuan-yuan out of the sedan and into the house, Wu

San-kuei, on cloud nine, walked alongside his prize possession. Once inside, he presented Yuan-yuan to his parents. Wu Shang uttered some welcoming remarks, but he harbored mixed feelings about what his son had done.

Prior to Yuan-yuan's arrival, Wu Shang had admonished his son that Tian Wang-yu was not a man to be trusted and said that the woman had had a dubious history with men. But the son was not to be dissuaded by anyone; he had made the quest for the most beautiful woman in China his lifelong pursuit. Now that he had achieved that goal, he was not about to let her out of his sight.

Wu San-kuei and Yuan-yuan were united at last. Dreams had indeed come true for both love-deprived persons. For him, it was finding his true love, a woman who would idolize him and put him on a pedestal. For her, it meant a powerful man who would love and cherish her and cuddle her in his arms. Wu San-kuei had encountered many female liaisons, but he found them undesirable and could not fulfill his sexual desires. Yuan-yuan had also had many sexual encounters, but they were mostly despicable, forced upon her by contemptible men.

The pent-up emotions of these two young lovers found liberation as soon as they were alone. She fell into his arms, his lips found hers, and they melted together in body and spirit. The voluptuous body of Yuan-yuan completely captivated the young general, so he disrobed her and himself, and they sank under the bedcover and drifted into never-never land.

Wu San-kuei had never encountered such a high level of sexual pleasure. He was reluctant to let go of Yuan-yuan, even though the sun had peeked through the window of his bedchamber for quite a while. Having a taste of pure love, both emotional and physical, for the first time, Yuan-yuan was also reluctant to let her lover go. At long last, Wu came to his senses and decided that he had better return north to tend to the urgent needs in his garrison; he had to let go of Yuan-yuan.

He urged his father to keep her temporarily in his house. The father agreed, but he was not comfortable with the arrangement because he feared retribution from Tian Wang-yu.

CHAPTER 14

The Truce

AS SOON AS HE ARRIVED BACK AT HIS GARRISON, WU SAN-KUEI began feverishly preparing to dispatch two thousand men to Peking to fulfill his end of the deal with Tian Wang-yu for Yuan-yuan. He also wrestled with the request from the emperor for ten thousand soldiers to help defend the Forbidden City. Last, and certainly not least, he needed to make arrangements to transport his woman from the capital to his garrison, without delay. As he was busy tending to these urgent demands, he was cornered by his chief of staff, who wanted to update him on the status of the garrison.

"The Manchus have stepped up their assault on us in recent days. They seemed to know that you were absent from our fortress. Thank goodness for those cannons. We were able to hold them off," said the chief of staff breathlessly. "General, welcome back! We sorely missed you!"

"Colonel, you are doing a good job in fending off those bastards," said Wu. "Do we still have enough cannonballs, in case they continue their attack on us?"

"Well, I am not too sure of that, General." The colonel sounded worried; he turned to his assistant, who stood next to him, "Major, go check that out and report back to me at once."

"Yes, sir," the major responded. He saluted and left the scene.

"Sir, how was your trip to Peking?"

"Good and bad," said Wu. The good, he thought was not the colonel's concern, so he gave him the bad news. "The emperor wants us to send ten thousand men to the capital to help him defend the Forbidden City."

"Did you agree to do that, General?"

"I told His Majesty that I will reevaluate our situation here before committing. Do you realize that I defied an order from the emperor by not acceding to his wish?"

"You were being sensible, sir," said the colonel. "Shan-hai-kuan is the major barrier that keeps the Manchus out of the capital. If our line of defense is broken, then the rebels are not his worry—the Manchus will be."

"I suppose you are right. That is what I said to His Majesty. But an imperial order is an imperial order, and I simply should not disobey it!"

The colonel suddenly reached into his side pocket and came up with an envelope. He handed it over to Wu and said, "I have a letter that was delivered by a messenger from the Manchus. It is addressed to you and marked Urgent and Personal."

"When did you receive this?" The general accepted the envelope.

"Two days ago. Since it was marked Personal, I did not see fit to open it."

Wu San-kuei furrowed his eyebrows and ripped open the envelope. He unfolded a letter and found that it was from his uncle. He quickly scanned the contents, and he pounded his right fist on the table near him. He was speechless, and his face instantly grayed. The colonel gave his superior a concerned look.

Ju Da-shou, uncle of Wu San-kuei, had been a general in the Ming army for more than thirty years. Wu had served under him when he was young, and he owed a lot of his success to the uncle. But the uncle, along with two highest-ranking officers in the Ming army, had surrendered to the Manchus in recent years. Many generals changed allegiance because they felt the emperor had abandoned them. More importantly, they sensed that the rapid deterioration of the Ming empire was irreversible.

When Dorgon, prince regent to the Manchu emperor, continued to encounter major resistance from Wu San-kuei in Shan-hai-kuan, he summoned Ju Da-shou from his post in Fushun, a Manchu garrison in the region, for advice in dealing with his nephew.

Upon arriving in Ningyuan, where Dorgon and his garrison were stationed, Ju Da-shou entered the command post. Finding Dorgon and bowing to him, Ju said, "Your Highness, may good fortune be with you and the Manchu empire!"

"General, welcome to Ningyuan!" Dorgon answered, pointing at a seat.

"How are things here at Ningyuan?" inquired Ju respectfully while taking the seat.

Dorgon got right to the point of his reason for summoning Ju. "Your nephew continues to be a thorn on my side. We have fought him rigorously for a long time, but we have made no progress in breaking through his fortress."

"Your Highness, my nephew is a battle-hardened warrior. The men under him are good fighters, well-trained and well-disciplined," Ju said with a touch of pride, as if he were proud that his nephew had learned much from him.

"I have to agree with you on that count," responded Dorgon, "but to make things worse, he's got those weapons that hurl fireballs."

"Those cannons are deadly," Ju muttered, "but I've heard that we are encountering fewer of them lately. My guess is that they are running out of cannonballs."

"Maybe so, but we must break through Shan-hai-kuan soon, before another cold winter descends upon us."

Ju Da-shou was a seasoned military man. Deep down, he knew that Dorgon was no match for his nephew. Dorgon was a good politician but lacked experience in tactical matters. His military was also inferior in logistics and manpower. But Ju dared not share those views with Dorgon. Instead, he said, "Your Highness, I heard that the rebels are fast approaching Peking. If that is true, then I think the Chinese emperor must deploy some troops currently under my nephew's command to rescue the capital."

"That might be the case," Dorgon agreed, "but Wu San-kuei has more than thirty thousand men stationed here, I'd be surprised if he would dispatch a large contingent to Peking. He knows that I still pose a major threat to him."

"Regardless of the number, any deployment will dilute his strength in the defense of Shan-hai-kuan."

"General," Dorgon said uneasily, "we have to decide on a course of action quickly. Either we withdraw back to Fushun or make another all-out effort to break through to Shan-hai-kuan soon."

"Your Highness, under the condition we are mired in now, I suggest that we pull back to Fushun and make another attempt on Shan-hai-kuan next spring," said Ju, tongue-in-cheek. "Hopefully, the rebels will do the work for us by getting to Peking first."

"That is precisely my concern," declared Dorgon, "I don't want Li Tzu-cheng getting to Peking before I do!"

Before Ju Da-shou could recover from his faux pas, Dorgon suddenly rose from his seat and said loudly, "General, do you think you can convince your nephew to surrender to me?"

Ju was taken aback by the question. He gathered himself and

searched for an answer. After a moment of silence, he summoned sufficient courage for a response. "Your Highness, Wu San-kuei is a person with a high standard of pride and loyalty. His father, Wu Shang, is also a man who has undying loyalty to the Ming emperor. I submit that it would be difficult to convince my nephew to turn his back on his emperor."

"I am in a position that I must try everything I can to neutralize him. I want you to go and visit with him and use your persuasiveness to convince him to join us, so that he can save his emperor from the ravages of the rebels."

Ju Da-shou bowed and muttered, "Your Highness, I am not optimistic that he will give up that easily. I will send him a letter and see if he will grant me a visit."

"My uncle, the one who surrendered to Dorgon, asked to see me on an urgent matter," the general said to his chief of staff.

"It is highly unusual, General," answered the colonel, "in time of war, to have an enemy agent request a visit—even if the agent is related to the commander."

"You might be right," Wu San-kuei said with mixed feelings. "To have my uncle act as the envoy, Dorgon must have some grandiose idea. I suppose there is no harm in seeing him, especially as he is coming to my camp." He instructed the colonel to send a reply to his uncle, via a messenger, and invite him to Shan-hai-kuan.

The day came. Ju Da-shou entered Wu San-kuei's fortress with an entourage of ten escorts. He came bearing a large wagon loaded with gifts. Welcoming his uncle at the portico of his mansion with his command staff, Wu San-kuei flashed a slight smile, his arms open. "Uncle, it has been a long time. You look well!"

The uncle reached for his nephew's hands and answered, "Yes, San-kuei, indeed it has been a long time! It is nice seeing you again! You also look well!"

While his officers escorted Ju's men away from the mansion, Wu placed his right arm around his uncle and ushered him into the reception hall. He then pointed at two chairs, placed side by side; as he took one of the chairs, Ju took the other. Two servants brought two cups of tea and handed one to each of the men. Wu dismissed the servants, leaving himself alone with his uncle.

"How is your father?" Ju inquired. "I have not seen him for a long time!"

"Thank heaven, my father is faring well."

The uncle let out a thin smile as he took a sip from his teacup.

"Uncle." Wu finally let his emotions flow. "When I heard that you turned your back against our emperor and surrendered to the Manchus, I was devastated!"

"Well, you were too young to understand. I was in dire straits at the time, as were many of our field generals." The uncle felt a touch of guilt as he tried to justify his desertion from the emperor. "Most of us were out of provisions, and with all our troops throwing down their arms or deserting our ranks, we were faced with certain death or captivity. Surrendering was the only viable solution for most of us. Besides, the Manchu khan treated us very well."

"You know that dying for the emperor is the highest calling for a true patriot!" said Wu San-kuei. "For all the high-ranking generals to surrender to the Manchus was despicable, to say the least!"

"San-kuei, if you were in our shoes, you'd see why we, the highest-ranking generals, all changed our allegiance to the Manchu khan."

"These high-ranking generals had all received benefits from the throne, some for generations. For them to desert the emperor when he needed them the most is the utmost disgrace."

"My nephew," the uncle fired back, "there is a saying: 'The wise knows how the wind blows!' The wind blows against your emperor, then and now!"

"It might be true for the time being. But winds can change direction quickly." Wu San-kuei was beginning to boil. "Uncle, you, as well as my family, received kindness and generosity from the Ming dynasty for a long time. To me, turning your back against His Majesty is a treasonable act, and it is unforgivable!"

Judging from his nephew's comments, Ju knew that convincing him to surrender to the Manchus would be a difficult task, if not an impossible one. So he turned to the second course of action that Dorgon had laid out for him: getting Wu San-kuei to agree to a truce with the Manchus.

"San-kuei, I have a document here that the prince regent of the Manchu emperor asked I present to you," said Ju Da-shou, handing a scroll to his nephew.

Wu took the scroll. He did not open it; instead, he clapped his hands twice. The head servant responded to the call and bowed to General Wu. "Sir, dinner is served!"

Wu rose and beckoned his uncle to follow him. Ju got off his seat and followed his nephew into the dining hall. Waiting there were officers from Wu's command staff and the officers who had accompanied the uncle. The two tables were filled with many dishes of food and many bottles of fine wine. Wu San-kuei placed himself at the head of the table, with his uncle next to him.

"Uncle, it's truly nice to see you again." Wu held up his glass and toasted Ju. "Here's the best to you. I hope that we don't meet on the battlefield!"

The uncle held up his glass. "We will not meet on the battlefield." He pointed at the scroll placed near his nephew. "If you accept the terms in that message from my master, then I am certain we will not meet in battle."

"We will drink to that," Wu said, and they both emptied their glasses.

After the dinner ended, Ju Da-shou retired to his guest chamber for the night. Wu San-kuei returned to his bedchamber. Before disrobing and retiring, he unrolled the scroll and read the message. It was a proposal from Dorgon for a sixty-day truce. Dorgon made a promise to fight with Wu against Li Tzu-cheng because, in his view, the rebels were the true enemy of the Ming emperor, not the Manchus. He further declared that his Ching dynasty, like the Ming dynasty, had the legitimate mandate to rule China, not the rebels.

Wu San-kuei was perplexed by Dorgon's message. On the one hand, he agreed with Dorgon that Li Tzu-cheng was an imminent threat to his emperor. On the other, he did not trust the Manchus, who had been his enemy for so many years. If he were to answer his emperor's call for reinforcements, it would weaken his defense in Shan-hai-kuan. But if he defied the emperor, then Peking was doomed. In that event, not only would the emperor be in peril, his father and the family would face the same tragic fate. And then there was Yuan-yuan, who he would certainly lose if the capital were to fall into the hands of the rebels. He tossed and turned in his bed, wrestling with the dilemma, before he fell into dreamland.

"My love, I am so happy to be with you at last. I pray to heaven to grant me one last wish," Yuan-yuan had said to Wu San-kuei on their first and only evening together.

"What would that wish be, my love?" Wu had inquired with a tender voice, cuddling her under the bedcover.

"I'd wish that we not be separated ever again!" she muttered, looking at him lovingly.

He kissed her softly and mumbled, "I will never let you out of my arms—never again, my love!"

Before she could respond, he held her tighter and kissed her passionately. The sweet taste of the kisses consumed the two lovers, and they floated in a cloud for a long time. But she finally broke away from his embrace and asked, "My love, are you going to take me away with you in the morning?"

Yuan-yuan's question jolted Wu back to the reality that he must leave her behind come the next morning. He must return to his post without delay, and he was not prepared to take her with him. So he said slowly, "My love, I must leave for my post without delay. His Majesty wants me to bring some troops here to help fight the rebels, and I will send for you as soon as I can make the arrangements to do so."

Wu San-kuei suddenly snapped out his dream. The thought of losing the love of his life was unthinkable, especially because it had taken him what seemed like an eternity to get her into his arms. He decided without further doubts to agree to a truce with Dorgon. By doing so, he could buy some time to not only deploy troops to save Peking from the rebels but also, more importantly, send a caravan to the capital to transport his woman to his garrison. And he also had to honor his commitment to help old Minister Tian.

He rose early the next morning and called for his uncle. When Ju Da-shou arrived at his office, Wu had already signed the document and handed it back to him. Ju was delighted that his nephew had acceded to Dorgon's wishes. "I will return to Ningyuan without delay. Now that we have become allies, I am sure His Highness will invite you to visit with him at his garrison in the near future."

Ju Da-shou left Shan-hai-kuan feeling like a man who had conquered the world. Wu San-kuei, on the other hand, felt like a man who had just sold his soul to the devil and his emperor down the river.

With Wu San-kuei's promise to lay down his arms for sixty days in his hands, Dorgon reached a comfort level and ordered the immediate withdrawal of all his troops from Ningyuan. He would use the respite given him by Wu San-kuei and return to Fushun to regenerate himself and his armed forces. He knew that the time would soon come for him to play a major role in a drama—the Drama of 1644.

CHAPTER 15

The Prince of Shun

BY THE BEGINNING OF 1644, LI TZU-CHENG HAD LED HIS SHUN army, with more than fifty thousand men, to within two hundred miles of Peking. The road to his ultimate objective was wrought with obstacles.

In the spring of 1642, on his initial attempt to march north from his base in Shensi, he was ambushed by a force along the way. The size of the force was unexpected. The force consisted of tens of thousands of men armed with weapons superior to those possessed by the Shun soldiers. In one fiercely fought battle, Li's army was routed because he was unprepared to take on such a big contingent. The prince of Shun was dealt a stunning defeat at the hand of an unexpected adversary. With his army in disarray, Li had no choice but to retreat and regroup. So he grudgingly gave back ground that he had gained and settled in the ancient capital, Sian.

The organizer of the force that blunted the Shun march was a retired general of the Ming army. He was one of the few remaining generals in the Ming army who maintained an undying loyalty to the emperor. Since he had some wealth of his own, he wanted to be the last bastion to defend the Ming empire against its adversaries.

Through much self-sacrifice and effort, he was able to galvanize small gangs of deserted soldiers and hangers-on into a mass. He fed them regularly and gave them money for extraordinary efforts. Within a few months, the general shaped the men into a formidable fighting force. Sadly for that patriotic general, this victory was a hollow one. His wealth was exhausted in one blow, and his force disbanded shortly after that one battle from the lack of continued support from him or his emperor.

Li Tzu-cheng was devastated by the setback, but it was mostly in spirit. He still controlled a sizable force in the former Kang garrison. Choosing Sian as his temporary station was not an accident, because Li knew that it was a capital of some ancient dynasties, especially one well-known dynasty named Tang. Moreover, Sian had been a major commercial hub in southwestern China, which facilitated his efforts to rebuild his force. While waiting for his army to rebuild, the dashing prince spent his days living like a king in the old palaces of the once-glorious Tang dynasty. He was not a student of history, but he had heard that the founding father of the Tang dynasty had been a man from humble origins, like him. And he also had the surname Li!

Ever since he took over the rebel force from the Brothers Kang, Li Tzu-cheng had a grand vision that, one day, he would be the emperor of China. He believed that was his destiny. He also believed that it was written in the stars. *So if I were to crown myself the emperor, where else is better than Sian?* he thought. But in order to realize his dream, he had one major hurdle to clear. And that hurdle was his good friend and comrade Liu Tsung-min. He had made a sacred vow to share the empire with him.

Li Tzu-cheng wrestled with his predicament for many days. With the help of his top aide, he devised a plan to deal with the Liu problem. The plan called for his aide to search the city for an expert in history and an astrologer. Within days, his aide found two men who met those qualifications and brought them in to see the dashing prince.

Li Tzu-cheng met the two men in a large but dilapidated old palace. Seated on an old and broken throne, he acted as though he were an emperor. Bowing to Li and singing his praises, the two men waited docilely for the prince to shower them with questions, which they hoped to be able to answer. After clearing his throat, Li Tzu-cheng pointed at the historian and asked, "The Tang dynasty belonged to the family with a surname of Li, and it occupied Sian as the capital. Do you think it is an accident that I am here in Sian, and my surname is Li?"

"Your … Highness. Er … Your Excellency—" The historian did not know how to address Li, so he stumbled. He soon recovered his senses. "I respectfully submit that it's not an accident. History often repeats itself. Perhaps history is repeating now, again!"

Li's face glowed, but he quickly became serious. "I have never tasted the bitterness of defeat since I took arms against the emperor. But the setback by that renegade general that landed me here really dealt me a humiliating blow."

"Your Excellency, a setback like the one you suffered was preordained! There are many setbacks like that in the long history of China. The most notorious example was one a renegade general handed the first emperor of the Han dynasty. After the setback, that emperor proceeded to found an empire that lasted for more than four hundred years."

The dashing prince was delighted to hear the historian's tale, but before he could react to the stories, the astrologer intervened.

"Your Excellency, I humbly submit that heaven is on your side!"

"How so?" Li was curious as he turned his focus to the astrologer.

"Some people reported seeing a star shooting up to the zenith of the sky from the horizon for many evenings," the astrologer reported, though he had no credible accounts to rely on. He felt, as the historian did, that offering stories the dashing prince wanted to hear would reap them handsome rewards.

"What does the shooting star in the sky mean?" asked Li.

"A star is born in Sian! That star is you, Your Excellency!" hailed the astrologer. "The throne is yours to claim!"

"Are these reports coming from reliable sources?" queried Li. Deep down, he really did not care because the stories suited his purpose. The stories by these two men would confirm his legitimacy to claim the throne.

After rewarding the two men with a handsome sum of cash, he dismissed them, saying, "Stay close to the palace grounds. I will be calling on you again soon."

The next day, Li Tzu-cheng called a meeting with his command staff, of which his good friend Liu Tsung-min was the leading member. As soon as the officers entered and found their seats, Li welcome them with a big smile. He declared, "I consulted two experts, one in history and one in astrology, and they both presented me with good tidings. They said that the sun, the moon, and the stars are in perfect alignment for someone to take the throne to succeed the failing Ming empire!"

No one was surprised by Li's comments, because they had expected the day would come for him to take the throne. They were only surprised that he would not wait until he reached Peking before doing so. The person most perturbed by Li's announcement was Liu Tsung-min. He had always taken the view that Li was, at best, a "best among equals" to him. He deferred to him because their late master, the Big Brother Kang, had favored Li, who had saved his life. Ever since he got a taste for power and luxurious life during his occupancy in Loyang, Liu had wished he'd be the heir to the throne. He thought that Li had forced his selfish will and whim on others to the detriment of the common cause: to take Peking and depose the emperor.

"These two experts urged that I take the throne, start a new dynasty, and be prepared to succeed the Ming dynasty," Li Tzu-cheng announced.

"Brother, the throne with legitimacy is in Peking. Creating one here for yourself does not render it legitimate in the people's view," Liu Tsung-min argued. He addressed Li as "brother" rather than "His Highness," as most of Li's subordinates did.

"Tsung-min, there were many instances in history, I was told, when dynasties coexisted, thus opening the way for many thrones at the same time," said Li. "Would you like to hear from the experts directly?"

Liu Tsung-min knew that his good friend was not to be denied and that he had the backing of most of the officers, so he declined the offer to see the experts. In the spirit of protecting the common purpose, he observed dejectedly, "I suppose founding a new dynasty will have one advantage. The people in China can come under our banner and be identified with us in our efforts to defeat the treacherous emperor!" Even though he was magnanimous, Liu really thought that he should be the one to be enthroned. Or, at least, share it with the dashing prince.

"Our troop level is almost back to normal. Perhaps the sooner you start a dynasty, the better it will be for our northern expedition," offered one of the officers.

"Has Your Highness given much thought to the name of your new regime?" asked another officer.

"I have given that much thought in recent days. But the strange thing is that it finally came to me in a dream!" said Li as he rose from his throne. "In my dream, heaven has bestowed on me a tiara with one word in its center. The word is *Shun*! I believe it means smooth and orderly! I will name the dynasty the Shun dynasty!"

Everyone got down on their knees to sang praises to Li Tzu-cheng. "Hail to the new Shun dynasty!" Liu Tsung-min grudgingly followed suit.

But before preparation to install himself as the emperor of the Shun dynasty could get under way, Li Tzu-cheng had a change of heart. He had sensed the antagonistic attitude from Liu Tsung-min toward his ascension. He also recalled that a deal had been made with Chang Hsien-chung, promising him that when Peking was conquered, the spoils would be shared equally. For these reasons, he decided to keep the title "prince of Shun" for the time being. He would delay his claim as emperor until he had reached Peking and deposed of the Ming emperor. By then, he would have attained the legitimacy to be the emperor. However, he did proudly declare that he was honored to occupy the grand palaces in Sian because his surname was the same as the rulers of the Tang dynasty who had previously occupied the palaces.

By the autumn of 1643, the prince of Shun was ready to resume his march to Peking. To soothe Liu Tsung-min's ego, he appointed him the supreme commander of the Shun forces, second in rank only to Li himself. Within six months, the Shun army, with more than fifty thousand men, had not only taken back the lost territories but conquered vast regions in the north. By late January of 1644, the Shun army was poised within two hundred miles of the capital.

CHAPTER 16

The Sacrifice

CHIEF EUNUCH WANG TUNG-YIN RAN BREATHLESSLY INTO THE inner chamber of the palace and found the emperor dressed in his nightgown, his long hair hanging loose. He appeared to be frantically looking for something. The eunuch bowed low to him. "Your Majesty, I have very, very bad news for you."

Emperor Chun-chen gazed at his trusted servant and answered softly, "How much worse can things get? How much more bad news can you bring me?" He resumed his search, moving from one end of the chamber to the other.

"Where is my saber?" he shouted. He appeared to gaze into emptiness.

"Your Majesty," the eunuch said with utmost urgency in his voice, "the rebels are within fifty miles of our capital. Most defenders of our gates have abandoned their posts. Those left behind are of little use, according to the last report."

"I need my saber to defend the palace, and ... myself!" the emperor mumbled. He scurried around the chamber like a man possessed.

"Your Majesty," the eunuch said in a caring but sad tone, "I believe you left your saber near your throne in the Throne Hall, the night you met with your ministers."

The chief eunuch was correct. Two nights ago, Chung-chen had called a meeting of his high ministers in the seldom-used Throne Hall to stress the urgency and importance of the meeting. Sadly, only three ministers had answered the emperor's call, Minister Tian Wang-yu one of them.

"Minister Tian," the emperor said in a very serious, quiet voice, "where are all of our loyal ministers?"

"Your Majesty, the rebels are within fifty miles of our capital. Many ministers are preparing to leave, for their own safety," responded Tian.

"Their own safety?" The emperor sounded annoyed. "The safety of the throne and the empire are not their concern? And what about the safety of the thousands and thousands of our people who live in the capital?"

"Your Majesty, I respectfully submit that you and your family should prepare to evacuate the Forbidden City," suggested Tian. The old minister himself had already made his own contingency plan to evacuate from the capital. He was still holding onto hope that Wu San-kuei would come to his rescue.

The two other ministers there murmured in agreement with the old minister.

"I am prepared to give my life to the empire," said the emperor. "I am not going to let the rebels ravage or torture me and my family." He reached back and picked up his favorite jade-handled saber, took it out of the scabbard, and waved it to show his grim determination.

One of the other ministers finally spoke. "Your Majesty, there is still time for us to consider other alternatives—" He was cut off by the emperor with a wave of his right hand.

"What other alternatives? The rebels are on our doorsteps, practically!" Chung-chen said acidly.

"Your Majesty," the other minister said, "are you still adverse to moving the throne to Nanking, for instance?"

"Peking has been the capital of our dynasty and our ancestral temple for over two hundred and fifty years. I simply cannot abandon it out of fear and desperation!" the emperor declared loudly.

"Then perhaps Your Majesty would consider sending the three princes out of the capital. In case Peking falls to the rebels, one of the princes can still carry on the Ming mandate."

The emperor had been leaning toward sacrificing all the members of the imperial family. He found the thought of moving south repulsive. But deep down, he could not disagree with his ministers. Even if he was ready to give his own life for the empire, it was his solemn duty to perpetuate the dynasty. If he could not survive the lifespan of the empire, then one of his sons should be given a chance to do so. "Minister Tian, do you think it is too late to have the three princes moved out of the capital?"

Tian Wang-yu was hoping that Wu San-kuei would come to the rescue by sending the troops that the emperor had asked for. "Your Majesty, we simply do not have sufficient time and manpower to escort the three princes out of the capital. The defenders of the Forbidden City are eunuchs and manservants. And none of them have military training."

One of the ministers said, "Why not disguise the princes as poor civilians? I will, with the help of some eunuchs, smuggle them out of the palace into the population."

Another minister echoed the minister's suggestion. "Good idea! After we get them out of the Forbidden City, then we can plan the next move south to Nanking or Kaifeng. Let's not wait any longer. Time is running against us."

The emperor hesitated for a moment, but he finally agreed

to the move. "Tung-yin, go and prepare their highnesses for the move tonight."

The chief eunuch bowed to the emperor and left the hall quickly to prepare the three princes for their journey.

The three ministers knelt and asked to be excused so that they could help to make the arrangements for the escape. Tian Wang-yu was more concerned with his own safety and the safety of his treasure. He already had a plan of escape, with or without the help of Wu San-kuei.

The three princes successfully escaped from the capital ahead of the advance rebel troops. They were escorted by a few loyal ministers and subsequently found refuge in Nanking. A few years after the fall of Peking, one of the princes established a shadow government there. The dying empire had found its way back to the dynasty's first capital. However, lacking financial resources and able administrators, the government quickly failed.

Emperor Chung-chen, left behind alone, felt insecure without his saber on his person. He quickly dispatched one of his attending eunuchs to Throne Hall to retrieve it for him.

In early April, 1644, Li Tzu-cheng' Shun army was outside the east gate of Peking, ready to enter the city. He had expected stiff resistance from the capital garrison, but none had materialized. People in the capital were bracing themselves for the horde of rebels, not knowing what would befall them. Rumors were inconsistent; some said that the prince of Shun was a strict disciplinarian and his soldiers a well-behaved bunch. Some reported that the Shun soldiers were nothing more than brigands and thieves.

Peking officialdom was basically divided into two camps: those who had decided to throw up their hands and kowtow to the new

master and those who had decided to hide or take refuge beyond
the capital. One who chose the latter category was Tian Wang-yu.
He had finally given up hope that Wu San-kuei would come to his
rescue, so he feverishly directed his servants to pack his treasures.
He moved out of his mansion in the middle of a night, heading
away from the advancing rebels. His destination was unknown,
even to him. He had not forgotten his favorite young women; a
few rode with him in his wagon.

The ominous report of the rebels' impending entry into
Peking had gotten to the emperor the day before the prince of
Shun entered the east gate. The chief eunuch told the emperor
that his palace guards were incapable of defending the Forbidden
City, and he urged him to take refuge while there was still time
to do so. Instead of heeding his trusted eunuch's advice, Chung-
chen ordered him to accompany him to the Hall of Ancestral
Altars. There he ordered that candles and incense sticks be lit
for each of his ancestors. He also ordered that bottles of fine
wine be placed in front of each of his ancestors' markers. Chief
Eunuch Wang directed the attending eunuchs in the hall to do
as ordered by the emperor. While waiting for his order to be
filled, Chung-chen drew his saber from the scabbard hanging
from his waist and held it high over his head. Then he cried
hysterically until the eunuchs had completed the arrangements
he had ordered.

The emperor proceeded with the ritual of paying respect to
each of fifteen ancestors, from the first emperor of the Ming dy-
nasty to his immediate predecessor. At each stop before a marker,
he prostrated himself and knocked his head on the floor nine times.
He then took a drink from each bottle in front of the markers.
When he got to the last marker, designating his elder brother, the
Emperor Tian-ti, the emperor suddenly rose and started shouting.
"You should not have died so young! If you had lived, I would not

have inherited this shambles!" He picked up the bottle in front of his brother's marker and emptied it in one big gulp. When the chief eunuch tried to stop him, the emperor pushed him away so hard that the chief eunuch fell to the floor.

Emperor Chung-chen got down on his knees in the center of the hall, directly under the temple dome. Tears flowed down his cheeks as he leaned on his saber in front of him. Looking up at the peak of the dome, he wailed, "I have been on the throne for seventeen years, but not by my own choosing. Now I must answer for the trouble that has befallen me. The misdeeds that created the troubles for our empire were committed by my ministers, not by me. Our empire and our ancestral altars are about to fall into the hands of our enemies. I have to accept the obligations that were charged to me by you, my illustrious ancestors. Since I cannot save the realm entrusted to me and perpetuate the glory of the Ming dynasty, I have only this measly life to give to you! Alas! I will never be able to face all of you, in hell or in heaven!" At the end of his confession, he pulled his saber from the floor and aimed it on his own neck. Chief Eunuch Wang got to his feet quickly and, with the help of the other eunuchs, wrestled the saber away from the emperor. The emperor apparently fainted and fell to the floor. The chief eunuch directed four eunuchs to carry him back to his chamber, a short walking distance away.

The next morning when the emperor came to, Peking was in turmoil. The rebels had begun their march through the east gate into the capital. The chief eunuch tried to rally his palace guards to rise for one last time for a showdown with the rebels. But much to his chagrin, most threw down their arms and deserted the palace grounds. Helpless and frightened, the chief eunuch brought a few eunuchs with him and rushed back to the emperor's chamber, trying to escort him out of the Forbidden City. But as they entered the chamber, they found Chung-chen sitting on the floor, dressed in his nightgown, his hair hanging down his face, holding a bottle of rice wine in one hand. Empty bottles were scattered around the floor. Chung-chen had apparently been drinking all night. He was in a stupor.

"Your Majesty," yelled the chief eunuch while pushing the emperor, "we've got to get out of the palace. Quickly!"

Chung-chen did not get up. He mumbled, "I have got to take ... care ... of ... my family ... my women. They cannot help ... themselves!"

"I have made arrangements to escort them out of the palaces. Some of my men are working on that right now," avowed the chief eunuch. "Sir, you've got to get dressed—quickly!"

Chung-chen ignored the eunuch's admonition, He pushed the chief eunuch's hands away. "I've got to ... take care of ... the empress and the princesses!" He staggered to his feet and at the same time emptied the bottle still in his hand.

"Your Majesty, the empress and the princesses will be in good hands, I promise you," the chief eunuch said, trying to coax the emperor to change his clothes and leave the palace. He had already arranged for the emperor to don the outfit of a eunuch as a disguise. The emperor grudgingly changed his clothes, three eunuchs helping him.

"Call a meeting of all the highest-ranking ministers ... in Throne Hall," Chung-chen declared loudly, sounding disoriented.

"Your Majesty, you have called many meetings, and few have answered your call," said the chief eunuch.

"You mean no one came to ... the meeting I ordered?" the emperor mumbled disjointedly. "I do not remember. Did I miss ... the meetings too?"

"Your Majesty, it did not matter! You did not miss the meetings. I was there for all the meetings, and not one of our ministers obeyed your order to show up!"

"Now you know ... why I will be blamed ... as the emperor who ... lost the realm of the Ming dynasty! Woe is ... me!"

To the last day of his life, Emperor Chung-chen absolved himself of blame, placing it squarely on the shoulders of his ministers. He asked for another bottle of rice wine; a eunuch looked at the chief eunuch and slowly handed a bottle over to the emperor. While the chief eunuch was frantically making arrangements to move him and his family, Chung-chen continued to drink until he fell into a deep slumber.

The emperor awakened when night was about to fall. Finding no one near him, he got off the floor and ran to the chamber where his empress lived. Finding her there with only two female servants, he dismissed the servants and handed his saber over to the empress. "If I were to die for the empire, I suppose that you should do the same!" he said somewhat cold-bloodedly.

The empress cried loudly and muttered, "Your Majesty, I will not shrink from my duty as the sitting empress. I will gladly die by your hand!" The empress handed the saber back to the emperor and held her head high, waiting for the saber to land on her neck.

He took the saber in his right hand. As he was about to raise it toward her, he suddenly stopped and cried, "My dear, I cannot do this to you!" After a pause, he untied the sash from the waist of the empress and handed it to her. "I will see you in heaven, my dear, hopefully!" He ran out of her chamber with huge strides, not looking back.

Running into the next chamber, the emperor encountered his older daughter there with two maidservants. Without uttering a word, he closed his eyes and swung his saber wildly at the women. They dodged. The emperor shouted, "Forgive me! I cannot bear to see you ravaged by the rebels." He continued to swing the saber wildly until he cut down the three women.

Moving to the next chamber, the emperor encountered his

younger daughter, his favorite, Princess Chang-ping. She was in
her room with three maidservants. The emperor waved his saber
and dismissed the other women; he apparently wanted to be with
the princess alone. He began to sob as he embraced the daughter.
She cried and held the father tightly. She was saddened by the appearance of the father. "Father, has the day arrived?"

The emperor gently pushed the daughter away and answered,
"Yes, my daughter, I believe the day has arrived. The day has
indeed dawned on your mother and your sister, and it will dawn
on me very soon!" He paused momentarily and continued, with
tears flowing down his cheeks. "How unfortunate for you, my
daughter, to have been born to this wretched family and in these
troubled times!"

"Father, if Mother and Sister gave their lives for our country, I
certainly am willing to give mine also." Princess Chang-ping held
her head high, expecting the father to land his saber on her.

The emperor raised the saber, but he stopped in midmotion,
crying out, "I cannot bear seeing you ravaged by the rebels when
they enter our palace." He froze as loud noises filtered in from a
distance. At about the same time, he also heard noises and footsteps
coming from within the palace. So Chung-chen closed his eyes
and thrust the saber toward the princess. He succeeded in hacking
off her left arm. As blood spewed from the princess's torso, the
emperor got down on his knees and embraced her. Frantically he
lamented, "My daughter, forgive me! I will see you under that
willow tree. The one in my garden. We will take flight to heaven
from that tree, together forever!"

The noises and footsteps from within the palace belonged to
the chief eunuch and his assistants, who were frantically searching
for Chung-chen and making arrangement to move the empress and
the princesses. Not finding him in his chamber, they had proceeded
to the next chamber and discovered the empress's body hanging

by the door. As they proceeded to the next chamber, they found three more female bodies in a large pool of blood. Following the trail of blood to the next chamber, they caught the emperor in the act of killing his youngest beloved daughter. The chief eunuch tried to stop the emperor, but it was too late to save the princess. The emperor appeared like a man possessed, and he was not to be detained. As soon as he saw the eunuchs, he dropped the saber and left the chamber, moving toward the nearest palace gate. The chief eunuch left the chamber and chased after him.

Catching up to him on the palace grounds, the chief eunuch slowed the emperor down and said, "Your Majesty, where are you going? We have a sedan waiting for you nearby."

Chung-chen was disoriented. He gave the chief eunuch a blank look and muttered, "I've got to get out of here. I have to get up to Coal Hill." He pointed toward the east, where the sky was totally engulfed in red. "The fire is fast reaching our palaces!" In reality, the red emanated from burning torches carried by the marching rebels and some sections of the city ignited by looters.

"Why Coal Hill, Your Majesty? You've got to come with me. You'll be safer with the escorts I have gathered to protect you. Being by yourself will court disaster!"

Chung-chen pushed the chief eunuch away and ran toward the nearest palace gate, the chief eunuch in hot pursuit. As they got closer to the gate, two guards who had remained on duty aimed their swords at the emperor because they did not recognize him. The chief eunuch yelled at the guards, "Open the gate for the emperor! Quick!"

The two guards looked at each other, and one shrugged and said, "Emperor? You?" he pointed at the chief eunuch.

"We have orders from the real emperor not to open the gate for anyone. I guess not even for him!" echoed the other guard.

The two guards blocked the gate and refused to budge, and the chief eunuch pulled the emperor away. They both ran toward one of the other gates. They spent many hours running from gate to gate, finding most of them either blocked by guards who refused to obey their order or the gates jammed shut. At last, they found an unguarded gate that was not bolted tightly, and the emperor and the chief eunuch forced their way out. Once they were outside, they encountered one mob of people after another, screaming and running from the east. Apparently the rebels were advancing toward the Forbidden City from that direction.

Pushing through the crowds, the emperor walked with quick steps toward a hill on the fringe of town. He was physically and mentally tired, but his adrenaline had kicked in, and he walked on without stopping. The chief eunuch followed closely behind; he, too, had found more than a second wind. As they reached the foot of Coal Hill, the emperor suddenly stopped and pointed to the top of the peak. "Tung-yin, I have a friend I must visit up there!"

"Your Majesty?" The chief eunuch gave the emperor an inquisitive look.

"My dear friend, the willow!"

CHAPTER 17

The Parade

THE NIGHT OF APRIL 25, 1644, WAS AN INFAMOUS NIGHT IN the history of China.

While Emperor Chung-chen and his trusted eunuch Wang Tung-yin were climbing their way up Coal Hill, the rebel army was marching triumphantly through the east gate of Peking toward the Forbidden City.

Leading the vanguard of the rebel army was Li Tzu-cheng, the prince of Shun. Under normal circumstances, it would have been General Liu Tsung-min who would lead the parade into a conquered city. But because entering Peking, the capital of China, carried a historical meaning, the prince was not about to let some-one else steal his thunder. He had worked too hard and for too long to get to this day.

Leaving his army of more than fifty thousand men outside the city gate, he entered the city in the twilight hours with a cavalry of a thousand. The rebel soldiers, wearing white hats and green uniforms, moved steadily through the city. Dressed in his light green garrison outfit instead of a costume befitting a prince,

Li Tzu-cheng rode high on his black horse, his signature green Stetson on his head.

The people of Peking began the day full of hope and trepidation as the east gate was thrown wide open to receive the triumphant conquerors. Most people had heard that the Shun soldiers were renegades who looted and raped the vanquished at will. At first, most people stayed indoors, and pedestrians hid on the side streets, watching the columns of horses moving by. An eerie silence enveloped the streets, broken only by the hooves pounding the street pavement. As the soldiers began to spread through the alleys, marking off billets, it became apparent to the people that the army was genuinely a disciplined force. Later, when leaflets were handed out by more soldiers, the population in Peking let out huge sighs of relief. The leaflets contained a promise by the prince that soldiers who committed atrocities or inflicted harm on the people would be punished by death, without exception.

As the prince of Shun rode further into the city, huge crowds formed and lined both sides of the wide avenues. They were yelling slogans like, "Welcome the prince of Shun!" "Long live the Shun dynasty!" and "Ten thousand years to Prince Li!" They were also waving banners and wearing hats displaying similar welcoming messages.

Li Tzu-cheng was emotionally touched. He wiped happy tears from his face and turned to one of his generals riding behind him and said, "Brother, this is worth living for and fighting for. I waited a long, long time for this day!" The crowd noises were so loud that it was doubtful that his assistant heard his comment. The prince moved slowly for no more than a few hundred yards before his path was abruptly blocked by a group of people. They were all on their knees bowing to him. Li jumped off his horse and got down to mingle with the group, and he heard one elderly man singing some verses; others shortly followed.

"Open the gate. Never too late. Welcome the new emperor. We will have no more fear. We will have no more lean years!"

As the group sang loudly, the crowd nearby soon echoed the verses. Li Tzu-cheng took off his green Stetson, laughing heartily and waving it in time with the singing. He then picked a young boy out of a circle of people and hoisted him high over his head. He shouted, "Brothers and sisters, I promise you—no more lean years! Your savior is here!"

In the midst of the yelling, singing, and hand-clapping, the prince of Shun jumped back in his saddle and placed his trademark Stetson squarely back on his head. He resumed his march toward the Forbidden City. Within a few more hundred yards, he came upon a high red wall. He pulled the reins to stop his horse and looked at the wall, awed and inspired. He said, "So this is what I had been fighting for over fifteen years!" He then turned his horse around and yelled, "Brothers, we have arrived!" In response, the troops echoed in unison, "Hail to the prince of Shun! Long live the Shun dynasty!"

As Li Tzu-cheng edged his horse closer to the gate of that tall red wall, he saw two large doors swing wide open, with two groups of people lining both sides of the gate. As he pulled his horse forward to the gate, ready to enter, two men came forward from the lines and knelt in front of his horse, blocking his path. The prince looked down and saw two men in impeccably colorful costumes. One appeared to be a high court minister, the other a eunuch. The one who dressed like a eunuch spoke first, in a high and squeaky voice. "Your Highness, welcome to the Forbidden City! I am the assistant chief eunuch of the imperial palaces. My name is Tang Jun. I am at your service."

Then the one dressed like a minister said, "Your Highness, I am the deputy chief minister of the court. My name is Do Wen-lung. Welcome to the Forbidden City!"

These men had been officials of the Ming emperor. For self-preservation and for future gains and security, they had decided to turn their backs on their former master and surrender to the Shun leader. Unlike many of their loyal counterparts, Do and Tang did not want to risk being caught and punished by the rebels.

The prince grunted loudly and waved his hand and said, "What are we waiting for? Let's proceed into the Forbidden City!"

The two men quickly got on their feet and led the prince through the gate with ten of his top officers. The rest of the soldiers were left outside the palace grounds for the night. As the rebel leaders rode past, the two lines of prostrate ministers and courtiers pounded their heads on the ground and shouted, "Welcome to the Forbidden City, the prince of Shun!"

Once he passed through the gate, Li Tzu-cheng could not believe what lay in front of him. The first thing that caught his eye was the huge, opulent palace called Throne Hall. Flanking Throne Hall were two smaller palaces, equally elegant, with golden-tiled roofs and red outer walls and many columns surrounding them. The assistant chief eunuch beckoned Li and his officers to dismount, so that he could lead them into the Great Within of the palaces behind Throne Hall.

As the prince got off his horse, his officers followed. He then turned and looked at them and let out a loud laugh. "Brothers, we really have arrived! This is beyond my wildest dream!"

His fellow officers echoed him with loud laughs, and Liu Tsung-min said, "Brothers, let's go inside and enjoy ourselves! We've come a long way and waited for a long time for this!"

Eunuch Tang ushered Li and his officers into a small palace behind Throne Hall. Inside the palace was a large round table with ten chairs surrounding it, and in the center was a larger chair that resembled a throne. The eunuch led the prince to that large chair; after Li took the seat, the other officers found theirs around the table. When Eunuch Tang clapped his hands twice, the other eunuchs waiting in the palace quickly began to pour wine into the glasses placed in front of each officer. While the glasses were being filled, fifteen pretty young maids appeared, holding dishes of exquisite gourmet food and placing them on the table. The men were famished because they had had a long and hard day. They had not tasted such delicious food for a long time. What most of them saw in front of them were gifts from heaven. They all felt an urge to pounce on the food, but they dared not do so before the prince had taken his first bite. There was an uneasy calm for what seemed to some an eternity as the prince exploded in a tirade. "Who's idea is it that you waste so much of the people's money on these dishes? My brothers and I have sacrificed our lives and our belongings to get here. We would be more than happy to eat rice and soup with vegetables, rather than these money-wasting dishes. Take them away!"

Eunuch Tang was speechless. He fidgeted and looked at Minister Do, who stood near him. The minister tried to make the best out of an awkward situation; he bowed and muttered, "Your Highness, we regret that we made the wrong judgment and wasted the resources of the people, but if you would prefer rice and soup with vegetables, we will order them prepared without delay." He took two steps back, waiting for a reply from the prince.

But the night was saved in one smooth maneuver by Liu Tsung-min. He held up his glass and tipped it toward his good friend. "Your Highness, let us drink to our triumph! Long live the Shun dynasty!"

When Li heard Liu address him as "Your Highness," his heart softened quickly. No one knew if the prince's tirade was an act or if he had spoken sincerely. Regardless, he calmed down and accepted his good friend's graciousness. He toasted Tsung-min. "Without your help and that of all my brothers here, I would not be sitting on this throne tonight. Let us all drink to that!" They hoisted their glasses and emptied them in one motion. Loud laughter followed.

As the prince took the first bite of food, everyone around the table was relieved, and they consumed the dishes in a short time. The two most relieved persons in the palace were the assistant chief eunuch and the deputy chief minister. They had survived the first tirade of their new master.

At the end of the dinner, Eunuch Tang, with the help of the other eunuchs and some maids, escorted the officers to their assigned chambers for the evening. Eunuch Tang personally escorted the prince to the most sumptuous chamber to rest for the night. With the exception of Liu Tsung-min, who had insisted on the company of some maids, all of his fellow officers found their soft beds irresistible, and they drifted into dreamland quickly. While the prince tossed and turned in his large bed for some time, thinking about programs for his new reign, Liu Tsung-min engaged in an orgy with a few of the young and pretty women he had forced into bed with him.

Emperor Chung-chen and his chief eunuch reached the peak of Coal Hill at about the same time the prince of Shun and his officers settled in for the night. As he staggered into the red pavilion, Chung-chen found his willow tree. He sat on the stone bench inside the red pavilion for a moment before he rose and gazed down the hill at the palaces that fourteen emperors, including himself, had called home for more than two hundred years. Uncontrollably, tears began to flow down his thin cheeks. He wiped his eyes with one of his sleeves so he could take another good look at the Forbidden City. He noticed that the redness in the sky cast a dullness on the glowing yellow tiles on the palace roofs. "What has this beautiful city come to?" the emperor asked himself. He recalled his younger days, when he was Prince Shen rather than the emperor, and he had wandered up this hill frequently to enjoy the panoramic view of the city.

On one of those occasions, at age twelve, Chung-chen had discovered a new friend on that hill. While his brothers were busy playing hide and seek and his father took in the scenic view of the Forbidden City, he spent his time under a lonely willow tree by a red pavilion. The tree was about ten feet in height, but the foliage was full, and it resembled a beautiful umbrella. The young prince, with the help of some eunuchs, would climb atop the tree to take in the panoramic view of the Forbidden City. It was breathtaking, he often thought. *If I become emperor,* he fantasized, *I would rebuild certain parts of the palace complex*; some parts were succumbing to the ravages of time. In reality, the lack of maintenance of the palaces was due mainly to the shortage of funds in the imperial treasury, a fact not known by the young and innocent prince. But he quickly dismissed those thoughts because he had three elder brothers, and the possibility that he would become emperor was remote.

Nevertheless, Chung-chen frequently ran up to the hill to enjoy the city view and be with his friend, as he called the willow. While the older eunuchs warned him to be more discreet and not expose himself to the common people so often, he ignored their warnings and stole out of the palace to run up the hill with an escort of only a few young servants. His reason for wanting to go up the hill was simple; he had no one to relate to in the palaces, and he found peace and happiness sitting below that willow tree.

Chung-chen's mind wandered back to the present. Those once-magnificent palaces had quickly turned into ghostly houses. Worse yet, the once-beautiful city of Peking was engulfed in smoke and facing imminent destruction. "My ministers failed me!" Chung-chen still held to that belief. "But I am the one who must answer to my forbearers." He then covered his face with a sleeve because he simply could not take another glimpse at the dismal view in front of him.

Wang Tung-yin, his trusted eunuch, looked at the emperor with sadness as he shivered in the cool spring night. The emperor's slender body was covered by only the thin layer of the robe of a eunuch. With his disheveled long hair blowing in the wind, Emperor Chung-chen struck a ghostly pose. The chief eunuch shook his head and said in a heavy voice, "Your Majesty, I will go and gather some logs to build a fire for you." Chung-chen did not react to the eunuch's remark; he remained in a stony repose. Seeing and hearing no response from his master, the eunuch quietly left to tend to the chore.

When he returned with an armful of small tree branches and logs, the eunuch could not find the emperor in the darkness. He dropped the wood on the ground and began to look for his master.

He found the emperor hanging from his favorite willow tree. "Oh, my heaven!" the eunuch screamed. "Your Majesty! No, no, no!" He let the emperor down gently, but it was too late to save him. Wang Tung-yin wailed, "Your Majesty, I have failed you! I should not have left you alone!" He wailed for over an hour, holding the emperor's corpse in his arms. Then, at last, he laid the body back down on the ground and untied the sash from his own waist and hanged himself on the same willow tree.

The body of the last emperor of the once-mighty Ming dynasty lay ignominiously under the feet of his faithful servant. The emperor wore a red shoe on his left foot, and his right foot was bare. His robe had two characters written over the chest area, in his own blood: *Tien Tze*, meaning "son of heaven." A blue shoe was found lying a few feet from his body.

Li Tzu-cheng rose early the next morning, eager to get to work on programs for his new reign. His first order of business was to locate the emperor. He ordered some men to search the palaces. After a morning of hunting, his men reported that they had discovered the bodies of the empress, the two princesses, and some maids, but the three princes and the emperor were nowhere to be found.

The prince hastily called a meeting with his officers to decide on courses of action for running the new government. In the meeting were the usual suspects, with Minister Do and Eunuch Tang also in attendance to assist in the transition.

The prince opened the meeting by saying, "We have got to locate the Ming emperor. The sky cannot have two suns if I were to become the emperor myself."

One of the officers said, "Your Highness, you should post a price on the head of the Ming emperor. The reward will go to the one who finds him!"

"Good idea!" Li Tzu-cheng declared. "Tsung-min, issue an order and circulate it around the city immediately. A reward of ten thousand ounces of silver for the emperor, dead or alive!"

Liu Tsung-min assigned one of his subordinates to carry out the order. Then he turned back to Li and said, "Brother, I understand there are many Ming officials still in the capital, and they are seeking placement with us. Should we not tend to that matter as soon as we can?"

The prince nodded and turned to Minister Do Wen-lung. "Minister, what General Liu has said seems to make sense. We need to reorganize the official ranks in the court so that we don't disrupt the function of the government."

"Your Highness, there are many officials, in all ranks, that expressed a wish to serve in your new regime. I should think that a process must be set up to screen them for placement in your government," Minister Do said respectfully. Deep down, he wished to be the person given the authority to administer the process. He, like the assistant chief Eunuch Tang, had chosen to surrender to the prince of Shun for personal reasons. They had both been stifled in their quests for power under the previous regime. Now that they had the chance to change their fortunes, they would grasp that opportunity enthusiastically.

"Minister, you will assist General Liu in the screening process," ordered Li, and he turned to Liu and continued. "Tsung-min, you will have total say in selecting who serves in our ministries."

"Your Highness, Minister Do and I will work on that at once." Liu bowed.

The prince then turned to Eunuch Tang and took up a rather mundane matter. "Jun, tell me. How many maids do we still have in our palaces that can be of service to us?"

Eunuch Tang stepped forward and bowed to the prince. "Your Highness, at last count, I believe we still have more than two hundred female servants under our control in the palaces."

"I'd like to assign them to our senior officers, as a reward for their faithful and loyal service to me. Round them up and have them available for my viewing tomorrow morning in Throne Hall," ordered the prince.

When he heard the order issued by the prince of Shun, Liu Tsung-min could not wait for morning to come.

CHAPTER 18

The Transition

LIU TSUNG-MIN AND HIS FELLOW GENERALS GATHERED EARLY the next day in Throne Hall and awaited the arrival of the prince of Shun. They were also looking forward to the arrival of the pretty palace maids, the ultimate prizes for their long and faithful service to the Shun army. Shortly before the sun reached its zenith, a parade of beauties appeared in front of the palace. The women had already been screened and ranked by Minister Do and Eunuch Tang before being presented to the prince and his generals. The ranking was based first on looks and second on age. Thus, the younger ones with the better-looking faces and bodies received the highest rankings.

When the prince arrived, everyone bowed low as if he were the emperor. After he had seated himself squarely on the throne, Eunuch Tang approached him and said softly, "Your Highness, I have just the most perfect woman to present to you!"

The prince scanned the ranks of the women and asked eagerly, "Which one?"

"She is not among those here. I will have her, along with

twenty of the most beautiful ones, delivered to your chamber this afternoon," Eunuch Tang said.

The prince found the eunuch's proposition pleasing to his ears, and he wanted the award ceremony to go quickly so he could return to his chamber and enjoy the company of the women the eunuch had chosen for him. "Eunuch Tang, are we ready to proceed with the ceremony?" the prince asked.

"Your Highness, yes, we are. When you give the signal, I will start calling the names of the generals. And they will identify the maids they wish to take to their chambers."

"Proceed!" ordered the prince.

"General Liu Tsung-min," yelled Eunuch Tang. As Liu stepped forward, the eunuch said, "General, point at the twenty maids you'd like, and my team will have them escorted to your chamber by this evening."

Liu Tsung-min walked down to where the young maids had gathered and selected the ones he liked the most. He was given first choice because he was the highest-ranking general. When he was done, the next ranking general was called, and the process went on until all ten of the officers had completed their selection. The process took more than two hours to complete.

After the selection was done, a team of eunuchs ushered the women away from the palace grounds. The prince rose and said, "Brothers, enjoy your rewards tonight! We have much to do in the days ahead." The officers bowed and cried out, "Your Highness, we are most grateful for your generosity! Long live the prince of Shun!"

As the crowd dispersed, Minister Do approached Liu Tsung-min and pulled him aside. "General, I have already set up the tents outside the meridian gate of the Forbidden City. It looks like we will need more tents to accommodate the number of officials we have collected."

"How many have we gathered so far?" Liu asked casually.

"At last count it was about two hundred 'clean' officials. As for the 'dirty' ones, I would guess that we have rounded up a hundred," Minister Do responded.

Those identified as "clean" officials were in the lower ranks of the Ming hierarchy, and the "dirty" ones were mostly higher-ranking corrupt ministers. Liu and Do had set up the procedure for a selfish reason. They would staff the new government with those in the lower ranks, the "clean" ministers, so that they could exert control over them. As to the "dirty" ministers, Liu and Do would punish them for the misdeeds they had perpetrated and confiscate the ill-gotten wealth hidden away by those men. The most notorious of the "dirty" ministers was Tian Wang-yu. Tian's attempt to escape the capital on the eve of the rebels' entry into the Forbidden City had been frustrated. He was apprehended by a team of rebels patrolling the city.

"Set up as many tents as we need," commanded Liu. "I will screen the office seekers personally tomorrow." He could not wait to get back to his chamber to enjoy the women he had been awarded.

When the prince saw the young women standing in front of him when he returned to his chamber, he could hardly suppress his lust and desire. He could not take his eyes off one of them in particular. The woman had the most beautiful face and a voluptuous body.

"Your Highness, I am Consort Tian," said that beautiful woman as she bowed to the prince.

"Consort?" the prince uttered in a puzzled tone.

"Yes, Your Highness," said Consort Tian. "I was the favorite consort of the emperor. I am now at your service!"

Consort Tian had survived the slaughter the evening Emperor Chung-chen was on his rampage. She happened to be with her father, Tian Wang-yu, as the old man was preparing to escape from the advancing rebels. Her father had urged her to leave with him, but ever faithful to Chung-chen, Consort Tian declined. When she returned to the palace the next day, she fell into the hands of Minister Do and Eunuch Tang. Unable to free herself, she became one of the captured women. Consort Tian was a clever woman, so she thought that if she played along with Do and Tang, she would be free, someday and somehow.

The prince was totally consumed by the exquisite beauty and personality of the consort. He quickly dismissed the other maids and opted to spend the night only with Consort Tian. The consort was attracted to the rebel leader; she found his gruff but masculine manners to her liking, unlike the emperor, who was tender and soft but lacked the sexual appeal of a real man like the prince. When they were in bed together, the prince, in his rough and fresh manner, fondled and caressed her, and the consort found it most pleasurable.

"Your Highness," the consort said teasingly, "how should I address you?"

"You can address me anyway you'd like," the prince mumbled, resting his head on the consort's soft bosom. "I have had the company of many women in my life. I'd dare say that that you are the best ... the best ride!" He let out a hearty laugh and kissed her passionately.

She hit him on the face gently and muttered, "Do you want to ride me again?"

"Of course, sweetie," the prince said, and he turned his body around and landed on top of her again. "How sweet it is!" he screamed a few minutes later, after another "ride" with her.

The two continued to frolic in the huge and sumptuous bed. Then the consort thought she should take care of real business before her man fell asleep. "Your Highness, I have a matter of utmost importance that I need your help with."

The prince continued to caress and kiss her. "Let me know what you have in mind."

"My father … you know who my father is, Your Highness?"

The prince perked up and said, "Eunuch Tang mentioned that your father is a high minister in the Ming court. And that he had given you to the emperor as a consort."

"Yes, my father is now in a difficult situation." The consort feigned sadness and lamented, "He has been incarcerated by General Liu in a camp outside the Forbidden City. My father is old and weak. I fear that he will not survive the treatment by your generals."

"What do you wish that I do?"

"I want my father to get better treatment. He does not deserve the punishment he is getting." The consort began to sob. "Please show mercy to him, an old and innocent man who was caught in a bad situation beyond his control!"

"All right! All right!" said Li, who really wanted to sink deeper under the bedcover against the consort's soft body and get a good night's sleep. "I will get on your father's case first thing tomorrow." He dragged her under the bedcover with him, and she complied.

The next morning, Li Tzu-cheng woke up happy and fresh after a night of fun and sleep, ready tend to some serious business. He called a meeting with his new brain trust, which included Liu Tsung-min, Minister Do, Eunuch Tang, and another general who had been a loyal member of his team for a long time, one Niu Chin-hsing. The meeting convened in a small palace that held the emperor's favorite conference room. Eunuch Tang wanted to use that particular hall because he thought the prince should begin acting more like an emperor than perpetuating his image as a rebel leader. Minister Do agreed.

When the prince entered the palace and found his seat, the four men bowed to him and sang out their praises. "Long live the prince of Shun! Long live the Shun dynasty!" They then sat in their assigned seats, the two generals sitting close to the prince.

The prince opened the meeting with a question that was on most people's minds. "Is there any news on the whereabouts of the emperor?" It had been three days since the rebels had entered the Forbidden City, and the emperor was nowhere to be found.

"As you know, Your Highness, we posted a handsome reward for finding the emperor. But to this day, no one has turned up for the reward," said Eunuch Tang.

"Your Highness," Minister Do chimed in, "I respectfully submit that it is time for you to take the throne and not wait any longer. We may never locate the emperor. He could be hiding underground."

"Your Highness, I agree with the minister," echoed General Niu. "The Ming regime was ended the moment you set foot on the grounds of the Forbidden City. I see no need to wait any longer."

The prince took a side glance at his good friend, but Liu Tsung-min avoided his eyes. Deep down, Liu Tsung-min still harbored the view that he and Li should head the empire as co-leaders, since Li had vowed that they would share the spoils when they made it to Peking. Without him, he thought, Li Tzu-cheng would not have survived to this day.

"If the emperor is still alive, then I cannot ascend to the throne," the prince insisted. "It is said, 'The country cannot have two emperors, as the sky cannot have two suns!'" In reality, Li Tzu-cheng was still keenly aware of Liu Tsung-min's feelings on the matter. And he had also made the same pledge to another ally, Chang Hsien-chung, when they struck a truce in Sian. Even though his intelligence sources had informed him that Chang's forces had been stalled in the march to Peking, Li was concerned that his ally would land in the capital eventually. In that event, his premature move to ascend the throne would bring major chaos.

"We should set a date for your ascension," Minister Do said. "The people cannot wait any longer for a rightful ruler."

All those present echoed a similar sentiment, except for Liu, who hesitated for a moment and then murmured, "I suppose the date can be changed, if events dictate."

Minister Do had already consulted with the almanac the night before and chose the first day of May, 1644, to be the day that Li Tzu-cheng would take on the title of emperor of the Shun dynasty.

The prince accepted the choice without further discussion. Then he promptly moved to the next item in the agenda. For the first time, he formally addressed his good friend by his title. "General Liu, I understand we have camps set up to house the officials of the former regime. How is the screening process going?"

"Everything is under control." Liu seemed annoyed at Li's intervention in a matter under his responsibility. He answered in a condescending voice, "Minister Do and I have been working diligently to staff our ministries with qualified candidates gleaned from the list of former officials. We also set up harsh punishments for those ministers who were corrupt and disloyal to the Ming emperor."

"Tell me about Tian Wang-yu." The name dropped from the prince's lips abruptly.

Minister Do and General Liu's eyes met; they were surprised by the question. The minister chose to respond first because he had more to lose and more to cover up then Liu did. "Your Highness, he is the father of Consort Tian, your new ... er ... lady-in-waiting."

"I know that. She was the one who told me." The prince sounded impatient. "I want to know who he was and what we plan to do with him."

Liu Tsung-min spoke up and related his recent encounter with
Tian Wang-yu to the prince.

"General, we have nabbed one of the high ministers running
from the capital!" An aide rushed into the camp and found Liu and
Do busy interrogating some minor ministers.

Both men dropped the matters at hand, and their victims were
rushed out of the tent. Liu turned to the aide and inquired, "Who
do you have?"

"We identified him as the chief minister of the Ming court,
one Tian Wang-yu," the aide answered.

"How did you come upon him?" Liu asked.

"His ten wagons were on the way out of the west gate two
nights ago. As he refused to stop for our inspection, we detained
him," the aide continued. "He kept ranting and raving that he was
the chief minister of the court."

"Where is he now?" Do queried.

"He is outside your camp, awaiting your disposal, General,"
the aide said.

"Bring him in!" Liu commanded.

"Yes, sir!" The aide left the tent quickly, and soon two soldiers
brought the old minister in, wearing shackles.

"Unchain him." Liu took one quick look at Minister Tian, and
he felt sorry for the old man. He appeared disheveled, gaunt, and
weak. "Minister Tian, take a seat." Liu pointed at a wooden stool
near him.

"Oh, thank you!" the old man mumbled.

"Tell me—you were the highest-ranking minister in Emperor
Chung-chen's court. Should you bear some responsibility for the
failure of the empire?" Liu got right to the point as he took charge
of the interrogation. Minister Do listened with undivided attention.

"I was only one of many ministers in his court. Why should I bear that burden all by myself?" The old minister sounded feisty.

"One ancient axiom says, 'A general in defeat should not speak of bravery! A minister who loses the realm should not live!'" Liu droned.

"I did not lose the realm, the emperor did!" Tian muttered.

"Nevertheless, you were caught running for your life with many wagons full of treasures while your emperor was fighting for his life! Much of those treasures belong to the emperor or rightfully, to the people. Saving your own skin I understand. But to steal from the people is unforgivable!" Liu charged.

"I worked all my life for the emperor. I even saved him from treacherous men like Wei Chung-yan. What I have accumulated I deserve to keep!" the old minister retorted. He was not about to give up his so-called "hard-earned" wealth without a fight.

"That wealth now goes back to the national treasury. In other words, the people of China," Liu shot back. In reality, he and his coconspirator, Minister Do, already had a plan in place to siphon some of the treasure for themselves. "Under the law of the new Shun government, former Ming officials who are found to be corrupt are to pay a price for their misdeeds. What punishment should you receive, Minister Tian?"

Minister Tian was speechless; he knew the ax would fall on him because the rebel leaders would not spare him. They needed to set an example by punishing former ministers, and he would be a perfect example: a wealthy and high-ranking minister who had a relationship with the emperor.

"Take him down!" General Liu shouted. "The punishment will be fifty lashes!"

The old minister pleaded for leniency, but to no avail. He was taken out of the camp to an area where punishments were administered to the so-called "dirty" ministers. Since the old minister was judged by General Liu to be one of them, he would receive his punishment in public view. For the past two days, dozens of former ministers had taken a beating from the rebel guards, to the applause and cheers of onlookers, including soldiers and meandering passers-by.

Soon Minister Tian's loud cry was heard in Liu's tent. The general and Minister Do looked at one another with satisfaction. For the general, the satisfaction was to hand out justice, his form of justice. For the minister, the satisfaction was to get even with a man who had done him injustices when he was serving under him, according to his own skewed standards.

While the old minister was incarcerated in the compound, Liu and Do secretly directed his men to divert substantial amounts of Tian's wealth to their personal coffers.

"Set him free!" the prince commanded.

"Set who free?" queried General Liu.

"Minister Tian!" barked back the prince.

"Your Highness, I beg your pardon," muttered Minister Do, "but why?"

"He is an old man!" said the prince. "He can do no more harm to us!"

"Justice must be carried out," argued General Liu. "Otherwise, how can we rule the country?"

"There are always exceptions to the rule," the prince said. "I said, let Minister Tian go!"

Liu was slow to take the order from the prince, and a tense atmosphere enveloped the meeting chamber. As the awkward moment lingered on, a soldier ran into the hall and interrupted the impasse.

"General," he addressed Liu breathlessly. But when he saw the prince sitting on the throne, he promptly changed his direction. He knelt and reported in a loud voice, "Your Highness, we have found the emperor!"

CHAPTER 19

The Omen

THE MOOD WITHIN THE FORBIDDEN CITY SUDDENLY CHANGED. It was April 28, 1644: three days after the rebels had entered Peking and three days before Li Tzu-cheng was to be crowned the first emperor of the Shun dynasty.

The discovery of the body of Emperor Chung-chen became a major event that consumed the otherwise disorderly and slow routines of transitioning the regime from the old order to a new one. Li Tzu-cheng was most eager to put the case of the deceased emperor behind him so that his path to take the throne legitimately as the emperor and the son of heaven would have one less obstacle. So he ordered that a viewing of the late emperor's remains be held the next morning in Throne Hall. He further ordered that all officials in his court be present for the occasion to pay their last respects to the late emperor. The order created quite a commotion because the official ranks of the new Shun government were in a formative stage, and most selectees for positions in the ministries had not been sworn in.

By nine the next morning, all had gathered on the palace grounds, awaiting the arrival of the prince and the bier of the late emperor.

The high-ranking officials, including the generals of the army, stood inside Throne Hall, while lesser officials were stationed outside the hall. When the prince arrived, all bowed and sang the usual praises to welcome him. After he had seated himself in the throne, he directed Eunuch Tang to bring forward the bier of the late emperor.

While a stifling silence permeated the premises as they awaited the arrival of the bier, a flock of large blackbirds swooped down and landed in front of the hall. The prince took that as a bad omen. He recalled that many centuries ago, one pretender to the throne had encountered a similar episode, and that man ended dying by the hands of his enemy. While the prince was pondering how that would play out in his own fate, some noise shook him back to the present.

A group of soldiers carrying the coffin with the late emperor inside had come on the scene. To the surprise of all, the coffin was a simple box made of pine, most unfitting for an emperor. It was placed in the center of the hall, directly below the platform where the prince sat.

The prince ordered the coffin opened. As soon as the cover was removed, the prince exploded in rage. "Who's idea it is that we treat His Majesty in such shabby manner?" He walked down the platform, approached the coffin, and saw the body of Emperor Chung-chen stuffed inside. The emperor's body was not in a state of deep decomposition even though it had remained in the open air for more than three days and three nights. But it was an ugly sight to behold because the emperor was cloaked in filthy soiled clothing, and part of his upper body was exposed. When the prince bowed down to take a closer look at the body, the stench hit him unexpectedly, and he quickly covered his nose and turned his face. He had encountered that stench many years ago from the bodies he had picked up as a soldier in the emperor's army and from the burning flesh consumed by the carnivores in his old home.

No sooner than he had turned away than Li Tzu-cheng turned back toward the coffin. He got down on his knees and cried, "Your Majesty, why did you kill yourself so quickly? I had hoped that we would rule China together!" He paused briefly, as if he were expecting a response from the body lying in the box. "I offered to share the mountains and rivers of China with you, but you rejected my gracious gesture," the prince wailed. "You left me with no choice but to take the domain from you!"

Everyone in the hall had found the prince's behavior strange. In all the years they had known him, the prince had not expressed a liking for the emperor. In reality, he had always regarded the emperor as a despot and an enemy of the people. So was the prince's strange behavior an act? Or were his true emotions on display? If it was really an act, then what was his modus operandi? No one knew.

The prince's emotional display finally came to an end when he rose and knocked his head on the coffin numerous times. Eunuch Tang took the opportunity and pulled him gently away from the coffin. Standing a few feet away from the coffin, the prince issued an order. He commanded his high ministers and generals to view the remains as a last tribute to the late emperor. The officials reluctantly obeyed the order; they formed a line and circled the coffin once before returning to their stations.

The prince turned to the minister. "Minister Do, His Majesty deserves a rightful burial. You are responsible for providing the ceremonial robes and a more suitable coffin for him. It must be done without delay!" With that, the prince ended the gathering.

Minister Do took the order, and he proceeded unenthusiastically with the task assigned to him. Within two days, Emperor Chung-chen was given a rightful but simple burial. He was interred on the foot of Longevity Hill, a short distance below where he had hanged himself.

The day after the burial of the late emperor was April 29, 1644, two days before the prince was to crown himself the new emperor. While Minister Do and Eunuch Tang and their men were busily preparing for the ceremony, the prince made a sudden announcement that surprised everyone. He canceled the ceremony until further notice.

Li Tzu-cheng did not sleep well for many nights after he viewed the remains of the late emperor. He had nightmares for two nights, and one particular dream haunted him; he read it as a bad omen for him to take the throne. He had dreamed of two large blackbirds flying over the late emperor's body, and they eventually swooped down and ate all of the remains in the coffin. To the prince, these blackbirds were the enemies of an emperor. In his case, the two enemies could be his disloyal subordinates, Liu Tsung-min and his ally Chang Hsien-chung, who intended to share the throne with him.

Then there was Wu San-kuei! The general had crossed his mind often. Wu San-kuei could be an obstacle to his ambition to become an emperor. But he thought that since Wu was stationed far north of the capital, he was not an imminent threat. He thought that Liu Tsung-min, his good friend and comrade, might be more of a threat because he was closest to the scene.

In response to the prince's decision to delay his enthronement, his brain trust requested a meeting with him. Li granted their request and met with them in his private chamber.

General Niu opened by asking the prince his reason for canceling the ceremony, and the prince related his nightmares and his interpretation of them. He finally confessed that he feared the consequences of having to deal with Chang Hsien-chung's claim to the throne and the threat of Wu San-kuei coming from the north. He did not reveal his concern from within the ranks: the threat of Liu Tsung-min.

Minister Do interceded. "Your Highness, there is much to be done. Unless and until you take the throne, we cannot set up a legitimate government. Without a legitimate court, we will not be able to carry out our programs in an orderly fashion."

Liu Tsung-min gave him a look of disdain. *You two-faced monster*, he thought to himself. *If I am the emperor instead of Li Tzu-cheng, you'll be in a better position to enjoy the spoils of the empire.*

Eunuch Tang added, "Minister Do is correct, Your Highness. Do you wish to set another date for the ceremony?"

"I have to give it some thought," the prince said. "Wu San-kuei—any of you know what he's been up to?"

"The last I heard was that he was planning to mobilize some troops to come to the rescue of the emperor," General Niu responded. "But now the emperor is dead, we have not heard what has become of his rescue mission."

The prince turned to Liu and asked a prudent question. "Tsung-min, whose responsibility it is to keep track of military affairs for us?"

"Well, I suppose …" He looked at General Niu and Minister Do and could not come up with a quick reply to the prince's inquiry.

"Regardless of where he is now, he will pose a threat to us. We've got to find a way to neutralize him. He's got a large army under him and is not that far from the capital," the prince said in a serious tone.

"I have an idea!" Eunuch Tang volunteered.

Everyone turned and looked at the eunuch intensely. Then the eunuch said, "His father is still in Peking."

"Whose father?" asked the prince.

"Wu San-kuei's father, Wu Shang," answered the eunuch.

"Yes, Your Highness," Minister Do said. "Call him in and ask him to convince his son to surrender to you."

"We can take him as hostage in exchange for Wu San-kuei's promise to turn his army over to us and surrender," suggested General Liu. His intelligence on the military status of Wu San-kuei was flawed, but his intelligence on the private life of the general was up to date. He had learned that hidden in Wu Shang's mansion was Wu San-kuei's beautiful consort, a woman reputed to be the most beautiful woman in China. He'd love to have the opportunity to get to the Wu mansion to see her. Liu completed his suggestion. "We can take his favorite consort as hostage!"

"We should not go that far yet, Your Highness," said General Niu, "but first we can see what Wu Shang can do to talk his son into surrendering to us."

"General Niu is right," Eunuch Tang said. "Your Highness, would you like to call Wu Shang in for an audience?"

Liu Tsung-min thought that the opportunity had presented itself for him to see the most beautiful woman in China, so he pounced on the chance. "Your Highness, Wu Shang, as a former high official in the Ming court, is on the short list to be interrogated by us." He then gave Minister Do a quick glance.

The minister got the hint. "Yes, Your Highness, General Liu is correct. Wu Shang, as a high-ranking officer and a former general in the Ming army, is to be interviewed and more appropriately interrogated by me and General Liu."

"Tsung-min, I'd like to see you have the first go-round with him," commanded the prince. "See if you can talk him into getting his son to surrender to me."

The prince's command was music to Liu's ears. He replied swiftly, "Your Highness, Minister Do and I will get working on that immediately."

As the prince began to call the meeting to an end, Eunuch Tang interjected, "Your Highness. Do you wish to select a new date for your enthronement?"

The prince paused and said, almost halfheartedly, "The eleventh day of May!" He moved his right hand, and the meeting came to an end.

❦

"Minister Do," Liu Tsung-min said when he met with the minister the next day in their camp, "let's see Wu Shang."

"General, shall we summon him to our camp for the interview?" the minister asked.

"Minister, I heard that Wu Shang lives in a relatively posh mansion. Wouldn't you like to see how much treasure he has stored in his home?" The general was most interested in one item of treasure in Wu's mansion: Chen Yuan-yuan.

The minister, a person with boundless greed, could only think of real treasure, like gold and silver; a woman was the least on his mind. "I agree with you, General. Let's go see him!"

In the afternoon, the two men paid Wu Shang an impromptu visit. The servant at the door was afraid to block them, seeing that they had come with a small entourage of soldiers. Instead, he turned quickly and went inside to announce to his master the names of the visitors.

Wu Shang was not surprised by the call, for he had expected to hear from the rebel leadership. He was most surprised that Liu Tsung-min had not incarcerated him in his encampment yet, as many of his former colleagues had been. Now that the day of reckoning apparently had arrived, he put on his best face and welcomed the callers into the parlor of his modest mansion.

"General Liu and Minister Do, welcome to my humble abode!" Wu Shang bowed, pointing at two chairs.

After they had taken their seats, a servant brought in three cups of tea, one for each of the men, and left.

"General Wu," Liu Tsung-min said after taking a sip from his

cup and putting it down on the table nearest him, "the prince of
Shun would like to have your service, if you would accept his offer
of a position."

"I am an old man who has outlived his usefulness," Wu Shang
said, a trace of sadness in his tone. "What do I have to offer to His
Highness?"

Do and Wu had served the Ming emperor together for a period
of more than ten years, so they knew each other quite well. "You
have extensive military experience that His Highness, the prince,
can tap into," said Minister Do.

Wu Shang did not answer the minister's obviously inane
statement.

Liu got right to the point of his visit. "General Wu, if you feel
that you cannot be of further help to His Highness, then how about
the service of your son, San-kuei?"

Wu Shang sat straight up on his chair after hearing the name
of his son mentioned. He knew that if the new master chose to
punish him, he need not dispatch two highly placed officials to
visit him. The offer of a position for him and for his son did not
surprise him. He slowly responded, "My son is a grown man. I
really have no influence on him. As a matter of fact, he and I have
not communicated for many months."

General Liu could not conceal any longer his real purpose for
coming to the Wu mansion. "His loving consort lives here, does
she not? I cannot imagine that your son does not keep in touch
with her."

"That's between the young people," Wu Shang replied. "I do
not have the energy or reasons to keep tabs on them."

"I heard she is a most talented singer." Liu could not contain
his desire to see the woman any longer. "I should like to hear her
sing!"

Minister Do finally realized Liu was primarily interested in seeing the woman and that the matter of Wu San-kuei was second-ary. But since Liu outranked him, he had no choice but to oblige. "Yes, I should also like to hear her sing."

Wu Shang also realized that Liu Tsung-min's visit had a hidden meaning, and he thought that by playing along with him could lessen the stress over his own fate and that of his son. He rose and ordered a servant to bring Yuan-yuan to the parlor.

When Yuan-yuan appeared moments later, Liu Tsung-min got to his feet. He could not believe what had hit him. That beautiful face and that gorgeous body were what he had come to see, and he could not care less about her singing talent.

Minister Do rose from his seat and took a quick look at Yuan-yuan. He could not believe that such a beautiful woman really did exist in this world. He had heard that many men had died in the quest for her, and he wondered if Liu Tsung-min would be tempting that same fate. In any event, his mission here was twofold: one, to convince Wu Shang to bring his son and his troops back to the capital and two, to steal as much treasure as he could find for his own enrichment.

Wu Shang broke the silence in the parlor. "Yuan-yuan, I'd like you to meet General Liu Tsung-min and Minister Do Wen-lung." He pointed at the two men and then turned and pointed at her. "General and Minister, this is Yuan-yuan, the consort of my son!"

The three exchanged greetings, the consort bowing low to the two men.

"The honored guests would like you to sing for them," commanded Wu Shang. "Would you be willing to oblige?"

"I'd love to sing, but we have no musical accompaniment at hand," said the consort in an apologetic manner.

The two visitors did not see fit to pressure Yuan-yuan; the general's interest was not her singing, and the minister's interest was altogether for something else.

"You will sing for us when our prince takes the throne as the new emperor!" said Do. "And oh yes, General Wu. My prince would like you to write a letter to your son and ask him to bring his troops back to Peking and serve him. If he complies with my prince's wish, your son will be given a viceroyalty of a province in China and a million pounds of gold and silver."

Wu Shang's first reaction was revulsion, but on second thought, he reckoned the decision was one for his son, not him, to make. Discretion might be the better part of valor in this instance, so he nodded and muttered, "I will do as His Highness wishes. A letter will be delivered to your office tomorrow."

The two men bade farewell to Wu Shang, and the host and Yuan-yuan bowed to the visitors. Liu Tsung-min took one long last look at the consort. He could not wait to put his hands on her.

CHAPTER 20
The Drama

THE DAY BEFORE THE REBELS MARCHED INTO PEKING, WU San-kuei was one-third of the way to the capital with twenty thousand soldiers. He had left Shan-hai-kuan two days before to answer the call of the emperor, hoping to help save his empire. He had previously expressed to the emperor his reluctance to part with his troops and leave his fortress undefended because of the imposing Manchu threat. However, after reassessing his position, he came to the conclusion that since he had subsequently agreed on a truce with Dorgon, the prince regent of the Manchus, it was safe for him to mobilize some troops to help save Peking. His decision was too late because while he was dawdling, Peking had fallen to the rebels. When that news reached him, he was still a hundred miles short of reaching the capital.

His first inclination was to return to Shan-hai-kuan. But his concern for the safety of his father and his family overcame that reaction. And the thought of Yuan-yuan transcended all else, so he decided to continue his journey to Peking.

His senior aide sounded a note of caution. "General, going forward to Peking might be a risky venture. I heard Li Tzu-cheng has an army of more than fifty thousand stationed near the capital. Our twenty thousand is no match for that."

"I understand," the general muttered, "but we cannot sit here and watch the Forbidden City go up in smoke!"

"I submit that it is too late to save the Forbidden City. With Shan-hai-kuan in good hands, we should pitch tents here for a few more days and see how events develop."

"I suppose we don't have too many choices," conceded the general.

For the next few days, Wu and his troops hunkered down and waited for further developments. He was eager to learn more about the fate of the emperor and his father. But he was on pins and needles, waiting for more news on the love of his life, Yuan-yuan.

Liu Tsung-min began the relentless pursuit of Yuan-yuan; Do Wen-lung had set his eye on the small wealth of Wu Shang. To Minister Do, no wealth was too small to sate his greed. After securing the letter written by Wu Shang to his son, the two men exerted pressure on the old general. They wasted no time in locking him up in their camps. Next, they began the process of relocating the family members from the mansion to more humble quarters.

Liu Tsung-min descended on the Wu mansion to hunt for Yuan-yuan. He barged into the house and found her alone in her room, packing her belongings, ready to leave with the Wu family.

"Yuan-yuan, I'd like to have you come with me," Liu Tsung-min declared. "You know who I am?"

Yuan-yuan was surprised by Liu's abrupt presence. "Oh! General ...?"

"Yes, I am General Liu. Remember?"

"Yes, General Liu!"

"Come with me, at once!"

"Where are you taking me, General?"

"To my mansion," Liu said, pulling Yuan-yuan away.

"No, General!" Yuan-yuan said, pushing Liu away. "Minister Do ordered that I leave tomorrow with the Wu family, for another house."

"No!" Liu spoke in a louder, stern tone. "You are to come with me!"

"General, you know that I am betrothed to Wu San-kuei," Yuan-yuan protested mildly, "and I am a member of the Wu family."

"No! You are not!" Hearing the name of Wu San-kuei, Liu Tsung-min began to rant. "Who the hell cares about Wu San-kuei?"

"If he finds out that you have taken me away, he'll be very upset!"

"Am I supposed to be afraid of him?" Liu yelled. "You are coming with me, now, to my mansion." Liu called out to the three men who had come with him. "Come and take her away!"

The men answered the command, rushed into the room, and forcibly took Yuan-yuan out. She struggled but was subdued by the brute force of the men. She was abducted by Liu Tsung-min to his mansion, the mansion that she had once occupied as Tian Wang-yu's captive.

Yuan-yuan's dream of living out her life happily with the young and dashing general named Wu San-kuei, was short: one evening. When she'd freed herself from lecherous old Minister Tian, she had not expected her life would take another turn for the worse. Much to her dismay, her new captor was by far the worst she had encountered. Liu Tsung-min, in her mind, made thugs like Ma Yi and Wang Kuang resemble well-mannered young gentlemen.

Once he captured his prize, Liu was not about to let it slip away. He guarded her with many maids and manservants while he was busy interrogating and torturing former ministers. Almost every night, he indulged in sex with his newfound beauty. He seemed to have an insatiable appetite for carnal activities. When Yuan-yuan resisted, he used force to subdue her, ripping off her clothes and assaulting her sadistically. Yuan-yuan was helpless. She could only swallow her tears and surrender her body to him.

"I have never seen a body as beautiful as yours," Liu said while he was straddling her in his sumptuous bed. He tried to impose his mustached lips on hers again, and she pushed them away.

"General, I am only a small woman," Yuan-yuan mumbled, full of tears. "I beg you to be kind to me!"

Liu exploded. "Have I been mistreating you? You can have all the luxury you desire here. All I ask of you is to take care of this general's bodily needs!"

Yuan-yuan was intimidated. But she thought this interminable abuse had to be stopped, so she pressed on. "General, you have many young and beautiful women in your possession. I beg of you, let me go home."

"You have no home to go back to," Liu shot back. "Wu San-kuei is two hundred miles away, and his father is confined in my camps. Your home is here with me."

Reality was bleak for Yuan-yuan, to say the least. She was like a wounded caged bird. She could only sing a sad song, swallow her tears, and continue to take the sexual abuse heaped on her by a wild and lecherous man. Her only hope for surviving the ordeal was for her one and only love to come to the rescue again. But the chances of that were slim.

Wu San-kuei's aide ran into his camp and handed him an envelope. "General, this was delivered by a special messenger from Peking!"

General Wu opened the envelope, took out a piece of paper, and unfolded it. It was a letter written in his father's hand. Wu recognized his father's handwriting, so he read it with intense focus. The letter contained a plea from his father for him to bring his troops to Peking and surrender to Li Tzu-cheng. He told his son that he himself had pledged his allegiance to the prince of Shun, and that if Wu would do the same, the prince promised to award him a viceroyalty and millions in gold and silver. Wu San-kuei received his father's plea with indifference at first. But his mood quickly changed. *This might be the only chance I have to save Yuan-yuan!* The thought of saving his father and the family did not cross his mind.

He pondered the possibilities confronted him for another day. "If I go forward to Peking, then I must abandon my position in Shan-hai-kuan," he muttered under his own breath. "I have no assurance that the Manchus will honor the truce." And he was concerned that he had no guarantee that Li Tzu-cheng would honor his word after he surrendered to him.

After much soul searching, he finally decided to write a reply to his father and, at the same time, mobilize his twenty thousand troops slowly westward toward Peking. His letter to his father stated that he was leaning toward surrendering to the prince, but he also gently chastised his father regarding the sacred honor and duty of being a former Ming general. His father should have died for the emperor rather than submit to a new master. But, as a pious son, he would take his father's advice as a last resort.

Before his letter to Wu Shang arrived, as his troops were moving slowing toward the capital, his own intelligence team returned with more bad news.

Lieutenant Pei, his private messenger, caught up with Wu and reported breathlessly, "General, Liu Tsung-min has incarcerated your father."

"Who?" General Wu thundered.

"Liu Tsung-min!"

"Who is Liu Tsung-min?

"He is the number two man in the rebel regime."

"Li Tzu-cheng, that devil, promised to treat my father well. If he lets his second in command mistreat my father, how can I expect him to honor the terms of my surrender?" At once, Wu San-kuei changed his stance on the issue of surrendering to Li.

"Lieutenant, I have an urgent journey for you to run," Wu ordered the aide. "I want you to leave for Peking immediately to do two things. One, deliver an urgent letter to my father. And two, find out as much as you can about what has happened to my woman!" He paused. "I will have the letter for you in about an hour. Be prepared to leave this afternoon."

In his letter, Wu San-kuei cursed Li Tzu-cheng for his quick reversal on the terms of his surrender by condoning the action of Liu Tsung-min. Unless Li Tzu-cheng ordered the release of his father and had him delivered to his fortress, Wu would take his troops to Peking to settle the score with the rebel leaders once and for all!

When Wu Shang showed the letter to him, Li Tzu-cheng was fighting mad. He promptly dispatched two regiments, with General Niu Chin-hsing in command, to take on Wu's forces. Wu was surprised by the confrontation, but his troops were well rested and primed for action. The two armies met in one fiercely fought battle that lasted for more than three hours, Wu San-kuei soundly defeated Niu Chin-hsing. The decisive edge in the battle were Wu's small cannons.

Wu San-kuei did not have much time to celebrate his brief victory. Niu Chin-hsing had suffered a humiliating setback and returned to Peking, much to Li Tzu-cheng's dismay. Wu San-kuei had suffered moderate casualties, and he regrouped to decide whether to press forward. He met with his second and third officers in command to discuss a strategy for the immediate future.

"General, I understand your feeling toward going forward to Peking," said the officer who was second in command, "but we've suffered some losses, and we are not up to full strength. We will need reinforcement before proceeding."

The third officer added, "General, I believe Li Tzu-cheng will lick his wounds and bring a larger force to fight us. I think he severely underestimated our ability in the last battle, and he's not going to do that again."

Wu San-kuei's dilemma became deeper in a hurry. He had given up the option to surrender to the rebel leader because he had taken arms against him. And if Li Tzu-cheng were to wage an all-out war against him, he would have to deploy all of his troops from Shan-hai-kuan; such an action would leave the fortress undefended against the Manchus. While he was agonizing over this deep dilemma, bad news struck again. His sources informed him that Li Tzu-cheng, apparently in revenge for Niu's defeat, had begun to march out of Peking toward Shan-hai-kuan with fifty thousand men.

Since he had agreed to take the throne as emperor of the Shun dynasty on the first day of May, Li Tzu-cheng had postponed the date three times. When the news of Niu Chin-hsing's defeat by Wu San-kuei reached him, he was furious and promptly decided on an expedition to confront Wu San-kuei personally.

On the eve of his departure for Shan-hai-kuan, Li Tzu-cheng decided to take the throne. He had finally come to the realization that he should not be intimidated by Liu Tsung-min and deferred to Chang Hsien-chung. On the twenty-second day of May, 1644, Li Tzu-cheng crowned himself the first emperor of the Great Shun dynasty. There was no fanfare because there was little time to plan for the occasion. Further, the new emperor wanted to demonstrate his desire to be the emperor of the people and delay festivities until China was unified. To accomplish the goal of unifying China, he must first defeat Wu San-kuei and then take care of the Manchus. Most importantly, he wanted to carry a legitimate mandate with him in his campaign against the renegade Wu San-kuei, and the barbarian Dorgon.

On the advice of Do Wen-lung, the new emperor took Wu Shang with him on his northern campaign. The hope was to put pressure on Wu San-kuei, knowing that his father would face great harm if he did not surrender to the new regime. Liu Tsung-min was left behind to attend to the affairs of the new government. That suited him well because he could attend to the personal matters of guarding his prize possession, Yuan-yuan, and the storerooms filled with gold and silver goblets and mountains of gold and silver coins and ingots. Further, he'd like to see his self-fulfilling-prophecy come to realization by eventually dividing the spoils between Li Tzu-cheng and himself. The sudden move by his good friend to take the throne all for himself not only surprised him, it infuriated him.

Ever since Li Tzu-cheng had shown his intention to be crowned the next emperor of China, Liu Tsung-min tried to obstruct him from achieving that goal. Now that Li had made the move without leaving him any alternatives, Liu sprang into action with the backing and help of his new comrade Do Weng-lung. Since Do had become close to Liu through their mutual fleecing of the former Ming officials, Liu recruited Do and a few generals in a secret effort to steal the throne from Li Tzu-cheng.

Do Weng-lung cornered Liu Tsung-min the day that Li Tzu-cheng announced he was to take his troops to confront Wu

San-kuei. "General, the time has come for you to take matters into your own hands."

"I know," responded Liu, somewhat dejectedly, "but he is taking almost all the troops we have up north with him. Even though I am the head of the army, I have no troops to command!"

"That might be the case," shot back Do, "but the generals friendly to you still have small units in and near the capital you can call on. Besides, a lot hinges on the result of the northern expedition."

"What do you think I should do while he is out of the capital?" queried Liu.

"Call a meeting of the generals and get a sense of their loyalty and commitment to your cause," Minister Do said.

The day after Li Tzu-cheng had taken his army out of Peking to challenge Wu San-kuei, with Niu Chin-hsing leading as vanguard, Liu Tsung-min called a meeting with three generals who had pledged loyalty to him, with Do Wen-lung also in attendance.

"Gentlemen, we must be careful to keep our conversations in utmost secrecy," warned Do before Liu had spoken a word. "There are eyes and ears in the palaces that are harmful to our cause, and they might even prove life-threatening to us."

"Minister Do is right!" Liu said, looking intently at the three generals. "Do you think it's time to make our move, now that he is out of the capital?"

"I don't think this is the right time," opined one of the generals. "We do not have sufficient troops to fight him should he win the battle in the north and come back triumphant."

"That's right," echoed another general. "We cannot rely on the scenario that he will lose his battle to Wu San-kuei. We have to find an option for how to deal with him if he wins the battle and returns in relatively healthy condition."

Liu Tsung-min nodded, and Do Weng-lung shook his head slowly. But neither had any solutions or thoughts to contribute.

The room was momentarily silent. Then the third general perked up and said, "I am sure Chang Hsien-chung must be most unhappy to hear that his ally took the throne before he has come to the capital."

The first general looked puzzled and queried, "What do we care about him? It's his loss for not being in Peking before us!"

"You miss my point," argued the third general. "Chang commands a huge army of his own. He can be helpful to us."

"But he is too far away to be helpful," Minister Do muttered, "although he might be a very viable option. Does anyone know where he is now?"

"I don't trust him!" Liu Tsung-min said loudly.

"But we need manpower to take on Li Tzu-cheng if he comes back with a relatively full force," the third general said. "Chang Hsien-chung is our solution."

Minister Do tentatively agreed with the third general's suggestion, but he could not figure out how Chang could be helpful unless his troops were closer to the capital. "Can we find out where he is now?"

"General Won," Liu commanded the second general, "send some intelligence out to survey the situation. Locate Chang's units and report back to me at once!"

"Yes, sir," General Won responded.

"Once we locate him, I'd like to be your envoy to meet with him," volunteered the third general. "I know one of the generals in his high command. He and I grew up in the same village. He can be a bridge between you and Chang, sir."

"Get on it, General Won," ordered Liu again. "We must act fast, before Li Tzu-cheng comes back, win or lose!" He raised his hand, and the meeting came to an end.

The first salvo fired by the Shun army was not a cannonball or an arrow but a letter by Li Tzu-cheng to Wu San-kuei. The news of a force led by Li Tzu-cheng, sixty thousand strong, had reached Wu first. When the letter finally arrived, he quickly opened it and read the contents. His face turned white. He yelled at his senior aide, who was standing nearby, "Captain, we've got to turn back for Shan-hai-kuan at once!"

"General?" the aide asked quizzically. "We are in striking distance of Peking!"

"Yes, but we are also within striking distance of sixty thousand rebel soldiers!"

"Sir?" the aide said. "Sixty thousand?"

"I said, we are turning back for Shan-hai-kuan. Our troop numbers are not sufficient to handle the rebel army coming at us!"

"General, may I know the contents of the letter?" The aide had never witnessed his superior in such a state of fear, so he knew the letter must be the reason.

"Li Tzu-cheng gave me an ultimatum!" said the general, his face now red. "If I don't surrender to him within three days, he said my father will pay a dear price for my defiance." With little time left before Li's army caught up with him, Wu decided to return to his home base to mount an effort against the rebels.

When he arrived at Shan-hai-kuan, he had only three days to organize a defense against the rebels. The distance between Peking and Shan-hai-kuan was about two hundred miles, and it would normally take six days for foot soldiers to cover the route. Unless the rebel army stumbled onto some unforeseen obstacles, like horrid weather, it would arrive at the gates of Wu's fortress in a short time.

"General, our provisions are running low," sighed his chief of staff in a hastily called meeting with Wu's command staff.

"Do you mean our rations or our ammunition, Colonel?" Wu asked, showing a trace of impatience.

"Our food supplies will last for about ten days, but our cannon-balls are running low, and I am afraid we will not have enough to scare off the enemy," the colonel responded.

"In other words, if we are under siege for ten days, we'll starve to death or have to surrender?"

"Sir, our troop strength is another problem we must face," echoed the second staff officer. "I learned that the rebel brigades consist of upward of fifty thousand soldiers!"

"What is our troop strength now?" queried the general.

"A little under thirty thousand, counting the casualties suffered in our last campaign against Niu Chin-hsing," answered the second staff officer.

"General, I know it is against your principals to ask for help from others," the colonel said contritely.

"Who would the 'others' be?" Wu asked, though he had a notion who the colonel was thinking of.

"Dorgon!" the colonel said unabashedly.

"I am afraid time is against us on that," lamented Wu.

"Do we really have a choice, General?" queried the second officer.

"Surrendering is the other choice," mumbled the colonel.

"I don't want to hear that word ever again!" the general said, showing minor irritation. "I will sleep on it tonight. Let's meet early in the morning." The meeting came to an end without a solution.

Wu San-kuei spent a sleepless night searching for answers to many thorny questions. One: he must find a way to survive a siege of his fortress should the rebel army get to him before he could mount an offense. Two: on his father's urgent plea, he had agreed to lead his troops back to Peking to serve the new ruler. To the desperate general, this was the only way to ensure his own survival. But that path had been closed when the rebel leader changed his heart. Three: as a high military officer, if not the highest, in the Ming court, his father had stood by and watched his emperor's demise without making a move to save him. He had violated a time-honored Confucian doctrine that a courtier should do all he could to save his emperor from losing the realm; failing that, he should pay for that failure with his own life. Last, but not least, Wu San-kuei's heart was where Yuan-yuan was. He simply could not let another man possess her.

The very thought of the possibility of Yuan-yuan being abducted and molested by some other men wreaked havoc in Wu San-kuei's mind, over and over. That eventuality would be real, unless he survived and retained his military capability. Without that capability, revenge for Yuan-yuan, and for his father, was impossible.

"General!" A voice shook Wu San-kuei out of his bad dream. His aide was standing next to his bed.

The general pushed his blanket aside and sat up, rubbing his eyes. Before he could utter a word, the aide handed over an envelope. "Sir, this just arrived by special carrier from Peking!" Wu ripped open the envelope, leaned closer to the candle on the table next to his bed, and pored over the message. His face turned gray. "You wicked devil! You son of ..." Wu San-kuei exploded. He jumped off the bed, pulled the sword from the scabbard by the foot of his bed, and, in one mighty motion, chopped off a corner of the table. Lieutenant Pei's special message from Peking reported that Yuan-yuan had fallen into the hands of Liu Tsung-min.

Wu San-kuei moved about aimlessly before he finally yelled at his aide, "Get me Dorgon!"

The aide looked at the general, bewildered. "Dorgon?" he muttered.

Dorgon had used the time he won from Wu San-kuei by signing the truce to regenerate his military. He used that valuable time to also consolidate his power base within the court as prince regent to the child emperor, Fu-lin. Conquering China was Dorgon's overarching ambition. The torch for achieving that goal had been passed to him by his father, Nurhaci, and his half-brother, Abahai.

As a practical matter, Dorgon knew that he was no match for Wu San-kuei. On many occasions when he'd encountered Wu's army, Dorgon had been soundly repelled by Wu's more efficient and well-disciplined troops. With Wu San-kuei preoccupied with the rebels, Dorgon slowly mobilized his troops back to Chin-chou, a garrison town about one hundred miles north of Shan-hai-kuan, to wait for opportunity to come his way.

Opportunity arrived in the form of a letter from Wu San-kuei on the twenty-third of May. When he opened the letter, Dorgon could not contain his excitement. "The day I have been living for has arrived!" He ordered his aide, who had delivered the good news to him and still stood nearby, "Bring Ju Da-shou and Fan Wen-cheng here quickly!"

Fan Wen-cheng was a high minister of the Ming government, well grounded in Chinese classics and an able and experienced minister. An opportunistic person, Fan had predicted the demise of the Ming regime, so he left Peking and surrendered to Dorgon. Dorgon, a student of Chinese classics and history himself, quickly appointed Fan to the highest political position in his court. Thus it was Fan Wen-cheng who was most instrumental in influencing Dorgon to intervene in the drama that was to unfold in China.

When Ju and Fan appeared as ordered, Dorgon gleefully handed the letter over to Ju and said, "Look here! What do you think I should do?"

"Your Excellency, this is the opportunity you have been waiting for!" Ju read the letter, handed it over to Fan, and said, "We should let him come and tell us what he has in his mind."

Fan read the letter and said, "Your Excellency, indeed, the opportunity has come!"

"Good!" snapped Dorgon. "Send him an invitation without delay!"

On May 25, 1644, Wu San-kuei arrived at Dorgon's head-quarters at Chin-chou with a small escort. Dorgon received him personally, with Ju Da-shou and Fan Wen-cheng in attendance. The reception was simple but formal.

Dorgon welcomed his distinguished visitor with respect. He extended his hands to him and said, "General, I have heard of your sterling reputation for a long time. It's my pleasure to meet you at last!" He quietly sized up the young general and found him to be handsome and dashing, but a bit short in stature.

"Your Excellency," responded Wu courteously, "the pleasure is completely mine!" He shook Dorgon's hands and sized him up; he was too thin but with an imposing bearing.

The four men found their seats; wine was served by two ser-vants. Dorgon held up his glass and made a toast to the young general. "Here's to you, General Wu!"

Wu San-kuei raised his glass and responded, "Your Excellency. Here's to our friendship!"

Dorgon got right to the point. "General, what can I do to help you?"

"Your Excellency. As you know, Li Tzu-cheng has usurped the throne, and I have the solemn duty to avenge my emperor!"

"General. I think it is more important that we oust him from Peking because he does not have the legitimate right to inherit the throne of China," Dorgon declared. "I believe my emperor of the Great Ching dynasty owns that legitimacy!"

Wu San-kuei was taken aback by Dorgon's audacious claim, but he did not have a response for him immediately. He knew he was here begging for help, so he was in no position to offend his host. But his uncle came to the rescue.

Ju Da-shou chose to address his nephew in a formal way. "General, Emperor Fu-lin of the Ching dynasty has heaven's blessing to be the ruler of China. Li Tzu-cheng is a rebel, and he does not have divine right to the throne!"

"You might be right, General." Wu also chose to address his uncle in a formal way. "In any event, he now controls the capital. We've got to take him out!"

Fan Wen-cheng knew that Dorgon's military force was inferior to the rebel army, at least in number. It was also inferior to Wu's force in Shan-hai-kuan. He offered an observation: "Your Excellency, I believe General Wu is correct. He has the solemn duty to take out the rebel leader. However, I speculate that the rebel force might be far too large for the general to take on. In my humble view, with your help, Li Tzu-cheng can be defeated because he has lost all his support. By overthrowing Emperor Chung-chen, he incurred heaven's displeasure. By abusing the former officials, he aroused political opposition. With your participation in this righteous venture, we will prevail!"

Dorgon was not a student of tactical matters, but as an adroit politician, he knew that without Wu San-kuei the Manchus would be unable to conquer Peking. On the other hand, he did not want to reveal his true ambition to the visitor for fear he might lose the golden opportunity that Wu had presented to him. So he acted humble and said, "General, are you planning an expedition to Peking soon?"

"Yes, Your Excellency," responded Wu without hesitation. "I've got to mobilize before Li Tzu-cheng gets to Shan-hai-kuan and puts my fortress under siege."

The uncle thought it was time for him to be the facilitator, so he chimed in. "General, if you need troop reinforcement from His Excellency, how much are you thinking of?"

"Twenty thousand!" Wu San-kuei blurted out.

"All right!" cried Dorgon resolutely. "General, it will take two days for my troops to get to Shan-hai-kuan. We should plan to join our forces there on the May 26."

"May 26 it is!" declared Wu San-kuei.

The meeting ended, and Wu begged to be excused from the reception planned in his honor because he wanted to return to his fortress to prepare his troops to meet Dorgon's deadline.

After his guests had left, Dorgon celebrated with his two confidants. He knew the golden opportunity he'd been waiting for had finally arrived. His father and half-brother had dreamed of entering Shan-hai-kuan and spent their lifetimes trying to achieve that goal, to no avail. But now Wu San-kuei was handing it over to him without a fight. He could not wait for May 26 to come!

⤷⤶

Meanwhile, back in Peking, on the eve of his departure to confront Wu San-kuei, Consort Tian confronted Li Tzu-cheng while dining with him in his sumptuous palace.

"Your Highness," began Consort Tian. "Oh! Maybe I should now address you as Your Majesty. I found out that my father is still confined in General Liu's camps."

"I have ordered him to let your father go," Li said halfheartedly because his heart was not into small matters like Tian. He was pre-occupied with the long journey up north to face the formidable foe Wu San-kuei. "You mean he had defied my order?"

"Yes, Your Majesty. The last I heard, my father is still in confinement!"

"That Liu Tsung-min is getting quite difficult!" Li barked.

"He has been acting very defiantly toward me I notice. I will talk to him before I leave tomorrow."

The next morning, Li Tzu-cheng left the capital with his troops, and the matter of Tian Wang-yu totally escaped his mind. Liu Tsung-min was among the group of officials seeing him off, but he and Li Tzu-cheng did not engage in any conversation.

Consort Tian waited a few days and learned that Liu Tsung-min still had not set her father free, so she decided to pay him a personal visit. Liu Tsung-min was totally surprised when his guard announced that Consort Tian was waiting outside to see him. Liu had learned that the consort had become the favorite of Li, and she also had a reputation as being beautiful and personable, so he was delighted that she had come calling. Liu ordered that the escorts who had come with her be dismissed so he could see her alone.

When she was being led by a maid into the private area of the mansion, Consort Tian already knew that she was to see Liu in his bedchamber. That large and opulent chamber had once been occupied by her father, Tian Wang-yu. When she entered the chamber alone, she saw Liu Tsung-min reclining on his huge bed, dressed in his night clothes. The consort bowed to Liu and stood a few paces in front of the bed. "General Liu?"

The general could not believe that heaven had presented him with another beautiful woman. "Yuan-yuan is beautiful," he muttered under his breath, "but this one is exceptional, to say the least." He surveyed the consort slowly and found that she possessed a fuller bosom; her rounder face and thicker lips were most enticing. He jumped off the bed and reached for her hands. The consort held her hands back, but Liu grasped them and pulled her closer to him.

"General!" Consort Tian protested mildly, trying to pull away.

"Now I know why His Majesty spent so many nights alone in his chamber and refused to mingle with us." Liu held the consort tighter in his embrace and at the same time imposed his thick lips on hers. The consort tried to wiggle free and forcibly turned her face away.

Liu was larger and stronger, and he pushed the woman in one mighty motion onto his bed. Without hesitation, he proceeded to rip off her outer garments. Once her breasts were exposed, Liu could not control his lust and proceeded to assault her. Much to his delight and surprise, the consort did not put up much of a fight.

When they were both settled comfortably in bed moments later, Consort Tian said in a soft voice, "General, if His Majesty finds out what just happened, he'll be most unhappy with me—and with you!"

Liu Tsung-min let out a hearty laugh and said, "He's gone! I am the emperor in his absence. It will be a long absence—trust me!"

"I don't understand," the consort said. "he will return one day, I am sure."

"When he comes back, he'll have to bow to me, the new emperor of the Shun dynasty!"

The consort was mystified by Liu's assertions, but she thought that it really did not matter who the emperor was. To her, they were no better than animals, only cloaked in regal robes. Her objective for being with Liu Tsung-min now and Li Tzu-cheng earlier was to find a way to survive and to find a way to extricate her father from the harsh environment that these animals had imposed on him.

She sat up on the bed and tried to speak to him about her father's case, but she found him soundly asleep.

She pushed him hard and yelled into his ear, "General!"

The man responded, perking up his huge bulk. "Oh! What's the matter?"

"General, His Majesty told me that he asked you to let my father go. Why is he still locked up in your camp?"

Liu stuttered, after letting out a big yawn, "Your father?"

"Minister Tian Wang-yu."

"Oh, yes! Minister Tian," Liu said, rubbing his eyes. "Oh, yes! Your father! I ordered Minister Do to let him go, but for some reason he is slow in doing so."

"General, I beg of you, let my father go," the consort pleaded in a soft voice. "My father is old. He will pose no threat to anyone."

"I will talk to Minister Do tomorrow. Let's get some sleep." Liu pulled the bedcover over his head and promptly snored away.

The evening was still young. Consort Tian tossed and turned in bed for a long time. Then she decided to get up and survey the mansion for sentimental reasons, because she had grown up in the house. She was curious to see how it had changed since she'd left it some years before.

She dressed and proceeded down a long corridor to the next bedchamber, the one she and her sister had previously occupied, Much to her surprise, when she pushed the door open she saw a young woman sitting on her bed, a maid standing next to her.

Consort Tian let out a shriek. "Yuan-yuan?"

"Consort Tian?" Yuan-yuan was equally surprised. "Why are you here?" She waved her hand to dismiss the maid and said, "Close the door behind you."

Yuan-yuan got off her bed and embraced the consort. They could not suppress their emotions and began to sob. They then proceeded to share their recent experiences and commiserate. They discovered that they both had a common goal to accomplish: to free themselves from the demons Li Tzu-cheng and Liu Tsung-min.

"Now that Li Tzu-cheng is out of the capital, all we have to do is to get away from this house," Consort Tian said in a very low voice.

"Yes! But it is not easy because he has guards surrounding the mansion."

"That might not be difficult. There is an escape hatch in this house," the consort said. "I know this house literally inside out."

"How do we get free from him?" Yuan-yuan said. "He is onto me almost every night. And now he's got you too. I am sure he will also have you under his nose!"

The two women spent a long time searching for a solution to free themselves from their captor. After much deliberation, Consort Tian finally broke the silence. "I have an idea! We might as well go the full distance!"

Yuan-yuan was puzzled. "Go the distance?"

The consort pulled her close and whispered into her ear at length. Yuan-yuan's initial reaction was a frightened look. Within a moment she declared, "Let's go for it!"

Consort Tian quickly returned to Liu's chamber. When Liu turned his huge body and found the consort still lying next to him, he clutched her and murmured, "Good night, my sweet!"

When May 26, 1644, arrived, Dorgon and his twenty thousand troops were ready and waiting at the gate of Shan-hai-kuan. Not far behind were another ten thousand men camped out about ten miles from the fortress. Dorgon was doubling down on the chance, perhaps the only chance, that was given to him to enter China without sacrificing a soldier.

Meanwhile, Wu San-kuei had spent a torturous evening agonizing over his fate in the drama that was about to unfold. Again and again, the thought of losing the emperor and his empire to the rebels haunted him. He blamed himself for not bringing his troops to Peking soon enough to rescue the capital, but, in reality, time and the size of the rescue party had been against him. Now, his father, Wu Shang, was in a precarious position, his life at the mercy of the rebel leaders. To make things worse, the fate of the love of his life, Yuan-yuan, was in the hands of one brutal rebel general, Liu Tsung-min.

Wu San-kuei realized that in a distraught moment he had placed his life and fortune on one Manchu, the moment when he got the news that Yuan-yuan had been taken by Liu Tsung-min. Was it moral for him to mobilize his whole army, with the help of his erstwhile enemy, to save a woman and not commit an equal force to save a desperate emperor and his realm? That question increased his feeling of guilt to a crescendo. He had reached the point of no return, the Manchus waiting at his doorsteps, so he decided to shut everything—morality, disloyalty, and all—out of his mind and let matters take their course. When he woke up the next morning, he ordered the gates to Shan-hai-kuan be opened wide to welcome Dorgon and his army.

Li Tzu-cheng and his fifty thousand strong had left Peking on May 22. Under normal circumstance, he would have reached Shan-hai-kuan before Dorgon. But for some unknown reason, his army had stalled, and when they got to within ten miles of the fortress, the armies of Dorgon and Wu San-kuei were lying in wait for them.

In one furious and hard-fought battle on a plain outside of Shan-hai-kuan, the joint forces of Dorgon and Wu San-kuei handed the rebels a major defeat. The rebel forces were not only overmatched by their adversaries, but they also endured fatigue from the arduous journey and inadequate provisions.

After receiving the news that Li Tzu-cheng had suffered a brutal defeat at the hands of Wu San-kuei, Consort Tian planned an exquisitely presented dinner for Liu Tsung-min to celebrate his claim to the throne. She'd also heard that the emperor might have been mortally wounded in the battle. She and Yuan-yuan would be the only guests at the dinner, and the women told him that after the dinner they would entertain him in his bedchamber.

Liu Tsung-min bought into the arrangement without a moment of hesitation; he could not wait to have the two most beautiful women in bed with him.

The evening came, and the dinner was served in the huge bedchamber rather than in the dining chamber. Even though the food was tastefully displayed, Liu's mind was more into the delicious dishes called Yuan-yuan and Consort Tian. He could not contain himself; he grabbed the women and kissed them incessantly. He reluctantly ate the food only when the women put some in his mouth.

Consort Tian picked up a glass of fine wine and offered to him. "Your Majesty! Ten thousand years to you!"

Liu Tsung-min flashed a big smile. "My love, I am not yet the emperor. But I will accept your blessing if we all drink together."

Consort Tian smiled, picked up two glasses, and handed one to Yuan-yuan.

Yuan-yuan accepted the glass and chimed in: "Your Majesty! Let's drink to your future. A bright and glorious future as the new emperor of China!"

Liu Tsung-min laughed loudly, tipped his glass, and emptied the contents in one motion. The women tipped their glasses and took small sips of the wine.

Moments after the toast, Liu tried to get up to grab Yuan-yuan, who was closer to him, but he fell back on his chair. The consort knew the poison had taken effect, so she beckoned Yuan-yuan to help her move the large hulk to the nearby bed. With some effort, they succeeded. The man began to vomit and choke at the same time.

They pulled a cover over him, picked up two small bags, and quietly walked out of the bedchamber. It was close to midnight; it was eerily quiet inside and outside of the house. Consort Tian led Yuan-yuan down to the cellar, and they snuck out of the mansion without being detected by the slumbering guards.

Liu Tsung-min, the man who had played with fire all his adult life, had finally died by fire. The fire of his potent desire for sex had finally consumed him. The cause of his death was a dose of poison Consort Tian had in her possession. It had been meted out to her and the other consorts by the Ming emperor the evening before the rebels entered the Forbidden City. His order was that all his consorts should have the poison available in the event that they were molested by the rebels.

Li Tzu-cheng survived his battle against Wu San-kuei. He brought his tattered army back to Peking and could not wait to take his frustration out on someone. He called the usual suspects, his so-called brain trust, into his palace as soon as he arrived in the Forbidden City. Noticeably absent was his good friend Liu Tsung-min. Li was saddened by Liu's death, but since Liu had brought the misfortune upon himself, Li rationalized that he did not deserve pity or sympathy from anyone. Besides, Liu's death had removed a thorn that had been frustrating him for a long time. What irritated Li the most, though, was the loss of Consort Tian.

"Wen-lung, I was appalled that our troops were not maintained in combat readiness." To begin his tirade, Li vented his irritation on Do. "We matched them in number, almost one on one, but we were routed in one battle!"

Do gave the two others in attendance a quick and painful look. "Your Majesty, our troops had won a major victory by taking the capital. I supposed they would still be in battle-ready condition." Do Wen-lung had made a bad comparison: the dispirited army of the Ming emperor was not at par with the well-trained army of Wu San-kuei and the reserve provided by Dorgon.

"Why are we so short of provisions? You know that we've been on mobilization status ever since we entered the capital."

Do looked at the others again, hoping that someone would save him this time. But no one volunteered, so he muttered, "Your Majesty, perhaps we did not anticipate that you'd mobilize such a huge force on such short notice!" Do knew that the treasury teetered on the brink of bankruptcy. The rebel regime had inherited an empty treasury from the Ming government to begin with. It was further depleted because of waste and corruption, with him being one of the major perpetrators, along with General Liu and Eunuch Tang.

"Wu San-kuei is not to be stopped!" lamented Li. "Now that he has me down, he will certainly continue to press toward our capital. Are we prepared to defend against him?"

Eunuch Tang Jun finally summoned sufficient courage to interject. "Your Majesty, our court is still in a formative stage. I am afraid if the enemy comes calling it will be chaos!"

The two colleagues sent the eunuch looks of irritation, but, to a man, they could not dispute the view he expressed.

"That is precisely how I feel about matters in our court too!" Li began to get more agitated as the meeting went on. He aimed his irritation at Do. "I admonished you and Tsung-min. The two of you took the internment of former high officials to the extreme."

Liu was not there to defend himself, and Do could not come up with a retort to Li's comment. Li had, on more than one occasion, chastised Liu Tsung-min on his excesses. On one occasion, Li had paid a call to the encampment and was appalled by the sight of several hundred men being tortured in the courtyard. When he turned his head to the opposite side, he had noticed more and more corpses being thrown into straw baskets and carried out of the campsite.

"Your punishment of the so-called 'bad' officials went too far, in my mind," Li said. "Your so-called 'clean' officials, those you placed in key ministries, were not up the task of maintaining order and efficiency in our court."

The three men hung their heads low and could not put up an argument. Li droned on. "We have little time to correct our missteps. We've got to regroup, especially our military capability, before Wu San-kuei comes to the gates of our palaces!" He then turned to Niu Chin-hsing and said, "General Niu, you've been kind of quiet. What do you think we should do to improve our chances against Wu San-kuei?"

"Your Majesty," Niu answered slowly, "you are still holding two valuable cards that you can use against him!"

"What cards?" queried Li.

Everyone was quietly anticipating Niu's response to the emperor's question. Niu Chin-hsing cleared his throat and blurted, "Wu Shang and Chen Yuan-yuan!"

Li Tzu-cheng let out a big sigh and pounded his hand on the table. "Indeed! But Chen Yuan-yuan escaped, I was told."

"But Wu San-kuei does not know that," Niu responded, hoping that Wu's spy in the capital also did not know that.

Li was not totally convinced that Wu San-kuei would fall for the ploy. "I am not sure your tactic would work this time around." But he must buy some time by deferring Wu from charging into the capital so that he could regenerate his army. Li grudgingly agreed to use Wu Shang and Yuan-yuan as bait to deter the young general.

"Why don't we give him another ultimatum?" suggested Minister Do.

"The ultimatum will say …?" the emperor asked.

"If he does not make peace with us, then we will execute his father and his woman!" answered Niu.

"I suggest, Your Majesty, we have Wu Shang write a last urgent letter to his son, asking him to come to Peking and surrender his troops," Eunuch Tang added.

"Get that done! Without delay!" the emperor ordered, and he stormed out of the palace and into his private chamber.

The next day, Eunuch Tang, with the help of Minister Do, went to their camp and coaxed a letter from Wu Shang. The old general had been confined again after returning to Peking with Li's army. The letter was written in Wu Shang's hand, but the words were dictated by Do and Tang. The letter admonished Wu San-kuei not to continue avenging the late emperor. By giving up his pursuit of Li Tzu-cheng and changing his allegiance to Li Tzu-cheng, he would not only save his own life but also the lives of his father and his consort. Further, the emperor of Shun would award him with a fiefdom and a huge cache of gold and silver. The letter was perfunctorily approved by Li Tzu-cheng and quickly delivered to Wu San-kuei.

While the court of the Shun dynasty was in a state of disarray, the ordinary citizens in Peking were in a worse state of confusion. They had gotten a false sense of security from their first encounter with the Shun army, seeing its soldiers were a disciplined group when they entered Peking. The people had expected life to be difficult but somewhat peaceful. Daily activities in the city streets continued, but in a more subdued fashion. Most people, however, had taken on a guarded approach to life and self-preservation.

But in the wake of their defeat by Wu San-kuei and Dorgon, these previously well-behaved soldiers, now fatigued and intoxicated, vented their rage upon the common people. They reverted to their cruel natures, sacking the ministries, looting the residents, raping the women, and setting fire to sections of the city.

Things rapidly took a turn for the worse when Do Wen-lung handed the letter from Wu San-kuei to his father, which he had intercepted, to Li Tzu-cheng. Li handed it right back to the minister and asked him to read it to him. In the letter, Wu San-kuei curtly rejected his father's plea to negotiate. He further promised that if

Li did not release his father and deliver him safely to his fortress, he would march to Peking and destroy the Forbidden City.

After listening to the reading, the emperor of Shun assumed a murderous rage. "Take Wu Shang out and execute him," he ordered. "Gather his whole family and execute them too. Put them all to death, at once!"

Do Wen-lung lost no love for Wu Shang, but he was in shock when he heard the order given by the emperor. He sounded a prudent warning. "Your Majesty, I am sure your decision will provoke a quick response from his son. Should we not wait a few days to let things calm down and give us some time to regroup?"

"Minister Do," yelled Li, "Wu San-kuei is spitting in my face, don't you see?" Li took a deep breath and continued. "Li Tzu-cheng is not to be intimidated by anyone! If Wu San-kuei comes to Peking, I will annihilate him. Personally!"

"Those are brave words," Do muttered to himself. Seeing that the emperor was still fuming, he waited a moment before issuing another warning. "Your Majesty, you know that Wu San-kuei has the backing of Dorgon's army. The two banded together become a formidable foe!"

Do Wen-lung touched on a sore spot for Li, reminding the emperor that Dorgon was instrumental in his recent defeat up north. Li fumed for another moment and then declared, "Minister Do, you are to carry out my order to kill Wu Shang and his family without delay!" Do was slow to react to the order, and Li Tzu-cheng yelled, "Oh, yes. I'd like to have the head of Wu Shang hung high in front of the meridian gate!"

"Yes … Your Majesty!"

"Oh, yes, one more thing," barked Li. "If you can hunt down Chen Yuan-yuan, she should be executed along with the others!"

"Yes … Your Majesty!"

"Go hunt her down!"

Yuan-yuan could not be found quickly, and she was fortunate to escape from the carnage.

By the first of June, the news of the murder of his father and the family had reached Wu San-kuei in his camp. The general fell to his knees and repeatedly knocked his head on the ground and wailed. When he got up, with the help of his aides, he took a sword from one of them and took his rage out on a wooden table. He continued his rampage for more than thirty minutes and finally screamed, "Li Tzu-cheng, you scum of the earth! I will come for your head!" After a few more moments of violent agitation, he turned to one of the aides and yelled, "What news of Yuan-yuan, my woman?"

None of the aides had any news to offer, but one of them reported, "Your personal envoy, Lieutenant Pei, is still hiding in the capital and trying to locate her."

"Is she alive?" asked the general urgently.

"We don't know if she was one of those murdered by the rebel leader," answered one of the other aides.

"Prepare our troops for a march to the capital," ordered Wu San-kuei. "I have a letter to be delivered to Dorgon."

"When will we begin our march, General?" asked the senior aide. "We've got to calculate the provisions we need quickly."

"Tomorrow morning!" the general declared.

Since their defeat of Li Tzu-cheng on May 27, Dorgon and Wu San-kuei had disengaged their joint forces. While Wu's army pitched camp within twenty miles from Shan-hai-kuan, Dorgon moved back to within five miles of the fortress. Dorgon was cagey, for he did not want to risk giving back Shan-hai-kuan, a

hard-earned piece of real estate that had eluded his father and
half-brother, even after they had given up a dear price in financial
resources and lives. While Wu was preoccupied with the rebels
and his family in Peking, Dorgon quietly built-up his manpower,
augmenting the ten thousand men he had initially stationed near
the fortress with another twenty thousand. The total strength of
his army had increased to sixty thousand strong.

When Wu San-kuei's letter arrived at his camp, Dorgon opened
it, read it, and threw up his hands in unabated joy. He was educated
in Chinese characters, so he could read the letter without help from
Fan Wen-cheng. But he quickly summoned Fan and Do to share
the joy with them. When they appeared in his camp, he handed
the letter over to Ju Da-shou and said, "Your nephew is playing
right into my hands!"

Ju read the letter and passed it over to his colleague. Fan accepted it and said, "Your Excellency, that's exactly how you predicted the outcome!"

"Since he is moving west on June 2, we will mobilize our
troops the next day," commanded Dorgon. "But I want to take our
whole force with us and leave a small group to guard the fortress."

"With no threat whatsoever at Shan-hai-kuan, I suppose five
thousand troops ought to do the job," General Ju suggested.

On June 4, 1644, the news of the combined armies advancing to within fifty miles of Peking had reached the capital. The
evening before, Li called an urgent meeting with his brain trust
and a few of the higher-ranking generals, but only two showed
up. Niu Chin-hsing and another loyal general answered the call.
The others, including Minister Do and Eunuch Tang, were busy
preparing themselves to get away with their treasures from the
Forbidden City. Thus, the emperor of Shun found himself alone.

"I now know how it feels to be an emperor on the run. Emperor Chung-chen was betrayed by his ministers! Alas, now, I find myself in the same predicament!"

He asked the two generals, "Why can't you help me to be a good ruler?"

"Most of our comrades feel the authority to rule was granted to you by them! But they all have the right to share the wealth with you!" replied one of the generals. Apparently, he expressed the prevailing sentiment of most of the rebel leaders. "Now that the empire is crumbling, they feel they have no obligation to defend it for you."

Do Wen-lung was the first to desert the Forbidden City, the Eunuch Tang Jun following closely behind. Neither had been an original player in the Li adventure, so the Shun emperor really could not expect either one to go down with him. Both men were in the game only for their own benefit, so when the going got tough, they collected many cartloads of their ill-gotten treasures and left the capital hurriedly. Minister Do even took a few women with him.

The emperor of Shun, Li Tzu-cheng, was left alone to guard the imperial domain that he had founded. As his once-mighty army spun out of control; the soldiers first plundered only at night, when a curfew was imposed on the city. Later, they forced open doors to the homes of innocent citizens, entering and seizing their gold and silver and violating their women. They even abused the owners of homes with whom they had lived. Peking was turned into hell for most citizens.

The next days, with his empire crumbling in front of his own eyes, Li Tzu-cheng had no choice but to take flight. He was hoping that his ally Chang Hsien-chung was marching closer to Peking so that he could take refuge in his camp. Moreover, he was hoping that perhaps he could borrow Chang's force to make another comeback for the Forbidden City. To surrender was to sign his own death warrant, he thought. He ordered the main palaces in the Forbidden City set on fire; he did not want to leave them in good condition for his enemies. He took a regiment of what was left of his army and rode out of the capital, smoke and flames filling the sky behind him. The dashing prince of Shun, who had occupied Peking for forty-one days, had been a self-proclaimed emperor of China for even less time: eight days!

On June 5, 1644, Wu San-kuei entered Peking without obstacle. Learning that Li Tzu-cheng had fled the capital, Wu was disappointed. He'd liked to have captured him alive to hang him by the meridian gate, the way he had done to his father. Without hesitation, he dispatched a regiment of his best soldiers to hunt down the rebel leader.

After settling in the palace where Li Tzu-cheng had resided, unbeknownst to Dorgon's movement Wu San-kuei got down to business—the business of Dorgon and Yuan-yuan! He had Lieutenant Pei continue the search for Yuan-yuan. As for Dorgon, Wu wanted to meet him outside the west gate to thank him for lending his troops to dismantle the Shun government. But little did he expect that the biggest blow to his plan was waiting to land on him.

On the same afternoon when Wu San-kuei was fighting with the remnants of the Shun army near the west gate, Dorgon and his army had gained easy entry into Peking, coming from the east circuitously. Before the two armies of Wu and Dorgon had reached the city, people in Peking had heard that there was a "great army" coming from the east. Most of them, including the officials freed from the rebel camps, expected to see Wu San-kuei or one of the surviving Ming princes. Instead, they found themselves greeting a large group of men with long pigtails down their backs and shaven foreheads: Manchus!

Wu San-kuei had planned to have the Manchu army be the reserve to reinforce his force. They were to be called on only if he encountered major resistance from the rebel army. Somewhat to his surprise, the rebel army put up a weak defense that his own army had easily overcome. So when Dorgon marched into Peking without his invitation, Wu San-kuei was stunned. He had planned to dismiss Dorgon when the mission was accomplished, after the rebel leaders had abandoned the Forbidden City.

Obviously, Dorgon had a plan of his own. As he neared the palace grounds, in front of the smoldering Throne Hall, he dismounted from his horse to the contrite adoration of the crowd. He climbed to the top of an imperial sedan waiting nearby to address the gathering. But that sedan had been placed there by some former Ming officials to receive Wu San-kuei or a Ming prince, not him.

"I am Prince Dorgon of the Ching dynasty. I am the regent to His Majesty, the emperor Fu-lin!" Dorgon declared in a loud voice. The crowd reacted with a hush; most observers did not know if they should applaud or keep silent. They were all startled and did not comprehend what was happening.

"I am here to help you avenge the loss of your late emperor of the Ming dynasty," Dorgon continued. "His eldest son, the crown prince, will be with you soon. And he will attest to the fact that I am the rightful ruler!" The crowd reluctantly applauded as Dorgon descended from the sedan. He had spun a lie, because the Ming prince was not expected to appear at all.

Escorted by a group of former Ming officials, Dorgon ascended the steps of Throne Hall. When he got to the top step, he turned and asked the most senior of the Ming officials to step forward. That official was one Li Ming-jui, who had survived the rebel torture chambers. If Tian Wang-yu had survived, he'd be the senior official answering the call. But he'd died shortly before Dorgon had entered the Forbidden City.

Old Minister Li walked slowly to the bottom of the steps where Dorgon was standing. He was full of trepidation. But, to his relief, Dorgon graciously asked him to be the senior minister in the court he would be forming. Li quickly declined the offer, saying that he was too old and lacking the virtue to lead the new government.

Dorgon declared forcefully, "Emperor Chung-chen was not given the proper rites of burial. All of you, especially you, Minister Li, owe your emperor that loyalty and honor. But without a leader to take charge of the affairs of the new court, your emperor's soul will linger on in perpetual limbo. Is that what you all want?"

Li Ming-jui was deeply touched by that admonition, so he got down on his knees and said, "Your Excellency, your wish is my will!"

With that one adroit move, Dorgon revealed his intention to have his nephew occupy the throne in the hall behind him. He only had to wait for the seven-year-old emperor to come to the capital to assume the Heavenly Mandate created by the Ming emperor's passing. To Dorgon, Li Tzu-cheng had not earned the blessing of heaven, so he could not inherit the throne legitimately, even though he had pilfered it for six weeks.

Wu San-kuei discovered what Dorgon had done behind his back, and he was furious. The Manchu prince had pulled a fast one on him, but he was powerless to have it undone. Worse yet, he had handed his base, Shan-hai-kuan, to Dorgon. So he licked his wounds and asked for a meeting with Dorgon. Dorgon invited him to a small chamber in Throne Hall that had not been damaged by the blaze set by the rebels.

Strangely, the roles between these two men of the hour seemed to have been switched. It had started with Wu San-kuei being the host who invited Dorgon to join him in the foray to the capital. But it ended with Wu San-kuei being the guest visiting Throne Hall, occupied by Dorgon.

Entering the chamber and seeing Dorgon perched high on a throne-like couch, with Ju Da-shou and Fan Wen-cheng standing behind him, Wu San-kuei found himself in a rather awkward position. He grudgingly bowed his head to Dorgon, and said, "Your Excellency, on behalf of the people of Peking and China, I'd like to express my deepest appreciation for your help in ousting the rebels and regaining the Forbidden City. The crown prince will come and reassume the mandate of the Ming dynasty soon!"

Fan Wen-cheng stepped forward and said, "General Wu, the mandate of heaven has passed to the emperor of the Ching dynasty! Li Tzu-cheng claimed that mandate fraudulently. Nevertheless, by taking the throne briefly, he, in effect, put an end to the Ming dynasty! Thus, the crown prince, a descendant of a defunct empire, does not have the right to reclaim that mandate!"

Wu San-kuei was livid, but he suppressed his temper and held his tongue. As he was searching for words, his uncle interjected. "General, I advise that you pledge your loyalty to the new ruler. The new emperor of China is His Majesty Aisin-Gioro Fu-lin of the Great Ching dynasty. I am sure if you submit to him, he will reward you handsomely!"

Wu San-kuei looked at Fan and Ju with utmost disdain; he was most disappointed with his uncle. In his mind, they were traitors who had abandoned their emperor and reaped personal gain and glory. *How can I bow to those barbarians from the north?* he reasoned. *They are here only on my invitation. Now that my need for them has been fulfilled, they should hold up their end of the agreement and get out of Peking.*

The thunderous voice of Dorgon jarred Wu San-kuei out of his reverie. "General Wu, take your army and go west. If you succeed in hunting down Li Tzu-cheng, the land you reclaim from him will be your fiefdom."

Wu San-kuei again had found himself in a difficult position. He had finally come to the realization that Dorgon was here to stay, and he had no real power, military or political, to alter that eventuality. Besides, his goal was to avenge the death of his emperor and his father, and that was not done. He must continue his mission to hunt down Li Tzu-cheng.

Then there was the urgent matter of Yuan-yuan. Since his private envoy had not located her, he would have to tend to that task personally. The thought that her love was wallowing in a sea of trouble continued to haunt him. These gut-wrenching problems persisted in wreaking havoc on him; Wu San-kuei had no choice but to give in to the Manchu prince.

At last, Wu San-kuei swallowed hard and said, "Your Excellency, I will leave the capital at once!" Then he gave a harsh look to his uncle and Fan Wen-cheng and declared, "And I shall return!"

With that cutting remark, Wu San-kuei bowed and left the palace. The next day, he took his regiments and marched out of the capital. He went west to pursue the former emperor of Shun, Li Tzu-cheng.

Within a fortnight, Aisin-Gioro Fu-lin arrived in Peking with much fanfare. Dorgon welcomed his seven-year-old nephew with open arms. The Manchus bathed in glory and staged a month-long celebration over their final victory in conquering China.

The Drama of 1644 took forty-one days to unfold. It had begun on April 25, when Li Tzu-cheng marched into Peking. It had ended on June 5, when Dorgon entered the Forbidden City. During the forty-one days, two dynasties had changed hands while another ruled in the interim. The Manchus, a minor race with a small population, had proclaimed themselves the masters of millions of

Han Chinese people, and many predicted that their occupation of China would be short-lived. But they proved the pundits wrong. They ruled China for 267 years!

The saga of Yuan-yuan continued for a period of time after the Manchus had gained control of China. The lives of most of those touched by her had met with tragic endings: Wang Kuang, Prince Soong, Ma Yi, Tian Wang-yu, Liu Tsung-min, Chung-chen, and counting.

The emperor of Shun, Li Tzu-cheng, fled Peking and went west, hoping to team up with his erstwhile ally Chang Hsien-chung to reestablish a base and mount another drive to recapture his lost mandate. But he lacked the resources, financial or human, to do so, even if he still had the desire. Chang Hsien-chung had encountered difficulties of his own as his drive north stalled, so he retrenched to the west and resettled in the capital of Sian. Soon, he died in oblivion and never came close to his dream of conquering China. Within a few months after his flight from the capital, Li Tzu-cheng was found and killed by Wu San-kuei.

After leaving Peking, Wu San-kuei spent most of the next few years trying to build a new base to rally the people in the south to challenge the Manchus. He succeeded in rebuilding his army and controlled a few provinces. But his efforts to overcome the Manchus were futile. He had also exhausted his efforts to find his woman. Since he had no clue where Yuan-yuan had gone, his task became impossible.

About ten years after he had marched out of Peking, Wu San-kuei and his army landed in a small town in Hunan province on their way to south China. One day he was tending to some small matters at his temporary post; his aide interrupted him and said, "General, there are two women outside asking to speak with you."

"What?" The general looked up, bewildered. "Women?"

"Yes. They look like nuns!"

Wu could not believe what he had heard. "Nuns?"

"Yes, sir, nuns!"

"All right. Show them in."

When they were led into his office, Wu San-kuei saw two women cloaked in what appeared to be nuns' habits. Standing in front of the general, the older of the two bowed and said softly, "General Wu?"

"Yes!" the general answered, also softly.

"General Wu San-kuei?" the older nun repeated.

"Yes. Wu San-kuei." the general reiterated.

"We heard a lot about you," the younger nun said, also in a soft voice.

Wu San-kuei found the encounter odd, so he asked, "Is there any way I can be helpful to you?"

"Someone in our convent prayed for you each and every night for over many years," the older nun reported.

Wu was truly befuddled. He was lost for words, and found the conversation odd.

The younger nun began to tell the story. "General Wu, we found a young woman outside of our convent some years ago. When we found her, she was very sick!"

"Yes, she was very sick and had not eaten for days. So we let her into our house," the older nun continued.

"Then?" Wu San-kuei began to show interest in the story, and he listened more intently.

"After a month, she finally recovered from her sickness and decided to join our convent and become a nun," said the younger nun.

"We asked her where she had come from. She either tried to hide her identity or she wanted to erase the past from her mind," the older nun said.

Wu San-kuei urged the older nun to tell him more because he had become very interested in the story.

"Over the next few years, she became a devout member of our convent. She'd pray all day and every day to the divine power." The older nun looked skyward and stopped to catch her breath. "The oddest thing, though, was that each and every night she kept to herself and prayed softly for one General Wu San-kuei!"

"We heard your name mentioned by the townsfolk. They said that you were passing through our town, and we decided to come and see you. We thought the woman might be related to you," said the younger nun.

Wu San-kuei was rendered speechless by the tale, and he froze in body and mind for a prolonged moment. Then he suddenly jumped up and yelled, "Where is she now?"

The nuns were surprised by the general's sudden move, so they took a few steps back from him.

"I'd like to see her!" barked the general. "Tell me, is she still in your convent?"

"I am sorry, General!" the older nun muttered, lowering her head. "You cannot see her!"

"Why?" the general asked impatiently.

The two nuns looked at one another for a prolonged moment before the older nun said in a barely audible voice, "She died a month ago."

The younger nun started to wipe tears from her cheeks. "Such a sad life!" she muttered.

"And she was still young and beautiful to the day she died!" lamented the older nun. She was also wiping tears off her face.

"Tell me what her name was," Wu San-kuei said finally in a low voice.

"We called her the Fallen Angel," reported the older nun, "but we found out later that she was a consort in the Ming palace. Her real name was Yuan-yuan!"

Wu San-kuei could not contain his sudden surge of sorrow. He covered his face, and tears began to flow down his older and thinner cheeks.

Wu San-kuei continued to drift in south China for another twenty years. His dream of avenging the deaths of the emperor and his father was fulfilled with his killing of Li Tzu-cheng. But the dream of taking the throne back from the Manchus and the dream of living forever with the most beautiful woman in China had eluded him. That last dream, which he had spent all his youthful years pursuing, meant he died at age sixty-three with a broken heart.

Like many stories of love, the love story of Yuan-yuan was a song of love: a sad song.

Printed in the United States
By Bookmasters